PRAISE FOR
THE NOVELS OF SARAH HEALY

House of Wonder

"With keen insight and rare emotional truth, Sarah Healy hits every mark with *House of Wonder*. It's funny, sad, hopeful, and heart-breaking and filled with characters that stick with you and make you care. If you've ever known an outsider or an oddball—or been one—this is a novel for you."

—Augusten Burroughs, *New York Times* bestselling author of *Running with Scissors* and *Sellevision*

"Sarah Healy's *House of Wonder* is an emotionally gripping tale of love, loss, and the universal convolutions of family. She paints her characters into life until you feel as if you've known them forever. I savored every delicious subtlety."

—Emily Liebert, author of *You Knew Me When* and *When We Fall*

"*House of Wonder* shows how family ties tend to worm their way from matters of obligation to matters of the heart, quickly and completely. The delicious dips into family history and the complex relationships in this book are as lovely as they are deep."

—Jennifer Scott, author of *The Sister Season* and *The Accidental Book Club*

Can I Get an Amen?

"A sparkling debut novel about dealing with family and finding love. An absolute treat!"

—*New York Times* bestselling author Janet Evanovich

continued . . .

"An emotional and satisfying novel that is as tender as it is funny—a fabulous debut that's fresh, honest, and addictive. Don't miss it!"
—*New York Times* bestselling author Emily Giffin

"Touching, funny, and full of heart. A highly entertaining novel about love and family, secrets and forgiveness."
—*New York Times* bestselling author Lisa Scottoline

"Funny, smart, wise, and refreshing . . . the work of a great new talent and an obviously gifted writer."
—Valerie Frankel, author of *Thin Is the New Happy* and *Four of a Kind*

"A soaring debut! . . . A beautiful story that will leave readers waiting breathlessly for her next book."
—*New York Times* bestselling author Beth Harbison

"Healy's supporting characters are charming." —*Publishers Weekly*

"More about starting over and learning to forgive rather than religion. . . . Healy delivers as many laugh-out-loud moments as touching ones, and with praise from authors like Emily Giffin, seems sure to join the ranks of women's fiction favorites." —Examiner.com

"Explores faith in an uncompromising, courageous manner . . . funny, thoughtful, provocative. . . . It's difficult to believe this is Healy's first book. One can only hope there will be many more." —Fresh Fiction

"Ms. Healy's funny debut novel is like Kim Gatlin's *Good Christian Bitches* swabbed with makeup remover." —*The New York Times*

HOUSE of WONDER

. . .

SARAH HEALY

 NEW AMERICAN LIBRARY

New American Library
Published by the Penguin Group
Penguin Group (USA) LLC, 375 Hudson Street,
New York, New York 10014

USA | Canada | UK | Ireland | Australia | New Zealand | India | South Africa | China
penguin.com
A Penguin Random House Company

First published by New American Library,
a division of Penguin Group (USA) LLC

First Printing, September 2014

LIBRARY OF CONGRESS CATALOGING-IN-PUBLICATION DATA:
Healy, Sarah, 1977–
House of wonder/Sarah Healy.
p. cm.
ISBN 978-0-451-23987-7 (paperback)
1. Brothers and sisters—Fiction.   2. Twins—Fiction.   3. Single mothers—Fiction.
4. Families—Fiction.   5. Life-change events—Fiction.   6. Domestic fiction.
7. Psychological fiction.   I. Title.
PS3608.E2495H68 2014
813'.6—dc23   2014001662

Printed in the United States of America
1   3   5   7   9   10   8   6   4   2

Set in Stempel Garamond   ·   Designed by Elke Sigal

For my husband, Dennis

Dogs never bite me. Just humans.

—MARILYN MONROE

HOUSE of WONDER

. . .

· · ·

The House on Royal Court

Ours were dinners of boneless chicken breasts, smeared and then baked in the congealed contents of a red and white can. My mother would have clipped the recipe from a magazine, using sharp orange-handled scissors, the type that can slice down a length of wrapping paper like a fin through placid water. Warren and I would sit waiting, eating our green bell pepper quarters filled with twisting orange strings of squirt cheese. They filled the role of vegetable, the bell pepper and cheese boats, but I'd lick out just the cheese. And then a timer would beep assertively and a steaming casserole dish would be pulled from the oven and set down in front of us. Portions would be scooped and piled on top of our plates, and then Warren would notice a desiccated piece of rice that was stuck to his fork from three dinners ago. His brows would draw together as he stared at it, and my mother would take the fork from his hands with a gentle tug. "For goodness' sake, Warren," she'd say, scraping the fleck off with one of her long, shiny magenta fingernails. "It's just rice."

My mother's fingernails were things of wonder. Each week she would go and have them wrapped in some sort of space-age material that made them as hard as drill bits. Then Sheryl, the manicurist to whom all the mothers went, would adorn them with snowmen or beach balls or abstract geometric shapes that my mother called "contemporary." "I love the contemporary design that Sheryl did this week," she'd say as she admired her fanned-out fingers. When we couldn't sleep, those fingernails would trace figure eights on our backs. We would close our eyes, feeling our mother's fingers skating across the planes of our skin, listening to her voice as she sang. Her speaking voice was soft and feminine; it was lapping waves of vowels. But when she sang, her voice was the type that would penetrate. It was the type that would make men stare as they ran their fingertips up and down the sides of their sweating highball glasses. But we didn't know that yet. We just knew that when she sang, we wanted to let the music seep inside us. When she won Miss Texas in 1972, she sang Anne Murray's "Snowbird," but with us, she tended toward old jazz standards. Her pageant songs were for brightly lit stages; they were for judges with clipboards. In our bedrooms at night, we heard songs for small, dark rooms.

We lived on a cul-de-sac in a town called Harwick, in the state of New Jersey. It was, in many ways, a brightly lit stage. So everyone knew about Warren. "How's your son?" they would ask my mother. And she'd crease her brow and soften her smile and reply that he was, *Good. Thanks for asking*, in a manner that made them feel benevolent and kind. "You know I asked after the Parsons kid," they'd say later that night over their own dinners of soup-can chicken. "Priscilla says he's doing well." And then they'd sink down in their seats, enjoying their armchair compassion. In that way, Warren performed a great community service. My mother had managed to make him, if not beloved, then at least accepted.

Priscilla Parsons had learned many things from the pageant circuit, but most important, she learned to play to her audience. And in those days, she still had the will to do it. In those days she would slick on some lipstick and arrange her bangs into a spiky waterfall and show up at my soccer games with a box of donut holes. She sat with the other mothers on the bleachers and they talked about who was going to be on *Donahue* and congratulated one another on enjoying that new show with the black woman, Oprah something. They talked about whose daughter was promiscuous and whose son was doing drugs. They talked about which male teachers were a little too effeminate and which female teachers were a little too butch. And then the mothers would clap when the game was over. And we would go to the mall. Well, my mother and I would go to the mall. Warren would walk circles around our neighborhood, flying his homemade radio-controlled airplane and listening to whale songs on his Walkman as our neighbors glanced out their windows.

The first time Warren ran away, everyone was sympathetic. The principal called, lasagnas arrived with nice notes, and friends' mothers implored me to tell my mom that *if she needed anything, anything at all* . . . And then their voices would trail off. I was never sure exactly what I was supposed to communicate. But when I would arrive home and see my mother pacing through the house, holding Warren's pillow, I knew it didn't really matter. And everyone was happy when he returned. Or they appeared to be, at least. But as Warren's childhood eccentricities lingered past adolescence, as he continued to disappear, as he reached the age when he was supposed to be "growing out of it," their collective goodwill became sapped.

"Goddammit, Warren," my father would mutter under his breath, as he nudged back the curtain from the front window. Warren would be standing at the end of our driveway, deaf to my mother's announcements that dinner was ready, immobilized as he stared at the pavement. "Jenna, honey, go out there and tell your brother to get in the house," Dad would say. So I'd grab a jacket and throw it over my soccer uniform, and push open the door, feeling the chill of the early fall air.

"Warren," I'd say softly as I approached, seeing that he was staring down at something, seeing some movement on the pavement.

"It can't get away," Warren would say, his eyes frozen. There wasn't terror in his voice, only a sad, tired resignation. "It's still alive, but it can't get away."

It would be a garter snake, a small one. And its tail would have been run over by a car, mooring it to the pavement. There would be no way it could have moved from that spot, but its body would continue to undulate in graceful, rhythmic Ss, its lidless eyes staring forward. In its futile attempt to keep moving, it would be doing the only thing it knew to do.

"It's okay, Warren," I'd say, putting my hand on his shoulder. "I'll tell Dad. He'll take care of it."

Warren wouldn't be fooled, but he'd come with me. The hair on his arms would be raised from the cold air and I'd see his breath cloud in small, vanishing white puffs in front of his mouth. And he'd turn and together we'd walk inside. But not before it could be noted that the Parsons kid had stood at the end of the driveway staring at a mutilated snake for at least thirty minutes. "Forty-five," Mrs. Daglatella would correct, her eyebrows raised and the lines across her forehead like ripples. "I heard it was forty-five."

"You have a way with your brother," my mother would say. "It's you and me that he'll listen to."

I didn't have to point out that she'd left out my father.

My father had very little patience for Warren. "I wish he'd just snap out of it," I'd hear him say to my mother on nights when I was supposed to be asleep. "I didn't think twins could *be* as different as Jenna and Warren."

"He's a late bloomer," my mother would say.

"Late bloomer?" There would be a humorless laugh, and when he spoke again, his voice would be somber. "I don't know, Silla. I think he should talk to someone."

"Why?" she would ask, a tinge of hysteria in her voice. "Because he's not just like everybody else?"

"He's not like *anybody* else."

"He is a smart, kind, wonderful boy. He just needs *time*," she'd say, her back to my father as she folded laundry, putting our things into nice, neat piles. Smoothing the creases and tucking in the arms and legs to form squares. "And maybe we should look into getting him a computer. I think he'd like that." My mother was always offering up such solutions. She wanted so badly for them to work. But when the computer arrived, Warren never did take to it. He seemed suspicious of its binary soullessness.

"Silla!" my father would shout as he walked in from the garage, and I'd see Warren tense. "When did you get a Bloomingdale's card?"

My father would set his briefcase down by the kitchen island and hang his suit jacket over one of the chairs. In his hands would be an envelope and a few sheets of paper with purchases itemized and listed in small black type—all that pleasure condensed into dry words and sums. My mother would remain facing the stove, her head tipped forward. "They were offering fifteen percent off with your first purchase and Warren needed a new comforter," she said, stirring, stirring, stirring a pot.

"But there are twelve hundred dollars' worth of purchases on here in the last month!" he'd declare.

"Fine," she'd say softly, still not looking up. "I'll take it all back." And the next day the frenzy would begin. She'd unearth her purchases from their hiding spots—the tucked-away closets and corners where my father never looked—and try to marry the contents of various bags with receipts. She'd try to determine what she could live without, what she didn't need. "It's not like we can't afford it," she'd say to herself as she held up sweaters and lamps and platters.

. . .

After my father left, things happened very fast. Without anyone to tell my mother to take things back, things didn't get taken back. And our house quickly filled with a great number of solutions. *I'm glad she's spending her alimony so responsibly,* I heard Dad snipe. And Warren, perhaps feeling a freedom he never felt around our father, perhaps feeling a rejection he never imagined, would fill the kiddie pool in the backyard and sit in it for hours.

"What are you *doing*, Warren?" I'd ask, as he sat with his thin, pale body submerged, his face turned toward the sky. He'd look at me with a glint in his eyes that were so much like my mother's, as blue as hers were green. "I'm reverting to a protozoan state," he'd say. And I couldn't help but laugh. He'd smile back at me, pleased. But an hour later, when I found myself once again outside, once again urging him to come in, it wouldn't be funny anymore.

"Get up," my mother would demand, as he lay in bed the next morning.

"Mooommmm," he'd reply. It would be a groan, a plea that was comforting in its good old-fashioned teenagerness.

"Don't you 'Mom' me. You need to get your butt to school."

And he would go.

Despite any bets against it, Warren graduated from high school. No one ever doubted that he was smart, but Warren's brand of intelligence tended to be a bit problematic. In eleventh-grade English, when we were studying the transcendentalists, we were instructed to write our own poems. Most—including my own—utilized nauseatingly common clichés and followed simple rhyming schemes, with lines like:

> My heart floats on the silver sea
> Will you ever see the real me?

But Warren's poems were different. Warren's were loopy, gasping compositions with a flamboyant structure that countered their restrained language. Anyone could see that they were special. Anyone could see that they were different.

"Did you write this?" asked Mr. Beeman, the principal, when Warren was called into his office. He sat at his desk, his fleshy red hand holding Warren's poem.

Warren replied that he had.

"I hope so," said Mr. Beeman, letting his words make their way slowly to Warren's ears. "Because plagiarism is cause for suspension at Harwick High."

Warren and I graduated together, accepting our diplomas one right after the other. My mother sat in the audience, a few rows away from my father and his new wife, whom I was now expected to call Lydia. And all the adults agreed that Warren should be allowed to take some time off. "To get his bearings," said my mother. "To grow up a little," countered my father.

I went to college that fall. And I was glad to be rid of Warren. When I made new friends at school, and they asked me if I had any siblings, I could reply, "Yeah, I have a twin brother," and leave it at that. They didn't need to know anything more.

If I had been back in Harwick, I might have been able to identify the exact moment when my mother's purchasing habits crossed the line from pattern to pathology. I might have been able to tell when the neighborhood's perception of Warren became something other than "oddball kid." As it was, I was young and unfettered. And I didn't want to think about Harwick or the house on Royal Court or anyone in it.

CHAPTER ONE

· · ·

Where's Warren?

I might have said that I was busy, that my family and I had grown apart, as families sometimes do. I could have pretended that our relationship was amicable but distant—one of pastel birthday cards and generic sentiment. I might have mentioned my four-year-old daughter, Rose, whom I was raising alone, or played for pity with the story of her father, of how he left and when. I could have trotted out any number of the excuses I relied upon to explain why I rarely went to my mother's house. But the truth was simple: I hated being there.

The house was too full of things, both tangible and intangible. Too full for me. In it, the past seemed to have mass and weight and form, crowding out the future. So when I did see my family, when we met to exchange our pastel birthday cards, it was anywhere but Royal Court. And I took solace in no longer belonging there. I had moved on. Or thought I had anyway. Because what rules us more ruthlessly than those things from which we run? I could have spent my life that way.

Instead, I got lucky. Instead, I got a phone call.

"Jenna?" It was my mother's voice.

"What's wrong?"

"Warren didn't come home from work last night."

In the silence, I remembered the way my mother used to look whenever Warren was gone, the way she would walk the house in circles.

"I'll come home."

I'll come home. That's what I always used to say—when I was at a friend's house or soccer practice or even at college, until Warren's disappearances dwindled and then ceased. *I'll come.* It was like a liturgy that I hadn't spoken in years, a response that came reflexively.

And so I canceled a meeting, picked up Rose at day care, and drove back to Harwick. (A shamefully short trip, I'll admit.) Warren going missing may have been the one thing that was sure to bring me back when little else could. Warren knew that.

From the backseat, I heard Rose's voice. "Are we here?"

I brought the car to a stop and, with my foot on the brake, found my daughter's reflection in the rearview mirror. Everything about Rose was red—her hair, her lips, even the dime-sized birthmark on her cheek. "Yup," I said. Then I looked up at the house where I had grown up, the house where my mother and brother still lived. I was Rose's age the first time I saw it. With its brick facade and white columns, I had thought it looked important, like the president of the United States could live there. I set the car into park. "We're there."

My mother was waiting by the front window, her hip jutting out as she leaned against the frame, the back of her hand holding aside the lace curtain. When she stood like that, like an old Hollywood starlet caught between takes, you could see the woman she used to be. When she stood like that, even I was mesmerized. I raised my hand in a greeting. Through the glass, Mom did the same.

From behind me, Rose yelled, "Hi, Nana!" and waved vigorously.

I got out of the car and opened Rose's door. Next to her was the evidence of the drive-through meal that we had eaten on our way over, at which our dog, Gordo, was staring with great interest. Rose scrambled down onto the blacktop and I squatted in front of her. "I don't know how long we're going to be able to stay," I said, tucking a curl behind her ear. And it was the truth. Now that I was here, I wasn't quite sure why. Now that I was here, I wanted only to leave.

Rose held up two fingers. "How about for two shows?" she said, as if we were in a heated negotiation and the currency was children's programming.

I rested my hand on her head. "We'll see, kiddo." I stood and opened the back gate of the station wagon for Gordo, who lumbered down, and we made our way up the path to my mother's battered-looking house.

The front door opened and Mom stepped out, propping it wide with the side of her body. She watched as Gordo passed her without hesitation and disappeared inside; then she looked up, her eyes meeting mine, and forced a smile. "How're my girls?" she asked as Rose and I climbed the front steps. There was a jitteriness to Mom's voice, shaky edges to her words. She was always anxious when Warren was gone.

"We're fine," I answered.

Mom glanced around the neighborhood, then rested her hand protectively on Rose's back. "Come on," she said to me, tilting her head toward the doorway. And it was only for a moment that I hesitated, just at the threshold, before stepping inside.

Mom led Rose through the foyer and toward the kitchen as I followed, navigating a path through a maze of boxes and bags, past towers of books and catalogues and baskets. There were long receipts—like ticker tape—scattered here and there. Many were from the department store where my mother worked. Their sums might be small, maybe only a few dollars, but the solutions ran cheaper these days. Under tables and lining the floor were bags of clothes with the tags still on them, boxes of infomercial inventions, and *But-Wait-There's-More!* extras still in their plastic wrapping and decoupled from the devices that could make them of use. Stacks of magazines were piled on each of the steps leading to the second floor, their covers showing women and houses and lives that were so perfect, you could stare at them all day. Some of those magazines had been there for years, becoming more and more dated.

Mom glanced back at me, reading the expression on my face before I had a chance to change it. And for one honest instant, we looked at each other. But the moment was too uncomfortable to let linger, and so I said, "The sugar maple's gotten huge." The maple stood in the park that abutted many of the backyards in King's Knoll, including my mother's.

"I know," she said, her face moon white. Then she turned,

letting her words trail behind her. "I remember when you kids used to climb it."

For the next hour or so we sat, not mentioning Warren's absence. Not really mentioning Warren at all. Rose drew pictures of whales and arrows and hearts while Mom watched, asking her quiet questions, complimenting her on her skill. With Gordo at my feet, I took out my phone and tried to scroll through e-mails, but found myself watching my mother instead. Until she looked up at me, the pretense of a casual visit becoming too much to bear. "He just hasn't done anything like this in so long." The words came out as if through a steam vent—only hinting at the pressure inside.

I put my phone down on the table and repositioned myself in my chair. "So, Fung said Warren left at his regular time last night?" I asked. Fung Huang owned Pizzeria Brava, where Warren worked doing deliveries.

My mother nodded, her lips tight, her arm resting on the back of Rose's chair. "At eleven p.m."

I glanced at the digital display on the stove. It was six o'clock in the evening.

"Are you talking about Uncle Warren?" Rose asked, as if we had tried to put something past her.

Mom and I exchanged a glance. "He just forgot to tell Nana where he was going," I said, seeking to soothe her.

But Rose was unruffled. "Oh," she said, as she processed the information. When she turned back to me, she did so brightly. "Can I watch a show now?" Though raising Rose without cable was a budgetary rather than an ideological decision, it had resulted in a child who could sniff out the Digital Preferred package like a terrier.

I got her set up in the family room, switching on the T.V. and selecting an addictive but vacuous cartoon, then came back into the kitchen. "Do you want a cup of tea or something, Mom?"

"I can make it," she replied, as she began to push herself up from her chair. It was more of an effort for her now. I hadn't noticed that before.

"It's okay," I said. "I got it."

As I waited for the water to boil, I stood in front of the window above the sink. The sun was setting, the trees turning into silhouettes against a watercolor sky. I looked out at the homes that lined the park, at the flickers and flashes of neighbors' television sets as they made their dinners and folded their laundry. King's Knoll looked exactly as it did twenty years ago. "God, nothing ever changes here," I said to myself, my face reflected in the window in front of me.

"I wouldn't say that," responded my mother, a strange lilt of warning in her voice.

"What do you mean?" I asked. Across the park, a deck light switched on.

"Nothing," she said, brushing some nonexistent crumbs from her lap. "I don't mean anything."

My eyes lingered on her for a moment before I turned back to the window, now noticing a framed picture on the sill. It was of Warren and me as babies, dolled up in our ridiculous his-and-hers twinsie ensembles. "Oh, God," I said, picking up the photograph. "Where did this come from?"

Mom leaned back in her chair to better see what I was holding. And though a smile came to her face, it looked as though it hurt just a little bit. "I found that picture when I was looking for"—her forehead creasing gently—"something else."

"How old are we here?"

"Three months."

I shook my head at the sight of us, with our big bulging eyes and infantile acne. "God," I chuckled. "We were such ugly babies."

With an expression of affection, my mother's head dropped to one side, her eyes on the photo as she considered my assertion. "No, you weren't," she said.

"Yes, we were!" I set the photo back on the sill. "We were so *skinny*."

"Warren was skinny," Mom agreed, the look on her face distant and fond. "But you were regular-baby-sized. The doctor said you got all the nutrients."

I felt the smile slide off my face. "That's a messed-up thing for a doctor to say."

My mother gave a shrug. "Warren was four pounds to your seven," she said.

"Still," I said, glancing back at the photo, at the way I dwarfed him in size even then. "It's not like I *denied* him something."

I saw her face change. I saw it sink with regret. "Coming into this world was just harder for him," she said, referring, I assumed, to the fact that I was born first and vaginally, while Warren was delivered sixty-seven minutes later via an emergency C-section.

I glanced at Rose, who was fully zombified by the television's flashes of color and sound. "Do you think the birth process"—I turned back to my mother—"hurt Warren in some way?"

Mom took a deep breath, her elbow on the table, her hand

propping up her head. "Your father did," she finally said, as if it were an inconsequential and commonly known fact.

"He did?" I had never been aware that my father faulted anyone but Warren for the way Warren was.

Mom's eyebrows lifted and she nodded steadily. "Umm-hmm. For a while he talked about suing the doctors."

"Why?" I asked. "Do you think they didn't act fast enough? With the C-section?"

She considered it for a moment. "No," she said ambivalently, "I just think you and Warren have a different makeup, that's all. You're more like a Parsons." Her head began to nod slowly at some inevitability. "Warren's a Briggs." Briggs was the maiden name of her mother, Martha, who died when she was five. My mother spoke of her very rarely and so I didn't know much about the Briggs side of the family, except that they had been wealthy by the standards of the day. My great-grandfather Benson Briggs had owned a small chain of department stores called Briggs Western that he sold for what was considered a very significant sum. The stores continued to change hands until they no longer existed, and the money from their original sale seemed to disintegrate through the generations. But when my grandmother was a young woman, there was enough of it left to guarantee that she and whomever she married would be quite comfortable.

"Were there people from the Briggs side of the family that were . . . like Warren?" I didn't know how else to phrase it. We didn't have a clean, tidy little label to put everyone at ease, so we settled on a description that was at once both inadequate and perfect.

My mother's eyes became as clear and lucid as I'd ever seen them. "Yes, honey," she said. "There were."

"Who?" I asked.

But whatever door had briefly opened to my family's past was closing, as my mother nodded toward the kettle. "It looks like the water's boiling."

It took me a full beat to turn and see the steady plume of steam, the water condensing on the spout. My desire to leave, to be free of the house on Royal Court, was attenuated by what had become a growing and real concern for my brother. *Because what if this time is different?* No sooner had I thought it than I heard the unmistakable sound of a car bottoming out at the entrance of the driveway. It was as if Warren had been watching some great cosmic clock, as if he had known exactly how long would be too long. *Dammit, Warren,* I thought. *Finally.*

My mother was on her feet at once. I followed her from the kitchen and into the foyer, Gordo announcing our procession with a series of clipped barks that held no menace. Pushing back the lace curtain, Mom peered out the window, lifting her chin to see past the glaring headlights from the car that was now parked in front of her house. Already I could see that it wasn't Warren's beat-up Civic. My mother waited, all her energy, all her attention, focused on the next few seconds. Then the passenger door opened. And there he was. Warren's face emerged in advance of the rest of his body, like an owl from the trunk of a tree.

Almost instantly, the front door was open and my mother was on the porch. "Warren!" she scolded as I stepped out behind her, my arms crossed over my chest. "Where have you *been*?" But past her shoulder, Warren's eyes found mine, and his lips curved into a small smile. It was as if we had planned to meet at this very spot, at this very moment, and I hadn't let him down.

Gordo had rushed ahead of us and was circling what we could now see was a green Jeep, his tail thumping against its body. I heard Warren greet him softly. *Hey boy,* he repeated, his voice high and gentle. *Hey.* From the driver's side came the creak of hinges and a face appeared that was disarming in its familiarity.

"Hi, Mrs. Parsons."

"Bobby!" said my mother, her voice an echo of my own surprise. Bobby Vanni had been Harwick's golden boy and my own most crippling high school crush. He had grown up down the street in the home where his parents still lived, and from what I knew, he was married to a lovely woman, had a lovely daughter, and was finishing up his medical residency. In short, he had turned out just as everyone had predicted he would: well.

Mom set her shoulders back and adopted her pageant smile. "What have you two been doing?" she asked, the slight quaver in her voice the only sign of her unease.

Bobby had only half exited the car. "Warren was walking down South Road," he answered. "So I gave him a lift."

Mom let out a small, almost inaudible gasp. "Well, thank you so much, Bobby," she said.

"No problem," he answered. And as he began to lower himself back into his seat, I felt the relief of having escaped unnoticed. Because Bobby Vanni was someone I only wanted to see when fully armored—with witty remarks and fresh makeup.

I didn't want to see him that night. I didn't particularly want to see him at all. As if he were alerted to the thought, his gaze met mine.

I dropped my head for only a second, then stepped forward. "Hi, Bobby," I said.

"Hey, Jenna," he said, almost to himself, as if he weren't quite sure it was me.

I gave him a polite smile. "It's good to see you."

"Yeah, likewise," he said. He stared at me for a moment before remembering himself. "Well," he said, "I really should get going."

Bobby made a farewell round of eye contact and got in his car. Then he slung his arm over the passenger seat, gave me one last look, and reversed down the driveway. I turned and walked into the house before he pulled into the street.

Standing in the foyer, my face humorless, I waited for my brother.

"*Warren*," I said when he stepped inside, my mother at his back. "Where have you *been*?"

Warren turned his head slightly, as if trying to see me from a different angle. "I went fishing," he finally said. He had a quiet voice, with words that came out unrushed, as if each needed breathing room. "After work."

I let my eyes slide shut for the briefest of intervals and took a breath. It was our grandfather—on our father's side—who had taught him that catfishing was best at night. "What about today, then?" I asked, my tone softer. "Where were you today?"

His chin dropped. "My car wouldn't start," he said. "When I was ready to go home."

I looked at my brother. His pale, almost ageless skin was

shadowed with purple under his eyes, and the bangs of his fine, rabbit brown hair brushed the tops of his brows. What would he do in such a situation? What would be Warren's solution if, key in ignition, his car remained lifeless? "And so what, War?" I asked. "You *walked*?"

He used the slightness of his frame to slide past me. "It wasn't so far."

"Where were you?"

"On the Raritan. Off of River Road."

"Warren," I said, my mind running over the route as I followed him. "That's got to be like *thirty miles*." Pausing, I waited for a response that did not come. "Warren, *this* is why you need a cell phone."

Warren shuffled into the kitchen. When he saw Rose, he shifted course immediately and headed to the family room, standing beside the couch on which she was sitting, and waiting for his greeting. She turned to regard him briefly. "Hi, Uncle Warren!" she said, before being reabsorbed into her show. Warren seemed reluctant to leave her, but physiological need trumped all else, and he walked quickly over to the sink, turned on the water, and pulled a glass from the cabinet. He filled it and drank it down in three long slugs. Then he looked at me, the corners of his mouth lifted so subtly that his smile was almost undetectable, as if he was enjoying a joke all his own.

"Warren, honey," said my mother, who had come in behind us, "are you hungry? You must be hungry." Our mother was always willing to forgive any and all of Warren's transgressions. To bury them quickly. "I can call for some Chinese?" Mom looked at Rose. "Rose, honey, do you like Chinese food?"

Rose looked over her shoulder and at me, as if the question were mine to answer.

"All right, you know what?" I said, Gordo's head emerging from between my legs. To Gordo, Warren's arrival was all excitement, all good news. "Rosie and I really need to get going. I have to be at work early tomorrow."

Rose let out a whine of protest. I looked expectantly at my mother, though what she could have said that would have satisfied me, I did not know. Her mouth opened as if in advance of speech, but no words came. "Come on, Rosie!" I called, turning my face toward the family room.

Rose and I were already in the car, my seat belt buckled, when my mother walked hurriedly out the front door, her arms crossed over her chest to ward off the cold. I rolled down the window and leaned my head out as she approached, letting the space between us fill with silence. It was night now, and the air had the cold calm of deep water. "Your poor brother," she finally said. "Having to walk all that way."

"He didn't exactly *have* to. He could have called someone."

"Well," she said. "Your brother has his own way of doing things."

I let out a sound that might have passed for a laugh. "That's one way to put it."

"Anyhow, you know what I was thinking?" she asked, her voice changing, becoming light and hopeful. "I was thinking that the block party is coming up this weekend." I didn't move, anticipating the request. "And it's been so long since you came. And I just know everyone would love to see you."

"Mom—," I started.

But my mother cut me off. "Please, Jenna," she said. There was desperation in her voice. "Please." And seeing her face, I couldn't deny her.

Since that night, I've often pictured Warren, sleeping in the backseat of his car, parked in a small dirt turnaround at the side of a wooded road. The interior would be damp with his breath and he'd have pulled the hood of his sweatshirt up for warmth. The sun would have shone through the windows early. And he would have set out at once, his belly empty, his body stiff. It would take him all day to walk from his favorite fishing spot back to Harwick. And it may have been a coincidence, the timing of his trip. It may be simply hindsight that lends it significance; a pivotal event requiring time to be seen as such. Or perhaps Warren knew exactly the right moment to bring me back home. Because when Mom called the next day to tell me that they'd recovered his car, I asked, "So, what was wrong with it?"

"You know, it was the darndest thing," she said. "As soon as Warren put his key in, it started right up."

CHAPTER TWO

• • •

All Alone

1952

Priscilla Harris's three-year-old fingers worked the peel of a
hard-boiled egg, tapping it against the kitchen table to crack
the shell, then pulling the fragments off until there was only
immaculate white. She shook some salt from the shaker over
the top, then took a bite. That's how she ate the egg, salting it as
she went. When her mother was there, she sliced it for her,
fanning it out. *Like a peacock's tail,* her mother would say. But
Priscilla had felt her stomach groan with hunger, and she hadn't
known when someone would be there to fix her egg the way
she liked it, so she'd pulled as hard as she could on the refrigerator door until it opened. Then she had taken the egg from a
bowl and sat at the kitchen table alone. As she ate, she had the

dull, gnawing feeling that she sometimes felt when she was by herself—a child's silent disquiet.

She heard Mrs. Lloyd's footsteps coming up the back steps, then the creak of the screen door as it was quietly opened, before it shut with a dull thud. Mrs. Lloyd was as thin a woman as Silla had ever seen and always moved like she was trying not to be noticed. She'd started working for the Harrises when Silla was a baby, after her husband lost his job and this time hadn't bothered looking for another. *At least she's white,* Silla's father had said with his good ol' boy smile, when his friend had teased him about hiring the wife of the town drunk. Mrs. Lloyd stood there now, the strap of her purse resting on her shoulder, her fingertips on its faded needlepoint flowers. She looked at Priscilla, who was still in her nightgown.

"Good morning, Priscilla," she said, her eyes cautious, her nod small.

Priscilla glanced up. "Mornin', Mrs. Lloyd," she answered, before returning her focus to the egg. Mrs. Lloyd looked concerned. And when Mrs. Lloyd was concerned, Priscilla was concerned.

Mrs. Lloyd took off her hat and set it on the rack by the door. "Where's your mother?" she asked.

Priscilla didn't respond, didn't acknowledge the question. One might think that she hadn't heard it. But, of course, she had. As she pulled in her lips and concentrated on salting her egg, of course she had. *Goddammit, Martha!* she had heard her father yell one night. *What am I supposed to tell people? That you lost track of time? When I don't know where the hell you are for an entire goddamn day?*

Mrs. Lloyd waited and watched for a few more breaths,

then sighed. "Lord have mercy," she said, shaking her head, as she walked over to the cabinet and pulled out a glass. She filled it with milk, then set it down in front of Priscilla, who waited a polite interval before taking three enormous gulps. She hadn't realized how thirsty she was. She hadn't been able to reach the glasses.

CHAPTER THREE

. . .

Block Party

There was a time when my father had thought it was wonderfully, delightfully apropos that he lived with his wife, the beauty queen, on a street called Royal Court. *I built a castle for you, Silla,* he used to say. And she'd turn to him with a smile so bright that the memory burns to white. But as I stood on my mother's porch before the annual King's Knoll block party, I stared at a lawn sign featuring the face of the woman who was now married to my father. With an excess of both time and confidence, my stepmother, Lydia, had gone into real estate when my half sister, Alexandra, went to college, and quickly became one of the top Realtors in the state. In nearly every neighborhood in the area, you could see a facsimile of Lydia's smiling face gracing the yards of homes that she had listed, including the one right across the street. *New listings went up thirty-five percent*, my father had said proudly, *as soon as she added that photo.*

"Is that Lydia?" asked Rose, following the direction of my stare.

Rose knew Lydia but not well, having seen her only a few times a year. But Lydia's appearance was as predictable as a habit, with freshly blown-out blond hair, light pink lips, and a black shirt that was undone one button too many. "That's Lydia."

Rose looked at the crowd that had assembled down on the cul-de-sac, where large rectangular tables held aluminum trays and brushed stainless Crock-Pots. Then she turned back to me. "Do you want me to watch Uncle Warren?" she asked.

Cupping her chin in my hand, I realized that she had understood more than I'd thought about Warren's recent disappearance. "And who's going to watch you?"

"You watch me and I'll watch Uncle Warren," she reasoned.

From behind us, the door opened and my mother, carrying a platter of Rice Krispies Treats, stepped out. "Okay," she said, sounding anxious, hopeful. "We're ready." She glanced behind her at Warren. "Fix your hair, honey," she instructed, after a quiet assessment. Warren took a moment to process the request, then used his fingers to straighten his bangs.

Leaning past my mother, Rose said, "Uncle Warren, you come with me."

A smile formed slowly on his face, though his expression remained quizzical. "You want Uncle Warren to come?"

"Yeah," she said, marching toward him. Mom stepped aside and I watched Rose grip Warren's pointer finger and pull him forward. Once she had his hand, she tucked it under her arm, as if for safekeeping. Warren gave a brief, suspicious glance toward the crowd. I often wondered how Warren, who interacted so oddly with strangers, held on to a job where he had to encounter so many of them each night. "Now you need *to stay where I can see you*," said Rose, repeating a line she'd heard me say countless times in parks and playgrounds.

Warren laughed. It was a quiet noise that sounded as if it had been turned out with a crank. "Are you in charge of Uncle Warren?"

"Yeah," she said, leading him down the stairs. "I'm going to make sure you don't get lost." My mother's eye caught mine and she gave me a grateful look.

As we made our way down to the party, we crossed the front yard, past metallic garden globes and faded pastel flags. Mom's yard was scattered with such objects, all looking like shells in the sand that had been washed from the house during the retreat of some great tide. We passed neighbors holding bottles of beer and cups of hot cider, heading to this house or that. They looked at us, gave a nod and a tight smile. But no one stopped for a conversation. I was surprised by how many homes were inhabited by strangers now, by how many faces were unfamiliar.

At the cul-de-sac a handful of the neighborhood's old guard were gathered—Bill and Carol Kotch, Shelley Ditchkiss, and, of course, Linda Vanni. Standing next to his mother with a red plastic cup in his hand was Bobby. A little girl who I assumed was his daughter clung to his side. No taller than Rose, she had thick espresso-colored hair that was pulled half back and secured with a grosgrain bow. It looked like Bobby had been cornered by Shelley Ditchkiss, who was one to drone on for thirty minutes about her son-in-law's promotion to partner or daughter's decision to be a stay-at-home mom, or something equally self-congratulatory and uninteresting.

The direction of my attention didn't escape my mother's notice and I felt her sidelong glance.

"You know, Bobby's living here now," she said, as we trailed Rose and Warren.

"With Linda and Sal?" I asked. It didn't make sense that Bobby was living in King's Knoll. Why would he need to?

"He moved back home so he could finish his residency," she said. "I guess they have him working all sorts of crazy hours in the emergency room, so he needs someone"—she nodded toward the little girl at his knee—"to help with Gabby." I had known that Bobby had started medical school a bit later than was typical, having spent a number of years in the corporate world first.

"What about his wife?" Several years ago I had heard Bobby had gotten married. I'd been pregnant with Rose and living with an increasingly distant Duncan at the time. I did an online search using the keywords *Robert Vanni Harwick NJ Engaged*. Photos of the wedding came up. His wife was named Mia. Mia Simon. I remembered thinking she looked exactly like the sort of girl with whom I had always imagined Bobby would end up—elegant and exotic and from somewhere other than down the street.

"They split up," answered my mother, with the sympathy of someone who had been through an ugly divorce herself. "They have a little girl, but . . ." She shook her head in the way you do when, try as you might, you can't make sense out of something. "I guess she stayed with Bobby. The mother is out west somewhere."

"Huh," was all I could say.

As the crowd grew denser, I scanned the surrounding homes, their facades like familiar faces on which the years had begun to show. For the most part, they had been well kept. But a bit of passé brickwork or an outmoded feature told the neighborhood's age, which was of that desolate stretch in the middle: not young enough to be desirable, not old enough to be classic.

My mother's house used to be the grandest and was now the most egregiously dated, with its chipped columns and monochromatic red bricks, its yard-sale lawn and crumbling pavement. The grass had been mowed fairly recently, but higher halos remained around the scattered ornaments—the garden flags and toad abodes and reflective orbs.

The block party, too, seemed to have lost something, with residents ambling out to the street to make their requisite appearances. The party used to be held in the summer, rather than the fall, until it was decided that it was just too damn hot in July to stand in the street all day. Back then we all went outside early with our mothers as they set up, arranging carved watermelon baskets and red and white coolers filled with cans of soda. Everyone would trickle out of their homes and by eleven the street would be a sea of bodies. The mothers would stand in a semicircle, laughing in their sleeveless tops and visors, their legs tanned and strong with the skin only just beginning to loosen around their knees. Occasionally, their eyes would cast about for their children, to make sure that we were present and accounted for. But for the most part we ran free, a pack of us, with burned shoulders and blackened feet. The fathers' voices would be louder than usual, boisterous and deep, as they reigned from their lawn-chair thrones, reveling in the suburbs' fulfilled promise—the pretty wives, the nice neighborhood, the happy kids—all under summer's hyper-color sun. Then we'd hear Mr. Vanni's voice. *The Seventh Annual King's Knoll Sack Race is about to begin!* he'd call, his huge arm waving above his head. And we'd all scramble over the smooth sunbaked asphalt, our lips stained red from the Popsicles that we were downing one after the other, taking advantage of the distracted adults and jubilant chaos that surrounded us.

Arriving at one of the folding tables, my mother moved aside a Crock-Pot to make room for her platter. "How are you, Karl?" she said to a man in a Windbreaker with a corporate logo, who was plowing a potato chip through onion dip. She squinted and rested her curved hand over her brow. "We got a nice day for this, didn't we?" With his face frozen in what must have been intended to be a pleasant expression, the man named Karl made a sound of noncommittal agreement before popping the chip into his mouth and turning away. A moment later, he engaged in a hearty backslap with a golf-garb-clad man whose huge convex belly gave him the look of a gestating aquatic mammal.

Once Karl was out of earshot, my mother glanced from Warren to Rose to me, then back out at the party. "It's good that we're all here together," she said, through her pageant smile. "We should walk around," she said. "Say hello to everyone."

My mother held Warren's upper arm protectively as we navigated the crowd, following Rose, who despite her best intentions was not doing a very good job of looking after her uncle

Warren. Mom nodded her hellos to the neighbors, mentioning that their new shutters "look great!" or that their chrysanthemums were "gorgeous this year!" They nodded polite thank-yous and kept walking. For the most part, they ignored Warren. Occasionally, the neighbors would steal glances at him, their gazes moving subtly in his direction as we continued to make our way down the street. But the conversation in which they were engaged wouldn't stop. And their assessment wouldn't last more than a moment or so. Some would offer a too loud and too enthusiastic, "Hi, Warren! How're your planes?" referring to the RC planes that he built and flew, walking endless loops around the neighborhood. *Hi, Warren!* It was the way people talked to toddlers. And dogs. That was the way they talked to Warren.

My brother used to have a friend in the neighborhood named Howard Li. Howard was a child prodigy whose parents were engineers at the enormous telecommunications company in the next town, and Howard was Warren's only real friend. When they moved into King's Knoll, everyone was nice enough, but made no real effort to engage the Lis socially, as Mrs. Li's seeming optimism, as manifested by her constant nodding smile, made everyone a little uncomfortable. "I don't understand what she thinks is so damn wonderful," I had heard Mrs. Daglatella say. But Howard and Warren seemed to understand each other. And I used to watch as Howard, a twelve-year-old sophomore, and Warren, a visitor from another galaxy, waged battle with defoliated forsythia branches in the backyard. Their skinny, shirtless bodies would leap and twist as they whipped their branches at a legion of invisible and invented foes, the forsythia humming as it cut through the air.

"Is she a Maglon?" Howard would ask Warren when I stepped out onto the deck, his forsythia aimed at me and ready to inflict its wrath.

"No," Warren would say almost coolly, having momentarily shed all geekiness. "She's an Aurotite." Howard would lower his branch and I would surreptitiously light the cigarette I had stolen from my mother, who still sometimes smoked back then—my small rebellion.

As we headed for the Kotches, who were now standing alone, Rose caught sight of Gabby Vanni tucked against her grandmother's side as she straightened up the buffet table. "Hey, Mom!" said Rose, pointing. "I see a girl!"

"Let's go say hi." I caught my mother's eyes. "I'm going to take Rose . . . ," I said, indicating Bobby's daughter and communicating my intent with a gesture. Mom nodded and I took Rose's hand.

As we approached, Mrs. Vanni gave me a fond smile. "I swear," she said, shaking her head. "You kids. You all grew up overnight."

"Hey, Mrs. Vanni," I said, surprising myself by how very happy I was to see her.

"Is this your little one?" she said, her eyes looking almost hopefully at Rose.

"Yup," I answered. "This is Rose."

Mrs. Vanni rested a hand on Gabby's back. Her nails looked as though they had been freshly manicured in a slick shade of red. She was the sort of woman who believed that you should keep yourself up, even after you'd put on a few pounds. "This is Bobby's little girl," she said proudly. She bent down toward her granddaughter. "Honey, this is *Rose*. Can you tell her your name?"

Gabby did as instructed and I waited to see if she would point at Rose's birthmark, scrunch her face, and lean away, as other little girls sometimes did. But Gabby just leaned in as Rose showed her the sparkly, probably magical rock that she had found in my mother's driveway. Once Linda Vanni was satisfied that the girls were properly acquainted, she turned back to me.

"So," she said, through an exhalation. "Everything good with you, Jenna?" Her brows were lifted expectantly, prompting me with a nod. Mrs. Vanni knew not to ask after Rose's father, Duncan—her tact a benefit, I supposed, of the King's Knoll rumor mill.

"No complaints."

"And how's Wonderlux doing?"

Wonderlux was the small design firm I owned with my business partner, Maggie. I smiled at Mrs. Vanni's ability to remember its name. The woman should be on a campaign trail, whispering facts about the constituents into her candidate's ear. "It's good," I said. "Thanks for asking." I gestured to the gathering around us. "It's great that you guys still manage to pull this off."

"Yeah. We've still got a pretty good group." Her head tilted from side to side. "Though I will tell you it was easier when Sal was more mobile."

"I heard about Mr. Vanni's . . ." I searched for the name of the ailment, rolling my hand in front of me as if beckoning it forth, and feeling ashamed that it wasn't on the tip of my tongue.

"Rheumatoid arthritis," she offered, not unkindly; then

she looked around at the assembled crowd. Her eyes lingered on a group of boisterous teenage boys who had positioned themselves in front of a Crock-Pot and were decimating its contents. Then she looked at me meaningfully. With a concessionary tilt of her head, she said, "Course it's not like it used to be." When my confusion registered, her face became troubled, as if she had said too much. "We've been having problems lately." She looked back out to the crowd with a sad and subtle nod. "In the neighborhood."

"What do you mean?" I asked.

She inhaled through her teeth, almost wincing. "There've been some thefts," she said, enunciating every consonant. "Lots of things going missing."

"Really?" I asked. "In King's Knoll?" Even though the neighborhood had become dated and somewhat down-market, I had thought it was regarded as safe and family-friendly.

Mrs. Vanni nodded, her chin moving slowly up, then down.

"My God," I said. "That's such a shame."

"Well, no one really knew they were thefts at first. Gina Loost thought she lost her watch and Perry Burt thought he misplaced his iPhone. Then enough people start missing things, and . . ." She opened her hand, as if to offer up the logical conclusion. "Just the other day, someone got into Beth Castro's garage and stole her son's mountain bike." It seemed to pain her even to think about it—theft being a problem in King's Knoll. "That's Zack right over there," she said, nodding toward the boys by the Crock-Pot. They were laughing and jostling each other like overgrown puppies. "He'd only just got the thing. I guess Beth said he paid for half of it with his lawn-mowing money."

"Poor guy," I said.

"The scary thing is that whoever is doing it seems to know exactly what to go for. There hasn't been any forced entry or anything," she said. "Lock your doors, that's what I've been telling everyone. *Lock your doors.*" Then her eyes seemed to narrow, tracking some logic I couldn't follow. "Your mother didn't mention any of this?"

"No," I said, thinking the omission inconsequential. "She didn't."

Linda paused for a moment, then swatted the air in front of her, as if it were an unwelcome thought. "Anyhow, I didn't mean to go on and on," she said.

I was searching for a more pleasant subject of conversation when Rose sprang up. Looking from Mrs. Vanni's face to mine, she began to bounce her knees as she held herself. "I need to pee," she said.

"Okay, Rosie," I said, grabbing her hand. "We're just gonna . . . ," I said, looking at Mrs. Vanni while gesturing up the street.

Mrs. Vanni nodded in understanding. "It was so good to see you," I said, as Rose and I turned away.

Navigating out of the crowd, with *excuse-us*'s and *pardon-me*'s, I glanced around for my mother. When I saw her, my feet became leaden. Though surrounded by groupings of neighbors— holding paper plates and plastic cups and talking about taxes and football and reality television—she stood alone, her hands clasped in front of her, her expression pleasant and hopeful. Like a girl who hadn't been asked to dance. As neighbors passed, they made sure they were looking anywhere but in her direction, suddenly finding the cloud formations overhead or the face of their watch endlessly fascinating. With an urgency I couldn't quite explain, I cast my eyes about for Warren and found him walking back up Royal Court. His pace was quick and purposeful. His head was bowed as if against the wind. He was going back to the house, of course. A house from which much that was of value had long ago been taken.

. . .

Lemonade Stand

1954

The sun hung fat and heavy in the sky, as if ready to be harvested, glowing the gold-to-orange ombré of late summer. Two months ago, the sun would have still been high overhead, proud and young. But it had settled into itself, no longer having quite so much to prove.

Priscilla looked at her mother's arms, which were draped over the table that they had set up next to the big oak in the front yard.

"Do you think we're going to get any customers?" asked Priscilla, her voice as tiny and lyrical as a bird's. She glanced at the pitcher of lemonade that they had made, the sugar still a thick layer at the bottom. It had been her mother's idea, the lemonade stand.

Her mother turned her head toward her, letting the warm, leaf-dappled light hit her face. "If folks are thirsty," she answered. Then she smiled, the small gap between her front teeth visible as she closed one eye, resting her cheek on the tablecloth, which was white with big fat red cherries on it.

Priscilla saw a car approach and straightened as it drew closer, waiting to see if it would stop, if the man driving would step out and with a smile drop a shiny nickel in the cup. Instead it only slowed and floated by—a blue-gray cloud passing on the horizon. "Maybe Daddy will buy some," she offered. But her mother's focus had gone elsewhere.

"Look, Silla," she said, rising from her chair, her gaze angled up toward the sky. Scooting round the table, her mother took a few steps closer to the street, her feet shuffling blindly over the dry, brittle grass. She raised her hand, pointing to a bird on a wire. "That's a scissor-tailed flycatcher." Her mother looked back at her. "See his tail? See how long it is?"

Silla nodded. The slender feathers that extended past his back were twice as long as the bird himself. "Why is it like that?"

"That's just how he was made," answered her mother simply, smiling as she watched her daughter study the bird. "Mama's gonna make him fly for you," she said. Then she turned, and squinting into the sun and bringing her hands above her head, she clapped loudly. The bird lifted off instantly, his wings flapping, his glorious tail spreading into a long, elegant fork. "Go on home, Mr. Flycatcher!" she said, her words long and unhurried. Beaming, Silla watched the bird until she couldn't see it any longer. Then she looked back at her mother, who was staring into the sky, her front teeth gently biting her lower lip.

Her mother was still standing like that when her father's bright red car approached. He peeled into the driveway and Silla watched him get out, slamming the door shut and marching over to her mother.

"Martha," he said, quiet and stern as he firmly took her upper arm. "What in God's name are you doing out on the front lawn dressed like that?"

Priscilla watched her mother look at him, as if she didn't quite understand the question.

"Goddammit, Martha," she heard her father whisper, as he took a step toward the house, pulling her mother along with him. She saw her lean toward his leading hand, as if to relieve the pressure from his grip.

"Daddy," Silla begged in a voice that wasn't loud enough to be heard, "we were just selling lemonade." The screen door whined as he pulled it open, and he forced Silla's mother in ahead of him. Inching closer, she heard her father's raised voice. "I have to get a phone call at work about you sitting in the front yard with our daughter in nothing but your *slip*!?"

"Lee," she heard her mother say. Her voice was always so innocent.

"This sort of thing has got to stop, Martha." Even at four, Silla understood the gravity in her father's voice. "One way or another it's got to stop."

CHAPTER FIVE

• • •

Painkillers

Gordo led the way down the empty sidewalk, trotting from Maggie's house to our car. Though Maggie and I spent our days sitting no more than eight feet away from each other in the Wonderlux office, Rose and I along with Gordo were frequent guests at the Dyer home, where Maggie lived with her husband and sons.

"Why do we have to go?" whined Rose, continuing the slump-shouldered, slack-jawed protest that she had begun in the house.

"You've got a big day tomorrow, Rosie." Duncan's parents, who had made an admirable effort to stay involved in Rose's life, were coming for a visit. And this time his mother, Miriam, had suggested that they take Rose to the Waldorf Hotel for the night. Though I was anxious about letting her go, it was the sort of indulgence that I couldn't easily afford, and therefore was grateful that Miriam and John were willing to provide for her. "You're going to live it up with your gram and gramp in New York."

Rose looked up at me, and in the dark, her pale skin seemed lit from within. "Is my dad going to be at the hotel?" she asked. It was a question of curiosity, rather than desire. As if she was trying to understand with what and whom she should associate her father's visits.

"No, monkey," I said. "He won't be back for a visit until Christmas."

Rose's brows drew together as she tried to process the information. "How many days is that?"

"About sixty," I said. Rose had recently become fascinated with numbers, always wanting to know how many days until her birthday or since she last went swimming.

"And how many days ago was the last time he came?"

"About three hundred," I answered, making my voice light.

"That's 'cause Tokyo is really far away," she explained, repeating the logic I'd offered her so many times before. *You don't get to see your daddy as much because Tokyo is really, really far away.*

Over dinner, Maggie had asked me what I was going to do while Rose was in the city, suggesting drinks and maybe dinner. Maggie loved drinks-and-maybe-dinner. And when I'd opted out, she'd given me the sort of look that seemed to insist there were better ways to spend a child-free Saturday evening than watching a movie in your fat pants. She had, however, let the subject drop.

The next morning, after Miriam and John picked up Rose, after I did the laundry and paid the bills and scrubbed the bathroom floor, I sat on the couch and looked around.

With my sock-clad toes, I gently poked Gordo in the side. "What now, huh?" I asked. He groaned and rolled onto his back, straightening his legs and arching his back. Objectively, Gordo was an exceptionally unattractive dog—something close to a chocolate Lab mixed with a sea lion. But he was a noble beast, loyal and true, who licked my feet and warmed the cold side of my bed, and whose small, slightly crossed yellow eyes looked at me with pure affection. I thought Gordo was magnificent. "Should we stick around here?"

The entirety of our little cottage could be seen from the family room. And compared with my mother's house, mine looked like the dormitory of a monk. Or would, if not for the small pops of color and life, all of which were related to Rose. Her toys, her artwork, her clothes. I never did like being there when she wasn't home. I never did like the way I could feel her absence as I passed through each room, seeing her shoes by the door or her chair in the kitchen. It was like walking through a cold spot in the ocean. So on impulse, I picked up the phone. On impulse, I called the one woman who would understand completely.

"Hey, Jenna," said my mother, sounding surprised to hear from me.

I hesitated for a moment. "Hi, Mom," I said.

"What's going on, sweetheart?" There was a twinge of worry in her voice, as if she was expecting trouble. And I realized how rare it was for me to call for a chat.

"I was wondering what you're doing tonight."

· · ·

A few hours later, I was in my mother's house, sitting on her couch, and watching a movie in my fat pants. Spread over my lap was a blanket and my slippered feet were resting on the edge of the coffee table. But despite those comforts, I had trouble relaxing. The house on Royal Court—with its memories, its things—felt like quicksand.

Objects had accumulated over the years, settled into their places like layers of sedimentary rock, but underneath it all, the bones remained the same. The same bulky television sat in the same oak entertainment center, the shelves of which were filled with the same boxes of jumbled VHS tapes. The right side of the same plaid couch had the same squeaky spring. And the same mauve lampshade gave the room the same dim light. I wondered if I was the same girl I had been when I watched my father walk out the front door with a suitcase in each hand, as if he were taking the last lifeboat off a sinking ship.

"Oh, Lord," said my mother, bringing a hand to her forehead with a pained chuckle. We were watching the beauty contest scene in the movie *Shag*, in which Bridget Fonda's character performs a scene from *Gone with the Wind* for a less than enthusiastic crowd. "That poor thing."

I shoved one of the sofa's many teddy bears behind my back as a pillow. "Did you ever do a dramatic interpretation for your talent?" I was clearly joking, but my mother answered honestly.

"No," she said, her head tilted as she watched the screen. "I always just sang." She took a breath, watching the girls parade around the stage. "I never did like the swimsuit portion, though."

Though I could think of dozens of reasons why that might be, I wanted to hear hers. "Why?" I asked.

She shifted, settled deeper into the corner of the couch. "In the bigger pageants, they used to announce your height and weight." She gestured toward the television. "When you first came out onstage."

I felt my expression turn incredulous. "They did?"

Her eyes didn't leave the screen. "Sure," she said, finding this bit of trivia wholly unremarkable. "The audience liked to know that sort of thing."

I looked at my mother, at the soft sag of her skin beneath her chin, and the rounding of her body. It seemed as though we often bumped into subjects from which she gently steered us away. Over the years, her beauty queen days had become one of them. "Did you get nervous?"

"Oh, yeah," she said. "I hated pageants."

I rearranged myself on the couch, angling my body toward her. "Then why did you do them?"

She looked at me for a moment, as though she wasn't sure why I needed to ask. "What else was I going to do?" she asked. When I didn't answer, she gave me a small, sad smile. "I wasn't smart, honey." She said it as if it were an innocuous fact. "And even if I was, your grandfather didn't think girls needed to go to college." Though she turned back to the television, her gaze remained soft and unfocused. "I got lucky," she said. "At least I was pretty. If I wasn't . . ." She shook her head. "I'd probably still be in Texas changing old Hattie's bedpans."

Hattie was my mother's stepmother. Whenever her name came up, it felt as though the air in the room became colder and thinner. She had married my grandfather when my mother was about seven years old, just a few years after my grandmother died. My mother didn't talk much about Hattie, though they were each all that the other had left by way of family. I had met her once, when my grandfather was still alive and they came to Harwick for their one and only visit. Though I thought Hattie was glamorous and beautiful, my mother's voice had turned shrill and angry when she was here. She burned dinner. She slammed doors. Warren wouldn't come out of his room, and spent their entire visit working on his planes. *Come on,* I had urged, as he put paintbrush to wing. *She's nice. She gave me ten bucks.*

"Oh, I love this part," Mom said, bringing my attention back to the TV. "Isn't Phoebe Cates just *gorgeous* in this movie?" she asked, her words slow and long as she pointed toward the screen. But I couldn't take my eyes off my mother.

We finished *Shag* and Mom dug through the racks of tapes near the entertainment center for another option, while I checked my cell phone for any calls from Rose. Without looking at me, Mom said, "It's a good sign if you don't hear from her. Means she's having fun." Then she held up another box. "*Steel Magnolias?*"

I opened my eyes, blinking against the dim light in the room. I had fallen asleep. On the television, the credits were rolling down a black screen. I looked at my mother, who'd also dozed off, her chin sunk back into her neck, dark smears of mascara having found their way into the lines around her eyes.

We both seemed to wake simultaneously. In those transient seconds between slumber and consciousness, I heard the sound of the front door being gently shut. Gordo let out a single, belated bark, then stared at me, as if covering up for his lack of vigilance. My gaze went to the digital clock display on the cable box. On Saturday nights, Warren usually got home from work within an hour-long window, depending on how many deliveries he had. I waited for some sign that it was him: his whistle, his footsteps.

My mother's face was alert, her body stone-still, and I knew that she was thinking about the thefts, about the things that had gone missing from Royal Court. There was a quiet creak of the floor and my mother raised one finger, a silent acknowledgment that she had heard it as well. Maybe whoever this was had seen us sleeping and assumed they could slip right in. I looked around at the room. *But what would they want in here?*

Then it came, faint but clear. A single bursting sob, like a crashing wave hitting the shore, then being just as quickly pulled back into the sea.

And my mother was up.

She walked quickly toward the foyer, her elbows pumped at her sides, as Gordo and I trailed closely behind. She saw him before I did, gasping and stopping in her tracks. Then I saw him, too. Warren was standing in front of the door. Blood caked his nostrils and was running in red rivers down over his lips, his chin. His nose was swollen, the bridge purple and tender. Another spring of blood came from a gash above his eyebrow and one of his planes was dangling from the hand of the arm that hung limp at his side. Startled, he gave us one brief, reflexive glance, the wide-eyed, frightened look of a solitary nocturnal creature. Then he dropped his head. "I'm okay," he muttered, walking quickly toward the stairs, as if he could make us believe we hadn't seen him.

"Warren!" cried my mother as she went after him. "*What happened?*"

Stunned at the sight of my brother, I remained still, feeling as though my muscles had begun to stiffen into rock, inch by inch, from the ground up. I heard their feet making their way quickly to the second floor. Then I heard Warren's door shut and my mother's fists on it. "Warren, honey, you need to tell me what happened to you!" she begged. "Please let me in!"

Still I couldn't move. *Mom,* I wanted to yell. *Leave him alone!* But I didn't. She couldn't see how embarrassed he was. How shocked and ashamed. All she could see was that her little boy had been hurt.

"Jenna!" my mother called from upstairs. I forced my feet to move. I walked more slowly than my mother, taking the stairs step by step, staring at the carpet that was as blue as the sky. When I reached the top, I looked at her agonized face. "Mom," I said firmly, my eyes widening instructively. I let my head bob in a slow, small nod. Then she covered her eyes with her hand, turned, and leaned her back against the wall.

Taking her place in front of the door, I spoke into its white wood. "Warren," I said, my hand on the knob. "It's me."

I waited for a moment for him to come. When he didn't, I swept my hand across the top of the door's trim. The straightened paper clip that I had always kept there was right where I'd left it. I stuck its end into the hole in the knob, released the lock, and opened the door. Warren was sitting on his bed, his feet flat on the floor and his elbows resting on his knees. He dabbed his bloody nose with his sleeve. He looked up at me, but said nothing.

I was always allowed in, even when no one else was.

· · ·

I drove while my mother sat in the backseat with Warren, her hand on his thigh. He was holding a washrag against his nose, his head leaning against the cool glass of the window. I thought of Rose. I thought of her standing at one of those big wide windows at the Waldorf, looking out onto New York, its lights looking like Christmas.

"Are you in pain?" Mom asked Warren quietly.

"I'm okay," he said, as he stared out the window, his mouth open slightly, from the swollen nose and heavy thoughts.

"Hey, Warren," I said. "Let me know if you get too hot."

I had the heat on high, and Warren was still wearing his thick Pizzeria Brava sweatshirt.

We rode in silence for a few more minutes before my mother asked almost hopefully, "Did this happen at work?" She tried to catch his eye, tried to evoke an answer, but Warren didn't move. "I remember when that one cook opened the pizza oven too fast," she said. "And knocked himself in the nose."

I turned up the radio just slightly, knowing that whatever had happened to Warren was not the work of a pizza oven. And as I stared out through the smooth, clear windshield, I remembered when Warren and I were eleven. He was shuttling an inchworm away from the peril of the Mt. Lewis School playground monkey bars over to the safety of the bushes. Scurrying with his shoulders hunched forward and hands cupped protectively around the worm, he passed a group of boys. I saw Seth Werlock's eyes become small before he casually, almost elegantly extended his leg. It met Warren's foot and Warren— who had been watching only the tiny green body in his care—flew forward, landing on his stomach, the inchworm disappearing into the grass. Warren turned his head to look at Seth, who looked away.

Acting on impulse, I yelled, "You stupid jerk!" and marched toward Seth and his friends.

"Hey!" called Mrs. Potchkit from the blacktop, alerted to the kerfuffle; Mrs. Potchkit was the lunch aide who everyone said rubbed Scope under her armpits.

I pointed at Seth. "He tripped my brother!" Warren was now on his feet and looking at me as if he wanted only for me to stop.

Seth scowled coolly at both of us. All I knew about Seth was that his mother worked at the local bar and his father lived in California and sent him postcards that he'd carry around until the white of the edges was soft and thick. "He fell," he said.

Mrs. Potchkit glanced from face to face. "If I have any more trouble with the three of you," she said, "you'll all be in the principal's office." Without acknowledging Mrs. Potchkit, Seth turned back to his friends. "Freak," he muttered, just loud enough so that Warren would hear, just quiet enough so that Mrs. Potchkit would not.

That was the first time I realized that the scale by which normal was judged changed as you grew older. That behavior that was quirky at seven would become odd at eleven. And that it wouldn't go unpunished.

There were a few more such incidents over the years. *Hey, Warren! Look! Maglons!* kids would shout in the hallways of our school. But by then, I had learned to pretend I didn't hear.

. . .

The silence in the car grew more complete as we approached the hospital. I turned smoothly into the entrance past an unchanging green light and across an empty street. The blacktop was freshly paved, the white lines in the parking lot crisp and new. I took a spot, then got out of the car, feeling awakened by the night air.

The hospital glowed bright through its sliding glass doors and I stared at the entrance as I waited for Warren to get out. But Warren just sat there, looking down at his knees. I felt my mother's eyes on me, so I leaned down. "War," I said, and that was all it took.

He unbuckled his seat belt. "I'm coming," he said, his lips barely moving.

Mom spoke for Warren as the tired-looking woman at a small wooden desk questioned him about his injuries. "He had an accident," she said. "We don't know the details." The woman continued to look at Warren, then pulled out a laminated chart with a series of cartoon faces in various degrees of distress.

"Point to the picture that shows how much you hurt," she said, her raspy New Jersey accent thick and unsympathetic.

Warren looked at her, then at the chart. He pointed to one of the faces in the middle. "Number four," he mumbled.

"All right," said the intake nurse. "Please have a seat. We'll call you."

When Warren's name echoed through the waiting room, we were brought to a curtained corral in the back of the emergency department. There was a chair beside the bed and on either side hung a thin cloth divider with pastel geometric shapes that I assumed were supposed to be soothing and stain resistant. There were two facing rows of beds in our area, and across from us, an elderly woman was moaning and delusional, saying that the doctors had taken her babies, that she wanted them back.

My mother looked deliberately away. "This is a horrible place," she whispered. My mother hated hospitals. She hated their brightness, their enormity. She hated that people went into them and didn't come out. Tonight, I could see why. I had been to the ER once with Rose when she was an infant and woke up with a cough so terrible, she wheezed and struggled for every breath. Then, we were taken directly to a private room. Here, we were in a stall.

A nurse rushed by. "Bed six," she said to someone I couldn't see. I heard a hushed, indiscernible conversation. Then a figure in a pair of scrubs that looked like a snatch of sky walked quickly toward the bed of the old woman across the aisle, lifted a clipboard from a hanger, and, after briefly consulting it, said calmly and kindly, "Mrs. Leroy, I'm Dr. Vanni."

Relief flooded my mother's face to meet the dread in mine. She looked from Warren to me and back again. *It's Bobby!* She was clearly relieved to have a doctor to whom our family would be familiar. Far more selfish, I sought the comfort of anonymity. I looked back at Warren, who was eyeing Bobby from below his brow, the rag still held to his nose.

After several minutes, Bobby turned away from the woman, whom he had calmed, and to the Parsons family—my mother, Warren, and me. His body stilled with recognition. "Amy," he called to a nurse, and gestured in our direction. She made a reply that we couldn't hear; then Bobby nodded. Giving a cordial but somber smile, he walked over to Warren's bed.

"Hi, Bobby," said my mother, with a sad smile. "Warren's . . . well, he's had an accident."

Bobby's eyes were already assessing my brother's wounds. "Warren," he said, almost to himself. "What happened to you?" Taking a pair of silicone gloves from a dispenser next to the bed, Bobby pulled them on. "Tell me if anything is too tender," he instructed, as he carefully led the hand that had been holding the dishrag away from Warren's face and lifted his chin.

Warren winced as Bobby's fingers lightly gripped the bridge of his nose. "We'll do an X-ray to make sure," Bobby said softly, "but that's broken."

"His nose?" gasped my mother.

"I don't think it needs to be reset," continued Bobby, ignoring my mother's interruption, not rudely but with professional focus.

Still not taking his eyes off Warren, he moved to the gash that intersected his eyebrow, competently probing it. After a few seconds he stopped, and I heard him exhale, then rub his rough chin with the back of his gloved hand. "You're going to need some stitches, Warren," he said. "All right?"

Warren met Bobby's eye and nodded. "Okay."

"We'll numb it up," said Bobby. "It won't hurt." He looked at my mother and me. "I'll be back in a few minutes to do the sutures." Then he disappeared past the cloth curtain.

No more than five minutes later, a nurse rolled up a metal tray. "You're lucky you got Dr. Vanni," she said, with the sort of admiration I imagined all the nurses felt for the handsome doctor. "He's the *best*."

When Bobby returned, he silently set to it, his face inches from Warren's as he made small, careful stitches. "When this heals, you'll hardly have a scar." My mother stood by the head of the bed near Bobby as he worked. I sat in a chair near Warren's feet. "Last one," I heard Bobby say, with a snap of the scissors. They made a small clatter as he placed them back on the metal tray, on which blood-soaked wads of gauze were scattered. Once his tools were back in place, he returned his attention to my brother. "Warren," he began, his voice low and calm. "Are you going to want to file a police report for this?"

Warren's brow immediately creased, as if the question were dangerous.

"Can he think about it?" I asked quickly, wanting to relieve my brother.

Bobby looked at me and nodded. "But with assault," he said, "it's best to involve the police as soon as possible."

My mother closed her eyes. I extended my hand. "Thank you, Bobby," I said, full of gratitude, and humbled by it. "Thank you so much."

Bobby clasped my hand, then brought his other up to meet it, so that my hand was between his two. Here, in the place of his work, what I might once have read as arrogance seemed like maturity. Perhaps the sort that was hard-won. "If you need anything, Jenna, just let me know."

We were given instructions about icing, painkillers, and potential problems against which to be vigilant. But really, Warren's injuries were not severe compared with many that the ER saw. It was their implication that was upsetting.

On the way out, Warren stopped to use the men's room and my mother and I hovered outside. With my hands stuck in my jacket pockets, I had that jet-lag-like sensation of not knowing to which time zone I belonged. At two o'clock in the morning, the interior of the hospital was as bright as day and my mind felt as though it were on a treadmill, with thoughts and memories coming unbidden.

I was sure that before tonight, Warren hadn't set foot in a hospital since Rose was born. Duncan had already been in Japan then; he didn't see Rose until she was three months old. But Warren came with my mother the very next day, in his Bill Cosby sweater and pleated khaki pants, ready to meet his niece.

Rose was swaddled tightly in a white, pink, and blue blanket. I was holding her in my arms, feeling how light she was, feeling that somehow in her, life had been distilled and concentrated down to its purest form. *What am I going to call you?* I whispered. Duncan and I hadn't settled on a name before he left, and his absence was as palpable as his presence might have been. *Huh, baby girl?* I rubbed my finger gently over the mark on her cheek and smiled. I didn't want her to see any tears so early in her life. *What's your name going to be?* It was then that I heard the squeak of Warren's sneakers on the brightly waxed floor of the hallway.

"I think it's right here," came my mother's voice from behind the shut door. There was a brief knock and the door opened before I could have voiced any protest, had I wanted to. My mother was holding Warren's upper arm and Warren was very still, looking at Rose from a distance with a guarded anticipation.

"Oh my goodness," gushed my mother. "Let me *see* her."

Warren hung back as Mom rushed the bed, her eyes immediately settling on Rose's birthmark. "Oh, it's not bad," she said, smiling softly. I had warned her on the phone about the birthmark. *It's called a hemangioma,* I had said, my lower lip quivering. *It's totally benign.*

"And I'm sure they can remove it if they need to," added Mom.

"They said it's small enough that it'll probably go away on its own." I smoothed a small lock of hair against her forehead. "But it might get a little bit bigger first."

It was then that Warren took a tentative step forward, leaning in to look at my baby's face while the lower half of his body remained a good three feet away. When he saw her, he seemed proud and pleased. "Hey," he laughed quietly, "she looks like a little rose."

A laugh sputtered from my lips. It was the first time I'd laughed since giving birth, and it loosened something in me, set something ajar, allowing emotions I had been trying to keep at bay to force their way up. I threw the crook of my elbow over my eyes and that laugh became a sob.

"Oh, Jenna," said my mother.

With my eyes still hidden, I shook my head, waiting until I could open my mouth without another cry escaping. "Maybe that'll be her name," I said, dropping my arm to look at my daughter. "Rose." It was the first of many decisions I would make without Duncan.

Warren's chest seemed to swell. "Rose," he repeated, as if the word felt strange but pleasant on his tongue. Then he stepped closer and leaned over her, his nose inches from hers. She made a face and moved her tongue against the roof of her mouth and Warren let out another quiet but expansive laugh.

"Hi, baby," he said, tapping his hand on the blanket above her belly. Then his face changed, softened slightly, as if he had to bravely break to his niece some difficult news. "You live in the world now," he said.

"Jenna," I heard my mother say softly, pulling me from my memory as we waited for Warren outside the men's room. Her eyes were fixed on an inconsequential point in the distance. "If you lived on Royal Court," she began, "and you didn't know us . . ." The question was coming slowly, like a twisty old creak. "What would you think of Warren and me?" She turned to look at me, her face full of knowing reluctance.

The house flashed into my mind, with its chipping trim and crumbling concrete steps; with the adult son who played with airplanes and was still living at home; with the mother who kept filling the house with more things.

"Oh, Mom," I said.

CHAPTER SIX

· · ·

Doll

1954

It was the first cold night of the winter and Priscilla lay in her bed listening to the gentle clanging of the radiator. Her eyes were shut tight, but sleep wouldn't come. Mrs. Lloyd always told her to talk to Jesus when she couldn't sleep. *Just tell him your troubles,* she would say. That evening before she left, Mrs. Lloyd had sat with her on her bed and sang "In the Sweet By and By." And Silla had sung with her. She had a pretty little voice.

Silla tried to talk to Jesus that night, but she couldn't think of what to say. She didn't know what was scaring her. She couldn't identify that it was some unnamed stirring in the world of adults that had upset her, only that things didn't seem right. The feeling was instinctual, like the way birds always seemed to know a storm was coming, the way they seemed to disappear from the sky half an hour or so before it grew dark with clouds. In the amorphous thing that was time to a four-year-old, Silla couldn't attach spans to the events of the past few weeks. She knew that her parents had gone away and come back, and gone away and come back again. She knew that her father had been spending more time at the house, pouring tall glasses of whiskey and sitting out on the front porch. She knew that her mother had seemed nervous, burning food and spilling things and staying in the bathroom for hours at a time. And that day, she had been walking around the house in circles. Just around and around the outside of the house.

Priscilla heard her door open. "Silla?" her mother whispered.

Priscilla opened her eyes to see her mother's face in the crack of the door, the hallway behind her as dark as the bedroom.

"Can Mama come in?"

Silla nodded and her mother, who was in her nightgown, came and curled up next to her on the bed, resting her head on her daughter's small stomach.

"Silla, they're going to try and fix me tomorrow."

Silla thought about this for a moment. "Are you broken?"

She heard her mother's soft breath. "I think so."

"Where?" asked Silla, looking down at her mother's hair, at her soft body. When things were broken, there were cracks and chips and fissures. Her mother looked perfect.

"I'm scared," said her mother.

Silla thought for a moment, twisting her fingers in one of her mother's curls. "Mrs. Lloyd says to talk to Jesus when you're scared."

Priscilla's mother pushed up with one hand, then the next, and looked at her daughter. "I don't want to go," she said, looking at Silla as if Silla might save her.

That unnamed fear surged up in Silla's stomach. "Are you coming back?"

Her mother nodded. And Silla felt the fear ebb. "Well," she said, reaching around for the doll that sat next to her on her nightstand. Her father had given it to her for her fourth birthday. She had round eyes with thick lashes, rosebud lips, and bright red hair. *She looks just like you,* he had said.

"Take Suzy," she said now, looking at the doll for a moment before holding it out for her mother. "She'll make you feel better."

• • •

CHAPTER SEVEN

Blue Pills

I sat on the cold edge of the tub and turned the water on, waiting for it to run hot before sticking the rubber stopper in the drain hole. It was an old claw-foot, with a green-tinged ring along the high-water line, and the beginnings of rust on the underside that no amount of cleaning would remove. The Nashes wouldn't be bringing Rosie back until midday, but after a few hours of heavy sleep, I had awoken at the usual time—six thirty a.m. That's when Rose always came bounding into my room, grasping a fistful of my white sheets and hauling herself onto the bed, her body vibrating with energy.

When there were a few inches of water at the bottom of the tub, I let my clothes drop to the floor and climbed in. Bracing myself for the shock, I leaned back, feeling the chill of the frigid enameled iron against my skin. It took a moment, but we were soon acclimated to each other, the tub and I. And I let my head nod back and my eyes close. I pictured Warren's face from the night before, the way he looked sitting on that hospital bed. And I thought of how Bobby had tended to him, gently assessing his wounds.

Looking at the dry, pink bar of soap in the dish, I reached for it, submerging it in the water, letting it become slick and quick, ready to slide from my grasp. I lifted my legs out of the water and looked at my long-neglected stubble. Reaching for the razor high up on the windowsill, I set to work. I was through with one leg when the phone rang. With a soapy hand, I grabbed the portable phone that I had placed on the closed toilet seat, in case the Nashes called. It was Maggie.

"How was your mom's?" she asked through a yawn. I heard her boys in the background.

Leaning back against the tub, I let my pink razor drop into the water and float there. Then I told her about Warren.

"Jesus," she said. "Is he going to be all right?"

"Yeah," I said. "I mean, physically, he's going to be fine."

Maggie heard the uncertainty in my voice. "But . . . ," she said, gently leading me to elaborate.

"But I guess it doesn't change that someone beat the shit out of him. If that's what even happened." With my free hand, I swished some of the suds out of the way to reveal the clear water beneath. "And we have no idea why."

After my bath, I sat myself down in front of my computer with the intention of getting some work done. But my mind veered continually off course until I heard the crunch of tires on our gravel driveway and rose to peer surreptitiously out the window. Miriam Nash stepped out of the passenger side of her husband's very British SUV and began unstrapping Rose from her booster seat.

"When you come to Connecticut," I heard her say, "you'll get to see your cousins Madison and Lincoln." Duncan's sister had subscribed to the convention of naming her progeny after dead presidents. "Would you like that?"

I waited, tucked out of sight, feeling disoriented by events of the previous night, and watched Miriam, whose silver bob was pushed back neatly by a headband, and Rose, whose chaotic red curls looked like tangled yarn.

Miriam took Rose's hand and led her up the stone path to the front steps of our tiny green gambrel cottage, which was once the residence of the caretaker to the large estate situated several hundred yards back. *Neat as a pin!* the ad had said. And despite its dated touches—the wood-paneled kitchen, the avocado-colored carpet—it was. The property was still criss-crossed with horse paddocks, though the Pritchards, from whom we rented, no longer rode or bred. Mrs. Pritchard's husband had suffered a punctured lung from a kick from a stallion, and after that, the stable had been sold off, animal by animal.

When the bell rang, I hung back for a moment, then strapped on a big, gracious smile. "Hi, you two," I said warmly as I opened the front door. Squatting down, I held out my arms and let Rose fly into them. "My girl," I said, holding the back of her head in my hand. "I missed you." With one of Rose's hands in mine, I stood. "Did you guys have a fun night?" I asked, looking from Rose to Miriam and back to Rose again.

"Yeah," answered Rose casually, as she walked past me into

our home, letting her backpack slide off her back, "I got to have waffles for dinner."

Miriam's gaze followed Rose inside the house, where she was riffling through a bag full of grandparent-acquired booty. Rose loved to gather trinkets, to collect coins and wrappers and ribbons. She was always bereft when I insisted on throwing any of it away. It made me worry that she had some of my mother's nature, that one day she would find herself a captive of it. "It'll be good for Rose," said Miriam, her head tilted affectionately, "to have her daddy back in the States."

"Yeah," I said, "she was just asking about when she would see him again."

Miriam let out a noise that signified her profound relief. "I'm *so glad* they're bringing him back to New York."

From the inside out, I felt myself stiffen. "You mean for the holidays?" I asked.

Miriam met my eye, her expression echoing the confusion in my own. "Well, he'll be back in time for Christmas," she explained, with a gentle smile. "But he's moving back to the States. He's done in Tokyo."

"Oh," I said, as if I were pleased, "that's great!"

Miriam's face twisted just a touch, as if she found my ignorance troubling. "I'm sure he'll be calling you about it soon."

"Oh," I said lightly, brushing away the slight, "I'm sure he will."

Miriam nodded. "When we spoke to him," she started cautiously, "we mentioned how nice it would be to have Rose come and spend Christmas with us up in Connecticut." My hand darted up to my chest and I began worrying my necklace, a single hammered gold disk with the letter *R* carved into it. It had been a gift from my mother. *And Warren,* the card had said. "It would give her a chance to get to know her cousins," Miriam explained. "And of course she hasn't seen Duncan very often over the past four years either."

I tried to smile. "I'm sure we can figure something out."

Despite his flaws, or perhaps in some cases because of them, everyone loved Duncan. When Duncan walked into a room, glasses were raised. "You're Duncan Nash's girlfriend?" people used to ask, and I'd proudly say that I was. When we first met, I was bartending to keep financially afloat after a round of layoffs at an ad agency I had worked for in New York. Duncan had an apprenticeship with a renowned English chef with a French name who was known equally for his skill and his vitriol. Duncan and some of the kitchen staff used to come into the bar to lick their wounds after their nights at the restaurant. They drained their drinks and admired their scars and mocked the chef whom they both revered and feared. Duncan did the best impersonation. "Motherfucking-cocksucking-stupid-American-cunt!" Duncan would quote in his best approximation of a British accent, his words sounding like a drumroll. I would listen and laugh with the rest of them, and Duncan would smile at me.

Then one night, I walked out of the bar to find Duncan waiting for me. He was leaning against a telephone booth with his arms crossed over his chest and smiling, like ours was going to be a romance from a movie. And for a while, it was.

Duncan was the first man besides my father to tell me that I was beautiful. He had snuck us into the pool at a posh hotel and as I came up for air after diving in after him, our whispers and giggles echoed around the dark room. I dipped my head back to let the water slide off my hair and I looked at him, only my head visible as my limbs circled under the surface that twinkled with the city's lights.

"You know you're beautiful," he said casually, the words hanging between us until his hand skimmed the water, playfully sending a small spray into my face.

When my father used to say those words, my mother would scold him. "Don't tell her that," I'd hear her whisper. "She's so much more than that." To my mother, beauty was a junk currency, one that lost its value almost as soon as you had finished counting it.

When she was younger, I understood that my mother's beauty was something to behold. "I was the first redhead to win Miss Texas," she used to say proudly. "They were all blondes and brunettes before me." One of the pictures still displayed on the wall by the stairs at 62 Royal Court was of my mother wearing her crown and holding an armful of flowers, her sash proudly announcing her new title. Her hair hung past her shoulders in thick, smooth curves and she had full, ripe cheeks that bespoke youth and health, and the ephemeral nature of both.

When Duncan told me that I was beautiful, it didn't come as a warning or a caution, but the most charming type of appreciation. Duncan was unconditionally charming. But the problem with a charming man is that everyone finds him so. And after several years, I started to notice something else, another ingredient that diluted the admiration with which people would ask if I was Duncan Nash's girlfriend. It would take me years and a few very unpleasant discoveries to realize that it was pity.

Then came the series of humiliating, tear-streaked arguments and the sort of theatrical relationship that plays well on television and in the movies, but not in real life. Like most women, I eventually realized that love is supposed to be quiet, not loud. It's supposed to make you feel whole, not broken. And like most women, I had to find this out the hard way.

When I became pregnant with Rose, my relationship with Duncan was in its death throes. We said that we were "taking a break," which is what men say when they'd like the option of possibly having sex a few more times, and what women say when they're having trouble accepting reality. And that's just what happened. I had stopped taking my birth control pills and hadn't seen Duncan in five weeks when the doorbell to my apartment sounded. Then the man who knew exactly the sorts of words I wanted to hear came in and said them.

The day I missed my period—before I even took the test—I understood that I was pregnant. And the knowledge felt like a cold, deep spring inside me. Once and only once did I have sex without protection. But sometimes fortune favors the reckless. Because in the end, I got Rose.

Three days later, finally ready to confirm what I already knew, I sat in the bathroom staring at two pink lines for a very long time—until my roommate pounded on the door. *Jenna, are you okay?* I told her that I was and I picked myself up and I opened the door and squeezed past her on my way to the kitchen, where I drank one glass of milk, and then another. The next day I went to my mother's house for our birthday and Warren looked at me as I was picking up bunches of discarded wrapping paper, his head tilted, his eyes searching. My mother was bringing the leftover cake to the spare refrigerator in the garage.

"What?" I asked impatiently.

Warren seemed to read my face and then his eyes widened almost infinitesimally. Something unspoken was exchanged between us, and I looked away, ashamed. What sort of woman would let this happen? I felt like a stupid teenager, accidently getting pregnant. Squatting down, I reached under the table for a shiny blue gift-wrap bow and I felt Warren crouch next to me. "Don't worry, Jenna," he said, his face as serious and grave as it ever got. "Warren will help you." He reached for a scrap of wrapping paper and put it in the garbage bag that hung from the back of one of the kitchen chairs. I felt him hesitate before lightly resting his hand on my back.

I folded forward as tears sprang from my eyes. Then, hearing our mother's voice call for someone to bring out the lasagna, I began wiping my face furiously, blotting it with the sleeve of my shirt. "Don't tell Mom, okay?" I asked, standing quickly as I grabbed the tray of lasagna and brought it to the garage.

In no small way, Warren was why I had Rose. For nine months, Warren and I had formed next to each other, cells dividing to become hearts and eyes and fingers. We had breathed each other in and out, more alike than different.

And then we were born.

As I grew, I developed a knowledge of the customs and norms and taboos that govern us, that tell us what to say and how to act and who to be. Knowledge that was added in layers, in strata, until I became a fully formed adult. And the further away from childhood I moved, the more I realized how poorly equipped Warren was, how naked. So when I became pregnant, I felt as if some cosmic die had been cast, and it was time to find out if what made Warren Warren was inside of me as well. It was time to find out if some penalty was to be exacted for my getting to be the normal one. I didn't think most people would understand that. In retrospect, I'm not sure I did.

Duncan, for his part, took the news stoically. We made one last attempt to become the couple we never could quite figure out how to be. For me, the effort was as compulsive and impossible as forcing together two magnets with like charges. I moved into his apartment; we talked about baby names; he went with me to doctors' appointments. When he wasn't in the restaurant and I wasn't at the agency, we'd take walks around the city. Through it all, he seemed like a barely domesticated animal whose true nature hadn't been entirely bred out of him. He'd sit silently, his mind miles and miles away.

Then one Saturday morning as I sat on the floor folding laundry, my belly spilling out over my lap, he came out of the tiny bedroom and settled on the coffee table next to me.

"Shep says they're opening a location in Tokyo." The sentence took too long to come out; I should have noticed that.

"That's cool," I said as I snapped a white T-shirt in front of me. "Maybe you'll get to go check it out."

The thick silence that followed made my hands, still holding the half-folded shirt, sink slowly down. "What?" I asked.

"They actually want me to run it."

The impossibility of such a monumental move overwhelmed me. "Duncan," I said, gesturing to my swollen stomach, "I can't move to Japan right now."

And from the expression on his face, I realized that wasn't what he was asking.

CHAPTER EIGHT

. . .

Maglons

Pressing the button on the lower left side of the screen, I shut off my monitor and lifted my laptop from its docking station.

"You taking off?" asked Maggie, casting her eyes at me from over one of her thin shoulders. Despite her birdlike frame and Catholic-school upbringing, Maggie used to be the type of girl who would get into fights, pulling hair and pressing nails into skin like a ferocious little mink. She referred to it as her "Bitch-Stole-My-Man" era, a fact I was occasionally reminded of by the suddenness of her motions.

I startled slightly. "Yeah," I said, zipping my laptop into its case. "I need to make a couple of stops before I grab Rose." Standing, I slung the bag over my shoulder. "We're going to head over to my mom's. See how Warren's doing."

"Tell him I hope he feels better." Maggie had met Warren only once, at Rose's third birthday party. I had warned her in advance that Warren was different, and I saw her discreetly watching him over the course of the afternoon, her dark eyes finding him as he hung back, away from the frenzy of cake and presents and balloons.

After my mother and Warren had left, when Maggie and I were in the kitchen shoving frosting-covered paper plates into the garbage, she said with her trademark frankness, "You know your brother's not just weird, right?"

I turned another plate out into the trash, pressing hard against its white underside with my palm to compress what was beneath it. Looking at the strata of belly-up plates, I took a small breath. "What do you mean?" I asked, though I was fairly certain I knew.

"I mean, he's probably on the Spectrum."

The *Spectrum*.

I rubbed the back of my hand hard against my forehead, then flipped on the faucet. "Yeah," I said. "Probably."

"Did your parents ever have him evaluated?"

"I don't know, Mags. I think it was different when we were all growing up," I said tersely, dumping the dregs of coffee from the bottom of the pot into the sink, watching the clear water wash away the muddy brown. "I know he saw some doctors," I conceded. "I don't know much more than that." In truth, I could replay every word of those tense conversations between my parents. I'd be lying still in bed, listening, praying that Warren was already asleep. *I don't know why you see our son as a problem that needs to be fixed,* my mother would say. But Warren didn't fit easily into any preexisting boxes, at least not any that were around when we were in high school. And after we graduated, Warren slipped out of the purview of those with the ability and will to find one.

Maggie leaned against the counter, her arms crossed in front of her as she rolled around a thought. "He totally reminds me of Lenny Martels," she said. Then she looked at me, realizing the statement needed explanation. "He was a kid I went to high school with."

Shutting off the water, I placed the coffeepot in the drying rack. "Every high school had a Lenny Martels," I said. "Ours was my brother."

Turning onto Royal Court, I saw a new real estate sign on the lawn of another home in the neighborhood with Lydia's smiling face and sharp-looking white teeth. *Jesus,* I thought. *If she was such a good Realtor, wouldn't she have sold a couple of these by now?* Though King's Knoll was one of the more affordable neighborhoods in Harwick, the glut of homes on the market had made buyers picky. And as I drove down the stretch of road to my mother's house, I counted four that were currently for sale, two of which were listed by Lydia. They all seemed to have freshly painted trim and porches graced with mums and pumpkins and big sun-bleached stalks of harvest corn. Their lawns were raked and their walkways swept and the brass of their doorknobs gleamed. They were all gussied up, as if King's Knoll were a singles bar. In that metaphor, I supposed my mother's house was the old lady at the end, in blue eye shadow and fishnet stockings, the one who'd rinse her dentures in the gin and tonic before telling you about the time she danced with Frank Sinatra, about what a looker she used to be.

As if to prove my own uncharitable point, I stared down the end of the street toward 62 Royal Court. At first, all I noticed was that something was very different. I found myself leaning forward, squinting toward what my mind read as a great collective absence as the car drew closer. My eye moving from void to void, I saw that the garden globes and lawn flags were all gone, the grass barren and brown beneath the spots where they had stood. On the porch, there were a few decorations—an autumnal wreath on the door, stone bunnies on the steps—but the bulk of my mother's things had vanished. *My God,* I thought. *Where'd it all go?* I was craning my neck in an attempt to gain a better vantage point when I caught sight of her, suddenly visible in the far corner of the backyard. Mom's hair was pulled back in a kerchief, she wore her maroon parka, and she was swinging a weed whacker, leaning back against its power as she annihilated unruly patches of turf.

I pulled up in the driveway and shut off the ignition, still watching her.

"What's Nana doing?" asked Rose from the backseat.

I waited a moment before answering. "It looks like she's cleaning up," I said, then opened my car door.

I moved to unstrap Rose, keeping my eyes on my mother, who had yet to look in our direction.

Rose and I padded together over the grass, which had begun to yellow with the cold nights. "Mom!" I called, though she couldn't hear me over the din of the motor. She was making wide sweeps, her face determined and eyes focused, like a child with a sword too powerful to wield. *"Mom!"* I called more loudly, my approach feeling oddly tentative.

Finally she swung around, aiming for the patch of foot-high grass that had circled a statue of Saint Francis of Assisi, and caught sight of us. Her surprise sliding into acknowledgment, she shut off the weed whacker and rested its bottom portion on the ground. "Hey, you two," she said, as she tried to smile, tried to catch her breath. "What are you doing here?" She didn't sound displeased to see us, but an underlying anxiety lined her face and rounded her shoulders.

I tilted my head toward the house. "We came to see how Warren's doing," I said. My face was expectant as I waited for her to explain the clearing of the yard, but she just smiled gently. "He'll be so happy to see you." Then she moved, preparing to go back to work.

"Mom," I said, resting my hand on her arm. She looked at me with her shocking green eyes, looking as if she feared the question that I hadn't yet asked. "Did you get rid of some stuff?"

She took a deep breath, her words drifting out the other end of it. "Yeah . . . I figured . . . It was time to clean up a little bit," she said, her gaze moving around the neighborhood as she smoothed down her kerchief. In it, she looked like a relic from a different time—when women rubbed their husbands' feet and got vacuum cleaners for Christmas and dreamed of being beauty queens.

Noticing my mother's eyes catch on something behind me, I turned to see Mr. Kotch on his bicycle passing along the street in front of our house, moving as silently as a ghost in the dim, clouded daylight. He was a slight man, with pale skin that seemed sapped of blood. His eyes didn't move from our house.

"What's he doing?" I asked. There was something disconcerting about his attention.

My mother looked unsettled by it as well, though she offered him a wave, which he returned with a single lifted hand. "He's been doing a lot of biking," she said, her face still tense. "In the neighborhood."

We both watched him pedal up the street until he turned onto Squire Lane. "You know, they're talking about reopening the quarry."

"Oh, God," I said. Bill and Carol Kotch's son Danny had been a year ahead of Warren and me, part of Bobby's graduating class. A week before he was to leave for college, he died after jumping into the quarry located past the woods behind the park. Bobby had been there. Since then, the quarry was sacrosanct. No one mentioned it, let alone discussed making it operational.

"I know," said Mom, shaking her head, her focus shifting back to the lawn equipment in her hands. "It's terrible."

"Here," I said, reaching for the weed whacker, "why don't you let me do this."

Mom swatted away my offer. "I've only got a little more left," she said. "You just go see your brother." She glanced at Rose, then squatted down so that they were nearly eye to eye. "You know your uncle Warren had an accident, right, honey?" she said, nodding as she spoke. She clearly wanted Rose to be prepared for the state of Warren's face.

"Yeah," answered Rose, "Mom said he's all like"—her

fingers swirled around her face—"*purple*." Rose clearly thought purple was a strange but fabulous color to be.

Pulling Rose into her arms, my mother buried Rose's face against her chest. "You are just the sweetest thing."

"Has he told you anything?" I asked. "About what happened?"

My mother looked up and shook her head.

Rose and I started toward the house while Mom went back to her weed whacking, as singular in her attention as before. Uncomfortable with what we did and didn't know about what had happened, I wondered if it was such a good idea to bring Rose after all—welcoming her into the house that sometimes seemed as if it could swallow you up. As we neared the front porch, I heard the steady build of an engine's motor, and looked toward the street to see the mail truck pull away; it always came late to Royal Court.

"Come on," I said to Rose. "Let's bring Nana's mail in for her." Rose found the efforts of the United States Postal Service thrilling and we made a ritual of getting the mail together at home. Her eyes would widen in delighted surprise as we opened the box and—lo and behold—it contained mail.

I slid out what appeared to be a large stack of bills atop an even larger stack of catalogues. "Can I carry it?" asked Rose, reaching and bouncing on her toes. I looked down at the top envelope, which bore the MasterCard logo. I sometimes worried about my mother's finances, as her job at the department store couldn't be very lucrative, particularly when you factored in the temptation of her employee's discount. But her house was paid off, and though she never discussed it in detail, my father's father had left her a sizable sum when he had died, a fact that hadn't sat well with my father or especially Lydia. Warren contributed, too, giving my mother any income that he didn't spend on his planes.

"Hold it like this," I said, helping Rose curl the stack against her chest. We began walking toward the house and Rose regarded her charge seriously, looking down at the mail instead of in front of her. "Careful, monkey."

I pushed open the front door. Rose stepped in before me. "It's us!" she called.

"Uncle Warren is probably in his room," I said. I was about to suggest that she wait in the kitchen while I went to check on him, but Rose had dropped the mail at her feet and was already bounding up the stairs.

"Uncle Warren!" she called. Getting to his door before I could, she swung it open and stepped right in. "Uncle *Warren,*" I heard her say, a sympathetic scolding. "I thought you were supposed to be purple."

The upstairs of 62 Royal Court was still wallpapered with the same blue floral pattern that had been there since we were children, and was still illuminated by the brass and etched-glass lighting fixtures. My old room had been turned into a guest room that was making the slow slip toward storage closet, but Warren's bedroom was still Warren's bedroom.

The walls were painted navy blue and his bed was neatly made with a forest green plaid comforter. There were still some posters from our childhood on the walls—a faded print of the solar system, and one of deep-sea fish with crafty lantern lures hanging in front of their jaws. On his bookshelf were rows of *National Geographic* in chronological order, their yellow spines lined up tidily. Our grandfather had given Warren his first copy when we were nine and had renewed the subscription each year for his birthday until he died when we were eighteen. Now the magazines were a gift from my mother. *And Jenna,* she'd always write. And arranged on his dresser and perched on the shelf of his closet, each angled just so, in their bright, candy-slick colors, were his planes. He built them himself and there were rarely fewer than a dozen. They weren't replicas or models; they were original flying machines, conceived of and designed in my brother's own mind.

I leaned against the doorframe. Warren was sitting upright on his bed, his feet resting on the floor in front of him. The bridge of his nose was swollen, and the tender crescents of skin beneath his eyes looked as though they'd been swept with purple. The wound that started at his forehead and intersected his brow was slick with ointment and pink where the stitches met. But all traces of blood were gone, and Warren appeared almost childlike, his hair light and clean, his skin freshly washed. He was looking at Rose, a curious smile on his battered face.

"How you doing, War?" I asked.

Warren ignored me, his attention focused on Rose, whose nose was crinkled with confusion and concern as she took in his injuries. "Did you fall off the swings?" she asked.

Warren's eyebrows drew together, and he gave a reluctant chuckle. "No," he answered, his hands at his sides and pressing on the mattress beneath him.

"Then what happened?" she asked, her voice a squeak.

Warren paused. "Maglons," he said. *Maglons.* Hearing the word was like time travel.

"What's a Maglon?" asked Rose, her stare darting between Warren and me.

"A bad guy," I said, the phrase drifting from my lips.

"Oh, I've got those in my class at school," said Rose, like she could tell us a thing or two about Maglons.

Warren gave Rose a playfully skeptical expression. "You have Maglons?" he asked.

"Yeah," said Rose, meandering over to one of Warren's planes, fingering its functioning door. "Tucker is the *biggest* Maglon ever."

"Hey," came Mom's voice from downstairs in the foyer. I hadn't noticed that the buzz of the weed whacker no longer sounded from the backyard. "Who left this mail here?"

"Oh," I called back, making my way back out to the hallway, my arms crossed over my chest, "we grabbed it on the way in." I leaned over the banister. "Rosie dropped it." Mom was bent over, quickly gathering it up, ignoring the catalogues but looking carefully at each envelope before putting it back into the pile. "Sorry, Mom."

"And this is everything?" she asked, not looking up. There was an edge to her voice.

"I think so," I said.

I watched her sift through the stack again; then, finally satisfied, she pushed herself up and briefly met my eyes. "Can you ask Warren if he wants a snack?"

Five minutes later, Rose and Warren were seated at the kitchen table, eating pistachios; my mother stood at the window, reading the instructions for a new electric sink buffer ("It says it removes surface stains *and* bacteria"); and I was leaning against the glass doors to the deck, flipping through e-mails on my phone and paying loose attention to the conversation.

Warren was explaining to Rose the physics of opening a

stubborn pistachio shell. "You just slide another shell into the crack," he said, as he demonstrated his method for using the leverage of a discarded shell. "And twist." And though his lesson fell on largely deaf ears, Warren seemed to appreciate being in the presence of someone who thought his face might look the way it did due to a fall from a swing. "Another," commanded Rose, still chewing, her palm outstretched.

"Can I have another, *please*," I corrected.

My mother plugged the electric sink buffer into the socket and squeezed in a generous dose of the complimentary cleansing gel. "It says to make sure the water is *off*," she said softly and to no one in particular before pressing a button and bringing the buffer to life.

She was thoroughly engaged in her task when the doorbell sounded. Warren made no outward acknowledgment, but his body stilled, as if to devote all his physical resources to the sense of hearing. I looked at my mother, who glanced back at me with what appeared to be an oversized electric toothbrush humming in her hands. *Who could that be?*

"I'll get it," I said with a sigh. I pushed away from the door and, sliding past Warren and Rose, made my way into the foyer. I expected UPS or maybe some lucky sap selling Omaha Steaks door-to-door. In short, I expected anybody but Bobby Vanni standing there holding a tinfoil-covered casserole dish.

"Bobby!" I said. Immediately, my mother's house and its things, the things I had begun not to see, sped to the foreground of my mind.

He looked at me for a moment before the corner of his mouth lifted into a smile. "Hey, Jenna."

"What's going on?"

"I came by to check on Warren." My eyes flitted down to the casserole dish in his hands. His followed. "My, uh . . . my mom wanted me to bring this."

My face warmed. There was something dear about Dr. Robert Vanni running around the neighborhood delivering his mother's baked ziti.

Bobby dropped his chin with a low, hushed laugh. And for just that split second, there was nowhere I'd rather be than standing at the front door of my mother's house.

"Bobby!" I heard my mother call from behind me. Clearly, since tending to Warren, Bobby had taken on hero status at 62 Royal Court. "You are so sweet to come. And, oh!" She had caught sight of the ziti; her hand was over her heart.

"It's from my mother," explained Bobby.

Mom looked at me as if to corroborate the goodness of the Vannis. "Bless her heart," she said softly.

For an awkward moment, the three of us stood in silence until Mom scooped the air in front of her toward her chest, beckoning Bobby forward. "Why don't you come in?" she suggested.

"Thanks," he said, stepping over the threshold. "I won't stay long." He looked at me, his eyes kind and knowing. "I'd just like to say hello to Warren."

Mom took a breath and smiled her pageant smile—it was her armor, her protection; her defense against judgment of any kind. "Aren't you sweet?" she said. And she led Bobby back to the kitchen.

"Here," I said, reaching for the casserole dish as he passed, "let me take that for you."

"Warren!" called my mother, in the June Cleaver voice that

she used only to address Warren while in the presence of company. "Bobby's here to see you!"

Bobby walked into the kitchen and I followed. "Hey, Warren," he said, as he approached my brother without hesitation, rounding the counter and already assessing his recovery. "Let's see how this is doing." Bending toward him, he swept his gaze over Warren's face, clinically, professionally.

Warren gave me a look from the corner of his eye, determined to hide his smile—to at least *seem* as though he minded the attention—as Bobby continued his inspection.

"This is looking good," said Bobby, focusing on the gash, on its spidery closures. Then he moved to Warren's nose. "You'll have some bruising for a while." His voice was low, as if the conversation was between only him and his patient.

"Hey," said Rose, her legs kicking playfully under the counter. "What's your name?"

He seemed to consider it for a moment. "Bobby," he answered. "I'm Gabby's daddy. I heard you guys had fun playing together at the block party."

Rose's eyes widened and she adopted the look of a hungry puppy. "Can Gabby and I have a playdate?" she asked.

"Rosie," I said, not wanting to seem presumptuous or eager or any of those things you weren't supposed to be when setting up any kind of date—play or otherwise.

Bobby chuckled. *"Actually,"* he answered, a temptation dangling on the tip of the word. He looked outside toward the park, then back at Rose, prolonging the anticipation. "I was just going to take Gabby to the playground." Rose's eyes widened in delight. "Do you think you and your mom would want to come, too?"

Rose scrambled down from her stool. "Yeah, yeah, yeah!" she said, nodding with her whole body. She turned to me. "Mom!" she said—a single word that had the capacity to be both a command and a plea. "Can we go?"

"Ummm, yeah . . . ," I said, my daughter's joy my own. "I think we can."

Then I glanced up at my mother. She was looking at Rose. And though she was smiling softly, her face was tensed in the way of those who have long endured pain so constant, they are no longer even aware of it. She was just about Rose's age, I realized, when her own mother died.

CHAPTER NINE

. . .

Jewelry Box

1954

At five years old, Silla sometimes still took a nap, settling down in the middle of the day to let her thick black eyelashes crisscross over one another, like delicate little briars. Consequently, she had trouble telling the days apart, not knowing when one ended and the next began. So she didn't know how long her parents had been gone. Only that it seemed like quite a while.

Her father had made arrangements for his parents to come and stay with her. She had met them only a few times before. They arrived with shabby suitcases and eyes that scanned the room, looking from object to object, possession to possession. Her grandmother picked up a vase that her father had always described as "oriental" and turned it over as if checking for a price tag. Her grandfather made his way to the living room and switched on the television, letting out a long, low whistle as the image appeared on the screen. They didn't speak much to Silla. Her grandmother made her ham and cheese sandwiches and told her when it was time to take a bath or go to bed. Her grandfather sat in her father's chair, watching her father's television. Her grandmother slept in her mother's room. Her grandfather slept in the guest room. And every once in a while, when Silla's small feet would move over the floor without enough sound to be noticed, she'd hear them talking. She heard them talking about what a damn shame it all was, about what a damn fool Lee had always been. But mostly, she heard them talking about what was going to happen to all her mother's damn money. *He could wind up without a cent!*

During the days, Mrs. Lloyd would come as she always had, and Silla would sit on the back steps while Mrs. Lloyd snapped laundry and set it on the line, squinting as she held the clothespins between her lips. She told Silla Bible stories, and Silla's favorite was the story of Daniel, who was cast into a den of lions as a punishment for his prayers. "But the Lord sent down angels," Mrs. Lloyd would say as she reached down into the basket full of damp clothes, "that came and shut the lions' mouths tight." And Silla would lift the toes of her saddle shoes up off the dirt, her hands holding her skirt over her knees, quietly delighted by the idea of beautiful winged angels that could subjugate mighty, ravenous lions.

A few times, Silla asked Mrs. Lloyd, "When is my mama going to come home?" And she would see Mrs. Lloyd's whole body seem to sink a bit, as if she were bearing an enormous burden. "Well . . ." was all she'd say, as she pinned up the end of

SARAH HEALY

a billowy white sheet, her thin body struggling against its weight. It was a long sigh of a word. *Well.* After a few moments she'd speak again. "Has anyone ever told you about the time that Jesus helped a blind man to see?"

Mrs. Lloyd was telling Silla the story—about the mud that Jesus mixed up and put on the blind man's eyes—when Silla heard a car roaring down the driveway, kicking up huge clouds of dry dust into the bright blue sky. She leapt up and ran around the side of their brick house to see her father's Cadillac come to a stop next to it. But her mother wasn't in the passenger seat. Silla lifted up to the tips of her toes, as if that additional inch might help her see something she had missed. Her father got out of the car and stood looking at her with his hands on his hips. On his face, he was wearing an expression that she supposed was intended to be a smile. "How's my Silla?" he finally called to her. But Silla didn't move, sensing something, some great culmination. "Come here, my girl," he said, clapping his hands together, his voice as sweet and as empty as sugar water.

Silla looked back at Mrs. Lloyd, who was purposefully minding her business by remaining focused on the basket of laundry in front of her; then Silla began walking slowly toward her father. As soon as she was within arm's distance, Lee Harris reached for her hand and pulled her close to him, bending down so that they were eye to eye. "Your daddy missed you," he said, gently pinching her nose.

But Silla's face was solemn. "Where's Mama?" she asked.

Lines formed across Lee's forehead. He looked like he was about to say something—then he suddenly straightened, lifting one finger. "Hold on, sugar," he said, opening the car door and reaching in. He pulled out a pink, rectangular box and squatted down in front of Silla. Holding the box to face her, he lifted its lid. Tinny, trilling music began playing instantly and a tiny ballerina began whirling and twirling in front of an oval mirror. Silla watched it, mesmerized. "It's for your jewelry, honey," he said softly, close enough that she could feel the warmth of his breath, which smelled faintly of drink. And while she was watching the small figure spin and spin in perfect, consistent circles, she heard her father say, "Silla, honey . . ." He hesitated, but her eyes remained on the ballerina, remained focused on her dancing. Until, that is, she heard him say, "Your mama's gone." Her eyes snapped to his and he nodded once. "She's gone."

. . .

CHAPTER TEN

The Big Hill

Rose and I stood on top of the Big Hill in the park, just above the pond in which Warren and I used to catch tadpoles and turtles, putting them in big plastic pitchers until Warren, his face creased with worry, insisted that we set them free. The pond was only five or six feet deep, so it always froze quickly, and on Christmas Eve the fathers would take the kids ice-skating while the mothers made dinner. Mr. Vanni would bring a thermos full of Irish coffee and the men would stand shoulder to shoulder, letting the whiskey warm their bellies, while we scrambled around on the slick ice, until our wool mittens were soggy and the knees of our jeans damp. Then our mothers' voices would call us inside, where we'd slip into hot baths, giddy and delirious with the wonder of what might await us in the morning.

After leaving my mother's house, Bobby had said that he and Gabby would meet us in the park in ten minutes, though it felt like it had already been fifteen. *I'll just go and grab Gabs,* he had said.

"Uncle Warren and I used to go ice-skating on that pond," I said to Rose, trying to keep her mind off the waiting and off the wind, which had begun to pick up.

"What's ice-skating?" asked Rose.

Anytime Rose was unfamiliar with something as common as ice-skating, I felt a stab of inadequacy. "Oh, Rosie. It's the most fun thing. You wait until the pond turns all to ice. Then you put on special shoes and go sliding around on it."

Rose smiled, almost with nostalgia for a pastime she had never experienced; then she turned back toward the Vannis' house just as Bobby and Gabby were exiting the back door. "Hey!" said Rose, pointing. "There they are!" She bounced onto her toes. "Hey, Gabby!" she called, though they were still too far away to hear. I hadn't realized how much she had enjoyed playing with Bobby's daughter at the block party.

Bobby bent down and said something in his daughter's ear, a permission likely, because Gabby came bounding toward Rose and me, her long, dark hair waving like a flag behind her. Rose rushed to meet her, leaving Bobby and me walking slowly behind our daughters and toward each other.

"Sorry," he said, closing one eye against the low, late-afternoon sun. "My mom's going out tonight and she needed to give me explicit instructions about reheating dinner." He seemed to find Linda's mothering amusing, if a bit overbearing.

"I bet," I said with a smile. "She always did like feeding you guys." Mrs. Vanni was a fusser. She fussed over Bobby and his sister. She fussed over her husband. And now she fussed over

Gabby, probably baking cookies for her class and setting up elaborate tea parties for her stuffed animals. My mother loved Rose. I knew that. But her heart was tethered elsewhere. *Hey, Mom,* I had said on the phone soon after Rose had started pre-school, *Rose's school is having this Grandparents' Day thing next Tuesday....* I remember the silence on the line. *Well, what about Warren?* she finally said. *Tuesday's his day off and I was going to go with him to get his haircut.*

Bobby glanced back at his mother's house. "It has its moments," he said, a nod to the fact that living with his mother at the age of thirty-six was not exactly what he'd had in mind. "But honestly, she's great," he added, "at helping with Gabs." I thought about Bobby's wife, Mia. What could make a woman leave a man like Bobby? What could make her leave her daughter? Wasn't it always the men who left?

Gabby and Rose had already headed off together toward the jungle gym, and Bobby and I followed.

"Hey," I began, feeling the rhythm of our steps, hoping it would, beat by beat, bring the right words to my lips. "I want to thank you ... for everything with Warren."

From the corner of my eye, I studied Bobby; he was focused on the girls, on their excited shrieks and squeals as they whipped down the slide. "I'm glad I was there," he offered. We came to the line where the grass met the wood-chip-covered playground floor and stopped—the demarcation between the land of adults and the realm of children. "Did he end up going to the police?" he asked.

I crossed my arms over my chest, not knowing how to explain that we didn't have the ability to make Warren do anything: not go to the police, not tell us who had hurt him.

"No," I said. "He hasn't even really told us what happened." I stared out at the line of woods past the park, at the colored leaves on the trees, which every fall seemed less vivid than I had remembered. It was wrong, what everyone said about memories. They didn't fade. They became sharper—brighter and more concentrated—making the present look diluted and thin in comparison. "So you think that's what it was?" I asked, dreading his answer. "Assault?"

"You never know, but . . ." Bobby's head dropped slightly, and I realized that he would never be the type of doctor who was comfortable delivering bad news. "I'd say so."

A burst of wind came, sent a strand of my hair across my face. I hooked it back behind my ear and nodded. *That's what I thought.*

Bobby might have said more. Or maybe I would have. We might have talked about the thefts, and now this trouble with Warren, and how we couldn't believe that things like this were happening in Harwick. But Rose called for me from the swings. "Can you push us?"

As we went to the girls, Bobby nodded toward the seesaws. "Do you remember the old wooden ones they used to have when we were little?" he asked. Like many things from our childhood, the old seesaws had been replaced with safety-tested plastic versions.

"Yeah," I said, smiling. Warren used to walk across them, seeking the spot in the middle where both sides were elevated equally off the ground. When he found it, he'd hold there for as long as he could, his arms and legs straining.

In the parking lot on the other side of the playground, I saw Mr. Kotch glide by on his bike, the wheels spinning as he looked at Bobby and me. Bobby gave him a wave. "Hey, Bill!" he called. Mr. Kotch nodded back as he began to make a U-turn, his lips forming a small smile that was covered by his thick mustache. I imagined that it must be difficult for Mr. Kotch, seeing Bobby and me grown and with children of our own.

"Mom says he's been riding his bike around the neighborhood a lot lately," I said.

Bobby squinted after him. "I think it has something to do with the neighborhood watch. I guess they have a meeting tonight."

And I wondered what the man who had already lost so much could be worried about losing now.

For the rest of our time in the park, we tended to the girls, spotting them, lifting them. And I found myself aware of Bobby's presence as I moved.

"Maybe we can get the girls together again sometime," he offered, after we had given Rose and Gabby the five-minute warning that it would soon be time to leave the park, then the three-minute warning, only to have to pull them off the jungle gym. We were now each gripping their respective hands.

"Yeah," I said lightly, understanding that *Let's get the kids together!* was often as rhetorical as *Let's grab a drink sometime!* "That would be great."

"Maybe this weekend?" he offered.

"Sure," I said, slightly taken aback.

Bobby took his phone from his pocket. "What's your number?" he asked.

As he entered it, I looked across the park, up to Warren's window, picturing the girl I used to be standing there. Picturing her looking down at us in disbelief.

"Did you have fun?" asked my mother, as she held open the back door for Rose and me. I shook off a chill.

"Yeah," I said. "Rosie and Gabby seem to have really hit it off." I slid Rose's coat from her arms and set it over a chairback. "Are you thirsty?"

"Yeah," answered Rose.

"Milk or water?" I asked.

"Orange juice."

I opened the cabinet and pulled out a plastic cup just as the oven beeped to announce that it was now preheated.

"Are you part of that neighborhood watch thing?" I asked my mother.

Her face changed as she slid the Vanni ziti into the oven. "What neighborhood watch thing?"

"I don't know," I said, sensing the intensity of her interest as she scanned the shelf above the oven where she kept her kitchen timers. "Bobby mentioned that there was a neighborhood watch and that they had a meeting tonight."

Mom selected the timer that was shaped like a cupcake and wound it. Setting it on the counter, she continued to stare at it as it ticked through the seconds, her hands on her hips, looking as though she was seeing something that she'd rather not. Then she turned to me.

"Do you remember how you and Warren used to call to each other?" Her face was urgent, as if something important hinged on my recollection. "When one of you was in trouble?"

I nodded. When we were little and one of us needed the other, Warren and I would rub our earlobes. And perhaps it was the alchemy of childhood, a magic that happened because I believed it could, but I swear it worked. When we were in first grade and Danielle Brewster, an angelic-looking third grader with a sadistic side, threw a rock at my head during recess, I hid in the bushes behind the school. I sat there, snot pouring out of my nose, the bump on my head swelling and bleeding—rubbing my earlobe and sobbing. Warren found me within a minute, quietly pushing aside the branches. *We'll tell Mrs. Plisky that you fell,* he reasoned, knowing even then that the truth could sometimes bring more problems, more rocks to the head.

"I remember," I said now.

Mom took a breath and squared her shoulders. "Jenna," she said, "I'm wondering if you can help me with something."

"What?" I asked, the word reluctant to leave my lips.

She turned to me and in her eyes was a surrender. "The house," she said. "I need your help with the house."

. . .

Timepiece

I yawned, my head resting against my palm, my elbow on the table, as I looked up from the printouts scattered over its surface to the room around me. The Wonderlux office was small, having to house only Maggie and myself, and furnished with a motley crew of used office furniture. But with its bright red door and dog bed in the corner, the space suited Maggie and me perfectly.

Maggie was pert and upright as she studied the handful of catalogue designs I had stayed up until three in the morning fine-tuning. "Ten bucks says they'll go with this one." She slid it across to me. "It's the safest."

Our meeting with the marketing department of one of our most important clients, Apothecary, was scheduled for tomorrow. We'd be showing them concepts for the catalogue (which I had done), along with packaging ideas for their new line of avocado-based skin care (which Maggie had done). Without a formal method for assigning projects, we divvied up work as it came in, always aware of what was on each other's plates. I glanced down at the sheet of paper. "It's my least favorite," I said.

"That's why they'll go with it." It was the cardinal rule of design, that the client inevitably chose the version you didn't even really want to show them.

I pushed away from the table, leaned back in my chair, and looked at the shelves on which we had samples of much of the packaging work we had done for Apothecary over the past few years. It was stacked and jumbled and largely in disarray, but I often imagined it on the shelves of a department store, the small white boxes in a brightly lit glass case. Apothecary gave their creams and lotions names like *Glow* and *Youth* and *Radiance*— tiny promises that could be bought and sold.

Maggie brought her hands above her head and stretched, making a sound that was almost like a purr as she let her muscles tense, then relax. "So," she said. "Do you want to meet at my house at nine?" We often carpooled to Apothecary's offices, which were about an hour away.

"I can't," I said. "I have to leave from the meeting to get Rose so we can be at my mom's before she leaves for work." My mother was closing the store tomorrow night, straightening up the piles of clothes and shuttling garments out of the fitting rooms after the customers had all made their way back to their cold, dark cars.

Maggie yawned; my fatigue was contagious. "What are

you going to your mom's house for again?" she asked, the back of her hand moving to cover her open mouth. It was a fair question; I hadn't exactly been a regular visitor to Royal Court in recent years.

I didn't know how to explain my unease with what my mother had asked me to do. Pulling another chair over the mint green industrial tile, I rested my feet on its metal base. "She asked me to help her get her house in shape," I said. Maggie's eyes held mine until I stared down at my beat-up old moccasins. "She says she wants to get the outside looking better. And maybe get rid of some things."

Maggie had never seen my mother's house, but she had seen the things she brought to mine: the chipped Christmas ornaments purchased on clearance in January. The sweaters with missing buttons or tiny holes in the seams. The dented lamps or picture frames with missing glass. She'd have found them in a forgotten corner of a discount store, with red sticker after red sticker assigning ever-lower prices—until she rescued them. When she and my father were still married, the things she bought were new and sparkling and full retail price. Now she bought what no one else wanted.

Maggie's mouth twisted a bit; she was shrewd enough to understand that Priscilla Parsons getting rid of her things was more likely to mean that something was wrong than that something was right.

The next afternoon, had Rose and I not been taking our time walking up the path to my mother's house, had we not slowed to collect the bright red leaves that had blown in from the towering maple in the park, we may have been safely inside 62 Royal Court. As it was, we had not yet reached the porch when I looked up and spotted a silver Mercedes, sleek and predatory, gliding down the street. Lydia.

It was too late to evade my stepmother, too late to slip discreetly inside. So, determined to look at something other than the car's approach, I glanced back over my mother's roof toward the maple tree. Every spring, it littered the deck with its seeds. *Whirligigs*, my mother used to call them. As kids, Warren and I would pick them up, reaching high above our heads before letting go, watching them twirl down, their twin pods looking like skydivers holding fast to each other during a descent.

I heard the engine cut.

"Hey, Mom," said Rose, sounding less excited than confused. "It's Lydia."

I turned to see Lydia opening the driver's-side door and gave her a wave. Then I started toward her, my pace unhurried, Rose at my side. I understood that Lydia had business on Royal Court, but it still felt strange to see her there. I thought about my mother, and what she must feel every time she drove down her street to see Lydia staring out at her from her neighbors' lawn signs. What she must feel to be constantly confronted by the image of the woman for whom her husband had left her.

Lydia rose out of the car and glanced quickly at my mother's house behind me, cinching the belt of her black trench coat. I half expected her to march across the lawn to meet me, but she didn't take a step over the Belgian blocking, and instead waited for me to come to her, her hands sunk into her coat pockets.

"Jenna," she began, as soon as I was close enough for her to avoid raising her voice. "Why didn't you tell me about *Warren*?" Her eyes were wide and expectant, her lower jaw hard. She must have heard that he had been hurt.

"It happened just a few days ago," I said, coming to a stop in front of her. I had been concerned about Warren going back to work so soon after the "incident," as my mother and I had begun calling it, but now I was grateful that he wasn't home; I didn't want him to have to see Lydia, not looking the way he did. I didn't want him to have to endure her questions.

Lydia made an annoyed little huffing noise, and rolled her eyes so discreetly that I wasn't quite sure I saw it. "A few days?" Lydia, who could go months, even *years*, without speaking to Warren, was suddenly vexed by a tardy update. "Jenna, this is the sort of thing your father and I need to know."

"Well, you know, Dad could give Warren a call once in a while. Maybe Warren could have told him himself," I said, knowing that this would never happen. My father wouldn't call. And Warren wouldn't have told.

We stood facing each other, the seconds feeling slowed, prolonged, until Lydia said, "Jenna, your father is hugely busy." She nodded her head, absolute in her position. "So we need to know that we can rely on you to communicate with us when necessary."

I let out a hard breath. "I'm sorry, Lydia. I should have given you guys a call."

"Well, that certainly would have been preferable to finding out when talking to a client about a potential listing." She shook back her frosty blond bangs. "It just doesn't look great when I'm not even aware that my husband's son was assaulted."

My chin jerked up at the term "assault." Warren hadn't yet

told us anything about what had happened; that he was assaulted was still speculative. "Actually, Lydia, we don't know what happened," I said. "Who did you say you were meeting today?"

But before Lydia could answer, Rose said, "Mom?" That was all. *Mom.* But it was enough to bring me out of myself, out of my anger. Feeling her small, warm hand in mine, I looked down to see that her eyes were wide. Rose seemed so tough, but since it was just her and me at home, she was unaccustomed to this sort of conflict, the sort that happens between adults.

I rested my hand on top of her head, her hair wiry against my palm, until I saw the muscles in her face fully relax. "Sorry, Rosie. Mom and Lydia were just talking about some grown-up stuff."

With her awareness brought to Rose, Lydia seemed to yield. "Hi, sweetheart," she said, with a reserved smile.

"Hi, Lydia," said Rose.

"Are you excited about Halloween?" Lydia leaned forward, trying at warmth.

"Yeah," answered Rose, tugging on my hand, swaying against the tension. "I'm going to be a cowgirl."

"Your cousin Cassandra's going to be Marie Antoinette!" *Cousin.* Cassandra was Lydia's daughter Lauren's little girl. Rose had met Cassandra only a handful of times. She was a barrel-shaped six-year-old who pushed her way to the front of every line and deemed almost everything "not fair."

Lydia turned her attention back to me, enlivened by talk of her granddaughter. "You should see the costume! It's this *gorgeous* brocade dress. And she has one of those big white wigs."

"Oh, how cute," I managed.

"So, anyhow," said Lydia, her tone becoming less effusive, "how is he?" She lifted her chin toward the house, a concession to her lack of clarity. "Warren, I mean."

I considered how best to answer her question. "He's doing all right," I said, but her eyes were scanning the yard, skittering to the empty spots where all the recently vacated bric-a-brac had once sat.

"How's your mother?" she asked, her eyes narrowing. Lydia occasionally asked about Mom, and the question wasn't unprecedented so much as uncomfortable. There was a time when the concern would have seemed perfectly natural, back when Lydia was Mrs. Stroppe, and my mom and dad played mixed doubles with her and Mr. Stroppe at Harwick Swim Club. Lydia would finish the game and change into her swimsuit, then wade into the pool with her visor and sunglasses still on. Her head never, ever got wet and her tanned upper body was entirely immobile as she glided through the water like a charmed snake.

"Mom's doing great," I said lightly. Then, eager to steer the conversation away from my family, I glanced at the homes around us. "So, it looks like you've got a lot of listings here."

"Well." Lydia's eyebrows flitted briefly. "I've been hoping that some would have sold by now." Looking around her, she coldly assessed the neighborhood. "But these properties just don't move anymore. And now with all these little thefts . . . And if what happened to *Warren* becomes some sort of trend"—as she said my brother's name, she extended her hand toward me as if we were somehow culpable in the depreciation of King's Knoll—"buyers are going to want nothing to do with it."

"I hope that won't become an issue," I said, aiming to draw our conversation to a close.

Taking her cue, Lydia reached for the door handle. "I feel just terrible for the people who absolutely *need* to sell." She paused, the door ajar. "The couple I just met with are desperate to get out of New Jersey."

With that, I could sympathize. After all, here I was, back in Harwick. And in some ways, I supposed we were all bound to a place. A place in time. A place in our memories. A place where we were loved or detested. A place where we got our scars. And as I thought about what it would take to leave, to truly leave, I glanced down through the window of Lydia's car. There, lying on top of her leather tote in a clear ziplock bag, was a watch. "Is that . . ." The words stalled as I studied its round gold face, its worn-looking, cognac-colored crocodile wristband. I hadn't seen that watch in seventeen years. "Is that Grandpa's watch?" Hit hard by a sudden and potent memory of my grandfather, I could smell his smell, see the spots on the dry skin of the back of his hand, hear the way he used to call Warren's name when he came to pick him up for a fishing trip. *Warren!* he'd call up the stairs. *We're meeting a catfish for dinner!*

"Yes, it was Martin's," said Lydia, her eyes lifting cheerfully, happier to be moving to a more pleasant subject. "I'm taking it to be cleaned up. We're giving it to Russell for his fortieth."

"Russell?" His name came out like the gasp after a blow to the gut. Russell was Lauren's asshole husband, who last Thanksgiving was on his BlackBerry all through dinner, looking up only to usurp the conversation with his booming voice, announcing how many miles he had logged on his bike the previous week or how his tax bracket had to bear the burden of single mothers and their "welfare kids." To be fair,

I'm not sure he had ever given enough thought to either me or Rose to realize that *I* was a single mother.

"But, Lydia," was all I could manage, shaking my head. "Russell isn't even . . ."

Lydia looked at me, as if waiting for me to make an inane point. "He's a collector," she said, as if that were enough to end the conversation. Then, for good measure, she added, "He collects watches."

"Lydia," was all I could say again. It was plea. "That watch would mean so much to Warren."

"Warren?" asked Lydia, truly confused. *What would Warren want with a gold Tiffany watch?* To Lydia, that's all it was, a nice watch.

But Warren would remember the look on our grandfather's face when he got it, his somber pride when his longtime boss, Mr. Barnes, handed him the box at his retirement party. Warren would remember that he wore it all those nights on the lake, when it was just the two of them in our grandpa's little green boat, the black water beneath them and the black sky above. I'd gone with them a few times, but never quite understood the draw. *How can the fish see their food if it's dark?* I'd ask. The only answer would be the gentle creaking of the boat, the lapping of the water against its small hull.

Finally it would be Warren who'd speak. "They smell their food," he'd say. "They have sensory organs on their whiskers." I'd look at my grandfather for corroboration, but he'd still be staring out into the water, a small, satisfied smile barely discernible on his face. Some nights they wouldn't catch anything. Some nights, they would bring home four or five enormous fish with tiny eyes, their mouths agape and their bodies slick and stiff as they lay on ice in a red Coleman cooler. But every time they went, come midnight, Grandpa would lift his arm and shake back his sleeve and look at that gold watch. *It's tomorrow, Warren. Time to head home.*

But I couldn't make Lydia understand. The only hope I had was my father. And unfortunately that wasn't much of one.

CHAPTER TWELVE

• • •

Briggs Western

1957

From the outside, the building revealed nothing of its contents. It was large and gray and stone, and took up an entire city block as well as a good portion of the air above it. It might have been an armory or an office building or a place where they made safety pins. But when you pushed through those glass doors—well, at the time Silla found it almost too wonderful.

"This used to be your granddaddy's store," said her father, bending to speak into her ear. And even though it wasn't called Briggs Western anymore, being inside something that once held her family's name gave Silla a sense that she had come from someplace special.

She leaned back, letting her gaze climb to the soaring ceiling, the lights above her looking like stars glowing in a sunlit sky. Around her were curved displays of glass and shiny metal, illuminated seemingly from within to showcase the immaculate rows of purses and gloves and scarves that they contained. Ladies with bright eyes smiled at her from behind the counters as their fingers moved over the buttons of the cash registers like they were the keys of a piano. Everywhere around her, there was color and sound and beauty.

"You can get anything you want, sugar," said her father. Today was Silla's eighth birthday and he had taken her back to the town where she was born to "tie up some loose ends," as he put it, before his wedding to Hattie. Silla supposed that meant standing in lobbies and sitting at desks while papers were signed and stamped and signed and stamped, as that's how they had spent their morning. But now that was done and she was here and it had been worth the wait.

She looked to the far wall of the store. Against it was shelf after shelf of stuffed animals, next to a display with bins of bright foil-wrapped candy. Her father saw her eyeing them. "Go on," he encouraged. "Go pick something out."

She took tentative steps, feeling the soft soles of her shoes meet that hard marble floor as her father walked next to her. She reached a round, tiered table, the perimeter of which was lined with dolls all looking out with a glass-eyed calm. "You like this one?" her daddy asked, lifting a blond one off the shelf. "This one's pretty."

She looked at it for a moment, but didn't know exactly how to answer. The blond doll looked the same as all the others— same nose, same lips, same arms that reached out to a person it couldn't see. Only its dress was different. From behind her came a gentle voice. "May I help you?"

Silla and her father both turned at once. There stood an older woman, small with a body that didn't look thin so much as deflated. Her shoulders were hunched forward over her flat breasts and her dark gray hair was pulled back into a small bun. She wore a skirt and hose that bagged a bit at her ankles, above the shoes into which her bent feet seemed awkwardly contorted. When she saw Silla's father, her eyes narrowed with recognition that seemed to try to slither from her mind's grasp.

"We're just having a look around," answered her father, stiffening slightly, giving a tense but polite nod as he angled his body back toward the display.

But Silla watched the lady, watched as her eyes drifted away as if with the tide of a memory. Suddenly, they snapped back to her father. "Excuse me," said the woman, "but aren't you Lee Harris?" The quaver in her genteel old Southern voice gave her an air of authority.

Silla's father looked down at his feet for a steadying moment before turning around with a cordial but restrained smile. "Yes, ma'am," he said with a nod.

She gasped, her hands clasped in front of her. "Why, I was at your wedding," she said, as if it was a thought she hadn't meant to speak aloud. "To Martha." Her eyes flickered to Silla.

"You don't say," replied Lee with a nervous chuckle, as he rested his hand on Silla's back, beginning to steer her away from the woman.

"Yes, I've been working here since it was Briggs Western," she said, as if he had doubted her. "I worked for Mr. Benson Briggs when I was just a girl."

"Isn't that something," said Lee. Then he nodded. "If you'll excuse us." He scooped Silla up onto his hip and began making for the door and as he did, Silla looked back at the woman. She was leaning against the display, looking at Silla with that troubled expression that she hadn't seen much since they'd moved away from here.

"She knew my mama?" asked Silla, bouncing with her father's steps. "Before she died?" But her father didn't answer. He navigated quickly through the enormous store and back toward those glass doors.

He had pushed through them and into the thick, hot air outside before he spoke again. Stopping on the sidewalk, he set Silla down and looked at her, his hands on his hips, his brow creased. "You know Hattie's going to be just like a mother to you, don't you, sugar?" Silla nodded and her father smiled, the relief rushing out with his breath. Then he pinched her cheek. "You're going to have the prettiest mother in the whole world."

. . .

Picture Show

Mom was seated at the kitchen table, looking at what appeared to be a thin catalogue, by the time Rose and I got inside. Her eyes stayed focused on the pages as we entered, and so I knew she had seen us talking to Lydia. This was how it had been when I was a teenager, trying to navigate the waters of loyalty after my parents' divorce.

"Hey, Nana," said Rose as she strode toward the table, dropping her backpack on the floor as she went. "Where's Uncle Warren?"

"He's at work, honey." Mom rotated on her chair, turning to face Rose, her hands clasped and dangling in the space between her knees as her forearms rested on her plump thighs. Everything about my mother was soft, forgiving. "He's bringing people their pizza." She said it as if it were the sort of job that children would parrot when asked by teachers what they wanted to be when they grew up. *I want to be a pizza deliveryman!* But that was the thing about my mother's admiration; she was unequivocally proud of Warren—a dedicated and reliable thirty-six-year-old pizza deliveryman who could explain the natal philopatry of sea turtles and spent his free time with his mother. A boy who was now a man, with a heart so fragile he had to keep it tucked away from the world. There was almost nothing Mom wouldn't do for him.

I nodded toward her catalogue, which I could see contained what looked like paint swatches lined in a grid pattern against the backdrop of an expansive wooden deck. "Are you thinking about repainting?" I asked.

She thrummed her fingers over the catalogue pages. "Well," she said, almost apologetically. "I was thinking that maybe we could repaint the columns out front. As the first thing we do."

"Oh," I said. I hadn't known what to expect when my mother had asked for my help with the house, and I was now beginning to understand the enormity of the task. "Okay."

Sensing my hesitancy, she turned away, smiling and gesturing for Rose to come sit on her lap. "It's just that . . . the quotes I got were kind of high," she said. "And I thought it would be nice to maybe do it as a family." Her voice was hopeful and uncertain.

"Yeah," I said, nodding. "No, I think that would be good."

She looked at me gratefully. "I guess you didn't really need to come today," she said. "I was thinking that maybe we could get started, but I was just reading online about what we need to do in terms of preparation." I nodded, listening. But she stopped, her head tilting to one side as she regarded me. "You're such a good girl, Jenna," she said, looking almost pained. "Everyone in this neighborhood has always loved you."

I hooked my hand on the back of my neck, letting it hang there. "Thanks," I said. I was uncomfortable with praise, especially the sort that seemed like a lament. Perhaps it was only the reflex of being a twin, but at once, I thought of Warren. If the neighbors had always "loved me," as my mother said, how had they felt about Warren?

Rose slid down from my mother's lap, her eyes focused on the forest green wire baker's rack between the doors to the foyer and the pantry. And though it was often difficult to pick out the new additions in my mother's house, the rack held a picture that I was sure hadn't been there before—a black-and-white photo of a woman, framed in thin wood with a small brass hoop on top. "Hey, who's this lady?" asked Rose, reaching for it.

"Lemme see," I said, resting my hand on her shoulder as I leaned in. The woman was staring into the camera. Behind her, in the soft, blurred background, was a picnic table underneath a tall tree that rose above the confines of the shot. She had a curious look on her face that wasn't quite a smile and her eyes seemed animated, as if she were seeing us as we saw her. She didn't appear to have a stitch of makeup on, and her bangs were shaped into a single, solid curl that looked like the barrel of a wave running across her forehead. One hand was resting on her hip, her wrist bending pliantly. She had my mother's full breasts and lips, and even in the black-and-white, I could tell her hair was red. "Is this your mother?" I asked, glancing back at Mom. I had only ever seen a few pictures of her mother, and they were all formal, posed shots, with crisp lines and good posture. This woman looked real. Like she might, at any moment, adjust the strap of the dress that was sliding down her bare right shoulder.

My mother shifted in her chair and crossed her legs, wrapping her clasped hands around her knee. "That's her," she said, smiling despite the tension in her brow. "That was taken the year before we lost her."

"She looks funny," said Rose goofily, probably meaning the hair or the clothes or the absence of color.

My mother made a soft sound that was almost a chuckle. "She was a little funny, I guess."

I was drawn back to the photo. "I've never seen this picture before."

"I just found it," said Mom. "I'd been looking for it for a while." She angled her head so that she could see around Rose and me. "I've been thinking about her a lot lately."

I didn't know much about my grandmother, only that she had died in 1954 after a complication related to routine surgery. My mother was five at the time and my grandfather met and married Hattie soon after. "You look like her here." I'd studied the other photos, seeking a resemblance that I was unable to find. But here it was clear.

My mother gave the photo one last look before straining to stand. "Well," she said, "I'd better get going. The store sent out one of those family and friends discounts, so it's going to be busy."

Her stare snagged on the open door to the pantry. "Oh, I forgot," she said, pushing the door open and entering. Like the rest of the house, it was chock-full. Dusty cans teetered in towers, and rows and rows of cereal lined the shelves. "It's just something I got at Costco," she said, her voice muffled by the soundproofing power of snack foods. "They're these bars. . . . They're supposed to be as nutritious as a meal," she said, pulling out a case of the raw vegan bars with deceptively delicious-sounding names—*Cocoa Almond Nut Chunk!* and *Banana Walnut Bread!* "I thought they'd be good for Rose's snack at school," she said, emerging from the pantry, her eyes lifted hopefully.

"Thanks," I said, as I took the box, Rose standing on her toes to peek down at what she surely thought were candy bars. I didn't tell Mom that Rose's school was nut-free. She looked too pleased about her contribution to disappoint her with talk of allergies.

Mom headed toward the front door. Guiding Rose with my hand on the back of her head, I followed through the foyer, listening to my mother as she told me about the cutest little sundresses that were on sale right now. "No one wants them because winter is coming, but they're just adorable. Do you think Rose would want something like that? For next summer?"

"That's okay, Mom," I said, picturing Rose's tiny closet. "We have like zero storage at our place."

I followed Mom out to the driveway and we each got into our respective cars. Backing out first, I paused to let her pull ahead of me. Never an aggressive driver, she stopped at the end of Royal Court, and seemed to be waiting for a break in the traffic large enough for a tractor-trailer to safely make a left turn.

"Come on, Mom," I muttered.

"Nana, *go!*" commanded Rose from the backseat.

As we were waiting, a familiar Jeep pulled into the development from the main road. Bobby's car passed and I gave him a friendly wave, which he returned. Then, in my rearview mirror, I saw his brake lights beam red, then the white glow as he reversed.

"Hey, Mom!" said Rose, just as my mother finally ventured onto the main road. "It's Gabby!"

Gabby Vanni's little fingers were gripping the top of the open backseat window, her mouth beneath the darkened glass, her eyes smiling and delighted. "Hi, Rose!" she yelled.

Rose tried to locate the button for the window. When she did, she rolled it down, and mimicked Gabby's posture. "Hi, Gabby!" she answered back.

I smiled into my lap, then looked up at the driver's seat to see Bobby leaning back, one hand on the wheel. His window slid down. "Hi, Jenna."

"Hey," I said, thinking to myself how very handsome he still was.

"So, Gabby is pretty excited to see that new rat movie," said Bobby, speaking in the loud, staged whisper that parents use when they intend to be overheard. *I heard Santa just lifted off at the North Pole.*

"Mom!" said Rose from the backseat. "I want to see the rat movie!"

Bobby smiled, and for a second, he was the old Bobby, the golden boy with white teeth and olive skin and the adoration of all. The Bobby who needed only to roll down his window and *hint* at an invitation to get a "yes."

I looked down, sliding my hand down the length of my ponytail.

When Bobby spoke again, his voice was polite, reserved. "I was thinking that maybe you and Rose would like to come."

"Sure," I answered.

"Great." Bobby smiled. Then he paused, as if to give what he said next consequence. "It's a date."

And though I returned his smile, I wished he hadn't called it that.

After Rose was born—after I'd found myself in my thirties and single and a mother—I'd let myself be set up and fixed up and partnered up at a few dinner parties. Most of the time, the men had been warned that I had a child, so they knew how to arrange their faces when I mentioned Rose. But their idea of dating a woman with a young child was often quite different from the reality.

Once, there was a man that I liked so much that I invited him to come in. I paid the sitter and made us some coffee. He waited on the couch. And when I set the cups down on the table, he gently took my wrist and pulled me onto him, kissing me, sliding his fingers through my hair. And I could feel myself thawing. His lips were on my neck when I heard Rose start to fuss from the crib in her bedroom. I froze. He stopped. "She's getting her teeth," I said, excusing myself to go comfort her. I hurried to her room. In my high heels. In my pencil skirt. *I'm sorry, Rosie. I'm so sorry.* And I wondered how I was going to do this, how I was going to *date* while raising a young child. When I opened the door, the cries that had been muffled were suddenly clear, and I shut the door behind me, seeking to contain them. Picking her up, I sat down in the rocking chair, rubbing my hand over the smooth cotton on her back. "Shhh," I said, as we moved back and forth together, chest to chest. "Mommy's right here." She lifted her red face to let out another shriek of protest and pain, then let her head collapse back into the crook of my neck. I rubbed her back for I didn't know how long. Until I inadvertently fell asleep. Until I awoke with a stiff neck and dry eyes and set her down in the crib to make my way back out to the family room, which was empty, aside from two cups of cold coffee. The man was gone. And I walked slowly back into my daughter's room and lay down on the floor next to her crib, my face against the carpet.

I realized, then, how it was that I would date while having a child. I wouldn't.

• • •

CHAPTER FOURTEEN

Flying Machines

Scattered over the porch were all manner of painting supplies: brushes and rollers and trays, everything we might need to restore the columns that graced my mother's front porch to their mid-1980s splendor. The thin brown plastic bags in which my mother had transported her haul from the home improvement store were weighted with paint cans, and packages of sandpaper had been torn open, the rough sheets peeking out. "They said we should sand off all the existing paint as best we can," said my mother, her hands resting supportively on the small of her back. "Before we put on the first coat."

I looked up the length of the column in front of me, my eyes following its grooves to the top, squinting as the trajectory of my gaze approached the sun.

"Oh! That reminds me," said Mom, as she disappeared inside the house. When she emerged, she was awkwardly carrying a stepladder, its metal legs bumping against her shins. "I thought we could use this," she said. "Rather than having to stand on a chair."

I took in the scope of the project, estimating how much would be involved in the sanding and repainting; it was likely to be more than either my mother or I had initially imagined. Then, angling my head toward the still ajar door, I called, "Hey, Warren!" waiting a moment for a response that I knew wouldn't come. "Warren!" I said again. "Do you think you can help us sand?"

After a brief pause, Rose answered. "We're playing Candy Land." She sounded annoyed at the interruption.

I rolled my eyes. Warren had always gotten a pass on chores, even though, if you asked me, he was perfectly capable of helping out. It was at least part of why my mother's house was in such bad shape. *He's been working on his planes,* my mother used to say when my father would ask why Warren hadn't mowed the lawn.

"Let 'em play," my mother urged, moving to close the door. "They love being together."

Rose did seem to view Warren as a playmate, the next-best thing to an actual kid. *When's he going to start acting like a normal teenager?* my father used to ask, when he would come home to find Warren in the backyard, fighting off Maglons or sending a tiny plane up into dusk's watercolor sky. And as I had sensed my father's growing distance, as his business trips increased in both frequency and duration, I used to look out the window and pray that Warren would suddenly straighten up. That his shoulders would become broad and solid. That he would brush his bangs back off his face, and stride confidently across the park. That he would become someone other than Warren.

I took a deep breath, running my hand up the back of my neck until it met the base of my ponytail. Then I pulled the stepladder over to the nearest column. "I can do the sanding, Mom," I said, reaching for a package of sandpaper. Having sanded a secondhand dresser prior to giving it a coat of bright pink paint for Rose, I knew that the task was tedious and tiring—not something I wanted Mom to have to do. "You can hang out with Rose and Warren."

"I can help," she insisted. But as she watched me climb the ladder, her voice grew less certain. "Maybe you can do the tops and I'll do the bottoms."

As we began working, running the rough paper over the already chipped paint, my arms fell into a rhythm. Heat rose in my muscles and my heart pumped steadily. Up and then down, the smooth, tender-looking wood appearing where it had been hidden. Soon my sweatshirt was covered in the thin, white dust, and despite the chilly air, I peeled it off, tossing it toward the welcome mat and looking down at myself. I had on a threadbare T-shirt with the logo of a noodle bar I used to go to in New York. I'd gone there the night Duncan left for Japan. I had stood on the front steps of our apartment as he got in a cab for the airport, wishing that I could cross and cross and cross my arms over my chest, wishing that I had rows and layers of arms, like the horseshoe crabs my father used to pull out of the water at the beach. He'd turn them upside down and their legs would be probing and reaching, warning you away. I watched

Duncan as he waved good-bye as the cab drove off, but I just rested my hand on my belly. And when he was gone, I remained on the steps for a very long time, my hand still on my stomach until, feeling the movement inside it, I forced my feet forward. Walking down the street to the noodle bar, I ordered an enormous bowl of soup. When the waitress came back to ask how I was liking it, she noticed that I was eating only the noodles, that much of the broth was still in my bowl. "Drink, drink," she said in a thick accent as she pointed to my belly. "Is good for the baby." And so I brought the dish to my lips, the steam meeting my face and masking the tears in my eyes.

"What time do you have to leave for the store?" I asked my mother.

"I should get going around one," she said, between slow, easy strokes of the sandpaper. "What are you and Rose doing the rest of the day?"

"We're actually going to see a movie," I said. I paused to scratch my nose with the back of my hand. "That one with the rat."

Mom clucked with recognition. "I heard that one's cute." There was the sound of a leisurely up and down with the sandpaper. "Too bad Warren has to work later. I'll bet he'd like to go with you." I pulled a fresh sheet of sandpaper from the packet. "Is it just you and Rose?"

I tried out the words that came next in my mind before speaking them aloud. "We're actually going with Bobby and Gabby Vanni."

"Oh," said my mother. "Oh," she said again. Though I was focused on the bare stretch of column in front of me, I could tell from her pleased-sounding tone exactly the look that was on her face. "Well, maybe Warren and I will go see it another time."

Rose soon came popping out the front door, Warren trailing behind her but hesitating at the threshold, keeping his body partially hidden as he held a white foam airplane at his side.

"Mom!" called Rose, standing at the base of the stepladder. She hooked her fingers in the tops of my boots. "I won Candy Land *four* times in a row!"

"Whoa," I said, staring down into her bright little eyes. "You must be *really* good."

I sensed Warren's attention, his smile. I glanced over at him. He lowered his head. "She just kept getting Princess Frostine," he said, shaking his head as if marveling at her luck, as if he hadn't found a way to slip the best card to the top of the stack. "I don't know how it happened."

"Uncle Warren!" said Rose, bouncing back to him. "Let's fly the plane!"

Warren assumed the expression of an affectionate old monk trying to remain stern with his enthusiastic apprentice, but his delight was clear. He made a noise of hesitation, like creaky old gears turning reluctantly. "I don't know," he said.

"Please, Uncle Warren!" she begged, looking as though total devastation were just a single "no" away. "I want to see it *float*."

His chuckle was mixed with a groan. "Okay," he said. Then beneath his furrowed brow, he glanced out at the street, and at the neighborhood beyond it. And as Warren took his first steps into the daylight outside the house, I was again aware of his injuries, which I had begun not to see. That's the way it always was with Warren; the more time you spent with him, the less apparent the anomalies became. But in the starkness of the bright outside light, they were once again very real.

"Hey, Rosie," I said. "You need to get your coat. It's cold out."

Rose scowled in my direction. "But *you* don't have a coat!" she whined.

"I have a layer of blubber," I answered, then pointed inside the house. "Go."

Rose pulled a little foot-stomp-and-turn combination as she rushed into the house.

"So what's that plane, War?" I asked, again sliding the sandpaper up the column.

My mother perked up. "Is that the one you've been working on?" she asked. "The one that can hover?" She turned to me. "That's hard to do," she said. "To make one of those planes hover."

Warren stood still, seeming almost annoyed that we were using such basic but irresistible means by which to draw him out of the house. When not fulfilling his duties for Pizzeria Brava, Warren seemed to prefer being indoors since the "incident." "You just have to use multiple gyros," he said, his lips barely parting to release the words. "On the canards and the rudders."

Rose came bounding back out the door, dragging her coat behind her by its sleeve. "Uncle Warren!" she said, as I climbed down the ladder to help her put it on. "Are you gonna fly the plane?"

Warren made another soft groaning sound. Again he glanced around the neighborhood. He seemed to start for the door, then changed his mind before taking a step. "You really want to see Uncle Warren fly the plane?" he asked Rose.

And all she had to do was nod.

Warren seemed uncomfortable as he crept out onto the lawn, his head sunk into his shoulders, his posture tense. But as he looked down at Rose, who was bouncing at his side, a smile inched onto his face. He said something to her that I couldn't hear, then set the controller down on the ground. Gripping the side of the plane with a single hand, he suddenly began spinning and spinning like a top, the plane held at the end of his extended arm gathering speed. When he released, it soared slowly, without ambition, until he darted down for the controller, and with movements that seemed instinctual, he directed the plane elegantly back into the air, lifting it out of the downward arc it had begun. The plane circled over Rose's head a few times, and she jumped and squealed when it swooped toward her—her very own air show. His hands moved quickly and the plane seemed to stop in midair, its nose lifting until it was almost vertical, hovering there.

"Look!" said my mother. "Warren says that's called 'high alpha' when it does that." She stared at the plane, marveling. "There aren't a lot of people who can make planes do that. He had to program that control panel and everything."

But as Warren stood there, his plane in a state of equilibrium, totally balanced between up and down, right and left, backward and forward, I saw his gaze move away from the sky and toward the road, and the car that was moving down it. Almost instantly the plane dropped, free-falling until it hit the earth, helpless and unguided. Warren walked over to it and scooped it up, his eyes focused on the ground two feet in front of him; then he hurried back toward the house. "Uncle Warren!" cried Rose, with a small, joyful leap, looking from Warren back toward the sky. "Make it go back up!" But he didn't respond; he kept moving as the car sped past, too fast for me to decipher much besides the fact that it was driven by a young kid and that he glanced discreetly but unquestionably at Warren—making it look so casual, so unintentional, so unremarkable—before disappearing down the road, the volume of the music coming from his car a blur of noise that lingered after him.

Warren kept his head down as he climbed the steps of the porch, silent as he brushed past us and went back into the house. "I knew it," whispered my mother as the screen door clattered shut. "Goddammit. I knew it." The words weren't meant for me, weren't meant to be spoken aloud.

"Who was that?" I asked.

Mom stared hard after the path of the car that had turned onto Mountain Road. "Zack Castro," she said.

I recalled the threesome of teenage boys hovering over Mrs. Vanni's Crock-Pot of sausage and peppers during the block party. "He was the one whose bike was stolen," I said.

"Yup." My mother's jaw tensed and she remained focused on the void at the end of the road. "That's him." She looked over at Rose, who had followed Warren to the steps of the porch, her small face weighted with matters she didn't understand. Then Mom smiled at her, made her voice light again. "Can you get Uncle Warren's controls, honey? I don't think he meant to leave them on the grass."

Mom and I looked at each other for one honest instant before, with pursed lips, she turned away. *That's him.* And the soft-sounding strokes of sandpaper once again sounded from her direction. *That's him. That's him. That's him.*

"I'll be right back." I stepped down from the ladder.

Distressed and curious, Mom looked at me. "Keep an eye on Rose?" I asked. Then I disappeared inside the house.

After gently knocking, I pushed open Warren's door. "Hey, War," I said, peering into his room. He was sitting at his desk, his back to the door, his hands efficiently and methodically dismantling his plane. "Warren," I said, padding toward him. "Hey, hey, hey."

"The gyros were overcorrecting," he said, shrugging away from my touch, continuing to pull at wires. "The plane wasn't stabilizing."

I rested my hand on his shoulder. "So you can fix it." It was the way I'd speak to Rose.

His hands slowed, and he gave me a discreet but suspicious look from the corner of his eye, as if making sure I was the person he presumed me to be. "That's what I'm doing," he said softly.

I lowered my head, feeling not like his twin, the person who understood him better than anyone, but like one of the people who tried not to stare at him as he flew his plane in the front yard, wondering what Weird Warren was doing now. For a moment, I listened to the sounds of his work. When I spoke again, it was without hesitation. "That kid was the one who beat you up, wasn't it? The one who drove by?" Warren seemed to contract, to pull his entire being into a thrumming center, and concentrate more intensely on his plane. "Zack Castro?"

I watched Warren's slender fingers work at pulling the tiny wires. When he spoke, he said only, "The plane is tail heavy in neutral." He pulled at what looked like a small secondary wing on the side of the plane. "So the canards need to be angled down." His focus seemed to narrow, his gaze to zoom in on the LED lights on the sides of the tiny aircraft. And taking a breath first, he said, his lips barely moving, "Sometimes after work at night, I fly in the park." And I knew I had my answer. The backyards of half the homes in King's Knoll abutted the park. That Warren hadn't denied it was Zack was as good as his admitting that it was. I pictured my mother's face. *That's him*, she had said.

. . .

Easter

1961

Hattie liked the Hooper boys. "They're just how boys are supposed to be," she'd say of the three young men who lived next door and were handsome and cruel in equal measure. "Their mama's raising them right." But Silla found them terrifying. And even though she stayed in her room when her daddy was traveling, which was most of the time, she avoided the window, which faced the fence that separated her own yard from theirs.

For each one of the three Hooper boys, there was an enormous dog, all three with muscled but hungry frames and the sort of matted brown and black fur that became burdensome in the heat. The dogs were kept tethered to an iron stake in the ground, where their world had a circumference of about forty grassless feet. Most of the time, no one went anywhere near them, but sometimes the boys got bored. Sometimes, they would wait until the dogs weren't looking; then they'd run up and try to kick them. The dogs would lurch around and begin their pursuit, their teeth bared, their snarls ferocious, as the boys would scramble away, laughing, their voices adrenaline-spiked. They knew exactly where the limits lay, when the dogs' lines would become taut, where they'd meet the resistance of their collars.

Hattie would head out as soon as she heard their game start, deciding this was the moment to shake out a tablecloth or prune the roses. Sometimes she didn't need the guise of a chore. Sometimes she'd just lean against the porch railing, her lips curved into a crocodile smile, one of her feet sliding out of the back of her high heel. Hattie always wore high heels.

Once they had an audience, the boys became a bit more vicious, a bit more daring. They rarely got bitten, but when they did, before they even assessed their wounds, they'd look to make sure Hattie had been watching. "Serves you right," she would say, her chin lifted regally. "You better go tell your mama to get the Mercurochrome."

Silla could hear the Hoopers outside now, so she sat on the floor between her bed and the wall, singing quietly. She did everything quietly, though she couldn't have told you why. And when she noticed the door to her bedroom start to open, her body stiffened, and her song hid in her lungs. But it was her father's face that appeared. "Daddy," she gasped, as she scrambled to her feet.

"How's my pretty girl?" he asked, as Silla hurried to him.

She wrapped her arms around his waist, noticing that his hands were tucked behind his back, hiding something from her view. It was then that she heard the chirping. "I got a surprise for you," said her father, as he brought around a small, lidless cardboard box.

Silla's smile was instant when she saw the chicks, when she matched their high-pitched peeps to their soft, butter-colored bodies. Their heads were lifted and eyes alert as they tried to grip the smooth bottom of the box and gain their footing with their tiny claws. "They're for Easter," said her father, as Silla peered at them. "You like 'em?"

She nodded.

"Then go on," he said, nudging the box toward her.

Silla slid the box from her father's hands and went to her bed, her eyes not moving from the chicks. She sat on the mattress, placing the container carefully on her lap. There were six of them. Six chicks. She counted them as they huddled to one corner of the cardboard, running her fingers over each of their tiny skulls. "Shhh," she told them, chuckling. "It's all right." Then she lifted her face to her father, blushing even before she spoke. "I'm singing with the choir tomorrow. At morning services."

"You don't say," said her father, staring at his daughter, who really had become quite lovely. "Well, well."

Silla bit away her smile and looked back down at the chicks, feeling her father's attention linger. "You know, you should probably keep those outside, sugar," said her father finally, giving his daughter a wink. "Hattie said she doesn't want any dirty ol' chickens in the house."

For the rest of the evening, Silla stayed outside with the chicks, on the other end of the house from the Hoopers' yard. She picked them up one at a time, cradling them into her chest, amazed at how light they were, at just how insignificant their bones felt. When her bedtime came, she put them in the shed with an old dishrag balled up in their box to help keep them warm. Surely, they needed something to do so.

The next morning, even before looking for her Easter basket, Silla slipped out of the house to check on them, a smile spreading instantly across her face as she opened the door to the shed to hear their greeting.

"You love those chicks, don't you, Silla?" asked her father, as Hattie massaged his shoulders after church. And Silla dipped her chin to her chest and smiled. "I'm glad, sugar," he said as he reached for his tumbler, then looked again at his daughter. "You sang pretty at church today." The drink was like liniment; you could see his muscles start to loosen. "You sang real pretty."

Hattie's hand slid slowly down her father's chest. "Silla, honey. Why don't you go out to the shed?" she suggested. "Visit those birds of yours."

That night, the rain started. Silla found its gentle persistence soothing. A thunderstorm was erratic. It would blow in and blow out, bringing spectacle and sensation. But a spring rainstorm would build gently, falling steadily until it passed through. And that night Silla slept soundly. The air was cool. Her father was home. And she heard nothing but the rain.

By the time she woke up in the morning, the skies had cleared and her father was gone again, back on the road. Still in her nightgown, she laced up her shoes and went out to the shed just as she had the day before. The ground was damp and almost bare in spots, and was still heavy with dew and a mist that would soon succumb to the sun. Before she reached the shed, she knew something was wrong. Before she had set her fingers on the handle, they started to quiver. And when the morning light filled the dark shed, it was the silence that she noticed first. Then she realized that the box was gone.

She circled the shed. She looked under the old workbench and behind the rusted-out washbasin. Once she knew for certain that the chicks weren't there, something instinctual, some impulse for self-preservation, took over in her. She walked back in the house, trying to move like a ghost, invisible and unnoticed. But Hattie was in the kitchen, standing at the sink when she entered. "What's wrong, Priscilla?" she asked, her voice too solicitous, too kind.

Silla couldn't bring her gaze up from the floor. "My chicks are gone," she whispered.

Hattie made a gentle *tsk* sound. "Ohhh," she said. "Ain't that a shame?"

Silla would never mention the chicks again and her father would never ask, as nothing held Lee Harris's attention for long, least of all six baby chickens. But later that evening, while Hattie was watching her television program, Silla went back to the shed. Scanning the area around the door, her gaze caught on a small divot in the dirt, still moist with the previous night's rain. She slipped her finger inside, feeling its boundaries. There weren't very many things that could make a hole like that. It would have to be something slender, something sharp. The heel of a woman's shoe, maybe. And as it turned out, they weren't uncommon in the yard. In fact, Silla followed a path of them, one by one, from the shed to the edge of the Hoopers' fence, where the world of the dogs met hers.

• • •

CHAPTER SIXTEEN

Chickens and Rats

Bobby propped open the theater door, letting the girls walk out ahead of him, then gestured for me to do the same. "So what did you guys think?" I asked our small group as we hung together, walking down the theater's dimly lit corridor, lined with posters of coming attractions and doors to other worlds. But Gabby and Rose were too absorbed with each other to pay any attention to the question. I smiled at Bobby, feeling a flash of discomfort as I found myself at a momentary loss for what to say next. Knowing each other since childhood had put us in an uncomfortable gray area between total strangers and blood relatives.

"Gotta love a good rat story," said Bobby.

Our footsteps fell into sync until we passed a poster for a campy horror movie that featured an enormous cobra—its body coiled, its hood spread wide. "Hey, do you remember Ron Frankney?" I asked, though I knew he did. Ron was part of Harwick lore in the same way Bobby was. In the same way Warren probably was. All figures from a shared youth whose myth was greater, more sensational, than their person.

Bobby chuckled, his chin dropping to his chest. "Yeah," he said. "I remember Frankney. He had that"—he glanced at the girls and lowered his voice, in the way parents do when they are about to use anything less than G-rated language near their kids—"big-ass snake. He used to feed it live chickens."

"It wasn't chickens," I said. "It was rats!"

Bobby stuck his hands in the back pockets of his jeans. "I'm pretty sure it was chickens," he said.

"It wasn't chickens!" I protested, relishing the feeling of being teased by a handsome man. "Where would he have even *gotten* live chickens in Harwick back then?"

"The Boorschmidts," he said, as if the answer were obvious. And I felt my head fall back with the sort of laughter that silently seeps through the whole body, warming it entirely. The Boorschmidts were another Harwick legend, a trio of brothers who had a small farm near the center of town and in my youth had seemed ancient, though they had probably only been in their sixties at the time. They wore jeans that they belted with lengths of rope, and sold corn and their own hybrid string beans out of the back of their pickup truck. When the property around them became more developed, they sold off all but a small square of land, but didn't relocate themselves. Instead they remained defiantly in their home—the yard complete with a half-dozen hound dogs and twice as many chickens—all in the midst of Harwick's suburban splendor.

We took a few more steps. "You know they finally sold the house," said Bobby.

I had noticed that the lot had been razed, but never thought to ask my mother what had become of them. "Where'd they go?" I asked, having trouble picturing the Boorschmidt brothers anywhere other than in their ramshackle home.

Bobby's tone was softer. "I heard they went to a continuing care facility."

"Oh, no," I said, watching my feet as they moved along the maroon carpet. I supposed I had always imagined that the Boorschmidts would die one day all at once, collapsing simultaneously into their bowls of oatmeal. "That's so sad."

We pushed out of the dark theater and into the bright expanse of the mall, with its light floors and atrium ceiling. "So I guess Lydia Stroppe was at our house the other day," said Bobby, his tone both casual and confessional. It wasn't lost on me that he didn't refer to her as Lydia Parsons; maybe we all had a tendency to allow the past to supersede the present, to overlay who someone was now with who they had once been.

"Oh, really?" I asked lightly.

"Yeah, my parents wanted to get her opinion on listing their house."

"You guys are moving?" I asked, hoping my voice revealed nothing.

As I watched my feet slide over the shiny floor, I felt an uncomfortable and unwelcome sense of loss. Yet Bobby's leaving Harwick shouldn't mean anything to me.

"My parents were starting to think about it, but now they want to wait until the market's a little stronger. My mom thinks moving somewhere warmer would be good for my dad's RA," he said. "But now that I've started talking to Hewn Memorial about staying on, I honestly don't think they'll end up leaving."

We passed a husband and wife with three little boys who all looked to be within a couple years of one another in age. I smiled at them and they smiled back. Suddenly Rose turned around. "Hey, Mom!" she said, her eyes wide and concerned. "Gabby says she's really, really hungry for ice cream."

Gabby looked as though this was the first she was hearing about it. "Gabby, huh?"

"Yeah," said Rose, all sympathetic nods. "She says it's her blood sugar."

I immediately halted. "Rose Parsons," I scolded. A boy in her class had type 1 diabetes and Rose's big takeaway from Miss Claire's lecture on the subject was that sometimes Conner might have to eat pudding if his blood sugar got too low, a fact she was trying to exploit. Rose gave me a hangdog expression and turned back around. Once she and Gabby were again oblivious to Bobby and me, I turned toward him, ready to offer an explanation, but Bobby said, "She's just like you used to be."

I softened. "She's way feistier than I ever was."

"I don't know," said Bobby. "You were pretty feisty."

We walked in silence for a few more paces until I asked, "So do you know the Castros, from the neighborhood?"

Bobby brought his hand to his jaw. "Over on Squire Lane?" he asked. Looking at me, he saw the degree of my interest. "I know who they are."

"What are they like?"

Bobby shrugged. "They seem nice enough. I think they're really involved in the town. I believe Rob is on the town council."

"What about their son?" I asked, barely waiting for him to finish. "Zack? What's he like?"

"I don't really know him." We took a few more steps. "He seems like your average teenager."

With my arms crossed over my chest, I looked straight ahead, into the crowd of the mall. "I think he might have been the one who beat up Warren."

I didn't need to say anything else. Bobby inhaled and righted his gaze, seeming to ponder the possibility. Then he nodded.

I let my hand fall helplessly to my thigh. "I don't know the kid," I said, "but would he *do* that? Would he really beat up a pizza delivery guy?" I looked at Bobby, as if he could explain it. "Just because he could?" I assumed it would be for no other reason. I assumed that Zack Castro could have no complaint with Warren other than his very existence.

Bobby lowered his head. "He's what, like seventeen years old?" he said, as if this were the sad but honest explanation.

We lingered in our thoughts until Rose pulled us back to the present with requests for things that were sweet and sparkly.

"It's Halloween tomorrow, Rose. You're going to have plenty of candy."

We pushed through the doors of the mall and it felt like leaving Oz. Gone was the anesthetizing warmth of retail. I blinked toward the parking lot, which was brightened by the towering, long-necked lights that ran in orderly rows up and down the asphalt. Then, from the deep chill of the late fall air, I felt an enormous shiver run through my body.

Without a word, Bobby reached around my back and pulled me into his side, rubbing my upper arm briskly and efficiently. And like a prim old schoolmarm, I stiffened. His hand stopped, and his arm dropped away. *It's just as well,* I told myself. And I reminded myself of all the reasons why.

"Where are you guys parked?" he asked.

I pointed toward our car. "Over by Lipman Teller."

"Come on, Gabs," he said, reaching for her hand. I had already taken Rose's. "Let's walk Rose and her mom to their car."

"It's okay," I said. "You don't need to walk us."

Bobby waved off my objection.

Once we arrived at my station wagon, he waited as I got Rose strapped in, letting the girls have one last moment together. "This was fun," I said, turning to face him.

"We'll do it again," he answered. And then he opened his arms and put them around me. And without having a chance to think about it first, I found myself hugging him back. It lasted only a moment, heart to heart, our backs to the rest of the world. We were at once holding each other up and standing of our own volition. At once strangers and old friends.

. . .

CHAPTER SEVENTEEN

Halloween

"Damn, it's cold," whispered Maggie, shivering as we stood on the sidewalk, watching as Rose and Maggie's sons, Sam and Henry, lifted their bags for one of their neighbors to drop in shiny little foil-wrapped candy bars. "I don't remember ever having to wear coats for trick-or-treating when I was little."

I held Gordo's leash, and smiled as I heard some older children across the street point and laugh at his costume, with its green body and purple spikes down the spine. Gordo was a dinosaur for Halloween and he seemed pleased by the attention it garnered him, his tail swinging spastically. Most dogs I knew hated to be dressed up in anything, but Gordo couldn't be more agreeable about it.

Rose, Sam, and Henry turned away from the door and

ran toward us, all bundled in down jackets and mittens over their costumes. Rose was a cowgirl, and Sam and Henry were two- and four-year-old clone troopers. "Thanks, Ann!" called Maggie as the older woman smiled, then let the door shut as she disappeared back into her house with her enormous bowl of candy.

"How are those bags looking?" I asked, peering into Rose's. "Holy smokes!" I declared, and Rose giggled, delighted by her haul. I gently pinched her chin, which was cold to the touch, her cheeks nearly as red as her little birthmark.

"All right," said Maggie. "What do you say to one more house. Then we'll go home and I'll make some hot cider?"

Rose wrapped her arms around Gordo's neck, which he minded only as it made licking her face more difficult. He swung his head from side to side as he tried to get to her. "Gordo, you're a *dinosaur*," she said, giggling.

Back inside, Rose and Sam peeled off their jackets and immediately lay belly down on the floor, sorting meticulously through their stash while making sure the contents from their respective bags didn't mingle. Little Henry found a corner and started unwrapping candy and shoving it in his mouth as fast as he could before Lance spotted him. "What!" Lance declared, as Henry's sudden urgency to swallow the sugary wad caused three half-chewed, saliva-covered Tootsie Rolls to spill out of his mouth and onto the floor.

Lance scooped him up and started tickling him mercilessly, his laughter so clear and bright and joyful that we all looked, including Rose, who often sought from Lance the fatherly roughhousing that she so craved.

"Now me!" she said, bouncing over to Lance and Henry.

"Now you?" joked Lance. He set down Henry and took Rose up in his arms, fluttering his fingers over her belly and sending her into a fit of giggles.

"Thank you," I mouthed to him, thinking of my own father: Stewart Parsons, Captain of Industry. I had been trying to get in touch with him since I'd seen our grandfather's watch in Lydia's car. But first he was in Europe for a meeting with the board. Now he was in Singapore for the global Snacks and Confectionary business unit conference. *He's just totally swamped*, Lydia had said. *And I think his cell phone acts up when he's overseas. What do you need to talk to him about?*

Maggie called us into the kitchen and we all took our seats at the table. Lance began ladling mugs full of cloudy, amber-colored liquid, which he had mulled with cinnamon while manning the door for trick-or-treaters. *"And . . . ,"* he said with great ceremony as he headed back to the stove and lifted the lid on another pot.

Maggie peered into it. "Ohhh," she said. She opened the overhead cabinet and reached for a stack of plates. "Guys, Dad made Grandma's meatballs. Are you all hungry?" Lance's mother was famous for making time-saver, stick-to-your-ribs recipes; dishes with unlikely combinations like Vienna sausages and pineapple or, in this case, frozen meatballs and grape jelly.

From behind Maggie, Lance wrapped his arms around her neck and kissed the top of her head as she sank a wooden spoon into the pot.

I pointed to each of the kids, waiting for their yea or nay on the meatballs. "I'll just get a big plate for the kids," I said.

Maggie gave me a happy wink as we passed, she on her way

to the table, me on my way to the stove. Then she groaned with delight as she took her first bite. "Oh my God, I *love* you," she said to Lance.

I was opening the cutlery drawer when I heard Rose's voice. "My mom loves *Gabby's daddy*," she teased.

Grabbing a handful of forks, I shuffled back to the table; I would face Maggie's inquisition later. "Rosie, honey, I don't *love* Gabby's daddy," I explained. "We're just old friends."

Maggie, who was wiping her smiling mouth with a paper towel, looked at me with a single raised eyebrow, while Rose pressed the palms of her hands hard against each other and moved them up and down, as if trying to create friction. "Then why did you smoosh together like this?" she asked, a mischievous lilt in her voice.

"We were just hugging good-bye," I said, as I pulled up a chair.

"I only hug people I love," said Rose, as she plucked a meatball from the pile, finally deciding that they were monochromatic enough to be palatable.

"You can hug people that you *like*, too," I offered. "You can hug people to say hello or good-bye, or to make them feel better—"

"I think you should love Gabby's daddy," interrupted Rose as she took a tiny bite. "He's nice."

And I was left staring at my daughter, whose small feet bucked under the table. I was left not knowing how to explain that love isn't that simple when you're a grown-up; that you don't meet someone who is nice, smoosh your bodies together, and decide to be in love. So instead I said simply, "He is nice."

. . .

Music by Vince Guaraldi was playing softly in the kitchen while Maggie and I cleaned up. Lance was reading the kids Halloween stories in the family room. We had changed them out of their costumes, wiped their faces and hands with warm, wet washcloths, and put them in their pajamas. Rose was leaning up against Lance and biting on her thumb, her pointer finger rubbing her nose. I was rinsing out cider mugs and wondering how long it would take before Maggie asked about the man I had smooshed my body against. It was halfway through the third mug.

"So," she said. "Tell me more about *Gabby's daddy.*"

I tutted dismissively. "He's just this guy I grew up with," I said, hearing the steady rush of water from the faucet. "He's got a little girl Rose's age and so we took them to see a movie."

Maggie was watching me closely, a small smirk on her face, her eyes narrowed. "Stop staring at me with your shrink smile," I said. That's what we called it, having discovered that all psychiatrists wore the same smug expression of vague amusement.

"I think it's great," she said with a shrug, reaching for a cup from the dish rack and returning it to the cabinet.

I moved to face her. "Maggie, it is *so* not like that," I said. "I don't even know what his situation is. He was married to this gorgeous woman and now I guess they're divorced, and she's out west and he's got Gabby. . . ." My head tipped from one side to the other with each point. "It all sounds very messy."

Maggie nodded as she arranged the mugs in an orderly line within the cabinet. "That's the way it goes. Things get complicated. We aren't all twenty-five anymore."

For a moment it seemed Maggie had been dissuaded from pursuing the topic any further, but after a few moments she asked, "So, what's his name?"

"Bobby Vanni."

She seemed to roll his name around in her mind for a moment, probably trying out variations of our coupling. *I asked Jenna and Bobby to dinner. Bobby and Jenna are having a barbecue.* "I like it. It's old-school." She nodded, warming to the person she was shaping in her head. "He sounds like a character in a John Hughes movie. Like a *Jake Ryan.*"

My laugh was low and full. "He was *totally* a Jake Ryan." I shut off the water and wiped the small splashes of water from the counter around the sink.

"Did you guys used to date or something?"

"*No,*" I said. "Definitely not. Bobby dated girls like Nicki Waldron."

"Who was Nicki Waldron?"

"You were probably a Nicki Waldron."

"No," she said. "I probably *beat up* Nicki Waldron."

I laughed, giving my friend a bump in the hip with my own as I draped the dishcloth over the handle of the oven.

I went back to the eating area to grab a few stray napkins from under the table. On my way back I said, "He did ask me out once in high school. To a party."

"And . . . ?" asked Maggie.

"And I got drunk, tried to kiss him, and spilled beer on his shirt."

"Parsons," said Maggie, shaking her head in pained amusement. "You are a disaster."

I remember the feeling of sinking and soaring all at once

when I saw him waiting for me at my locker on the last day of school in junior year. *There's a party Friday. At Rick DeSesso's.* That phrase was repeated to all of my friends, countless times, as we analyzed the intonation, the possible meanings behind its nuanced delivery. The length of the pause between sentences, the emphasis on Rick DeSesso versus Friday—we examined these details with nearly unimaginable intensity.

At the party, Rick played master of ceremonies, nodding his approval at Bobby's unconventional choice of a date for the evening. "Parsons," he said, giving Bobby a high five as I passed in front of him. "Nice." Rick DeSesso's house had a detached garage with an empty apartment above it, so he used to have epic but exclusive parties to which his parents would turn a blind eye. With the cool music and dim lights, the wonderfully shabby little space seemed to exist in a sort of eight-millimeter haze, outside the influence of parents or teachers or authority of any kind.

There was a pony keg of some terrible yellow beer that I drank without restraint, feeling the effect of the alcohol make its way slowly through my body, sinking down into my legs. I was smiling and nodding my head to the music, surrounded by the popular kids and their drunken laughter. And I was there with Bobby Vanni. *He's just going to try and get in your pants,* my friends had said. And I hoped they were right.

When I stumbled out of Rick's strange little bathroom— which had a toilet and a shower, but no sink—and Bobby was standing outside the door, leaning coolly against the wall across from me, his arms folded over his chest, one hand holding a red plastic cup full of beer, for a moment I thought I was a different girl. For a moment, I thought he had been waiting for me. I took a step toward him, lifted my chin, and closed my eyes. My slight stumble, one I couldn't blame entirely on the alcohol, caused me to bump him, sending a slosh of yellow beer onto his sleeve. Still, I wrapped my arm around his neck; I pressed my lips to his mouth, feeling them answer once before I felt the heat of his hand on my shoulder, firmly but gently pressing me away. At the sound of his chuckle, I opened my eyes. "You're pretty hammered, Jenna." He was looking at me with amused affection. "We should probably get you home."

I just stood there, blinking dumbly. "Oh," I said. "Okay." My mind was working slowly, but the thundering hooves of humiliation were drawing closer. I didn't want to be little Jenna Parsons anymore. I didn't want to be the girl from the neighborhood.

Nicki Waldron, who throughout our senior year would claim to have been offered a modeling contract that she opted to turn down, leaned her head into the hallway, her tiny pink T-shirt lifting on one side to reveal a stretch of tanned stomach. *Finster just called and said his parents are in the city. We're all going to hit his pool.* She was speaking to Bobby, not me.

I stood there staring at the floor. "Cool," he said. Without taking his eyes away from Nicki's very pretty face, he nodded toward me. "I'm just going to make sure Jenna gets home first."

Then, with as much dignity and nonchalance as I could muster, I waved him off, telling him I had a ride. That I was all set.

"Are you sure?" he asked, skeptically.

"Totally," I said. "I'll see you later."

Warren met me at the end of the street. I sat tucked behind a shed, twirling a small blade of grass between my fingers while

I waited for him to pull up in my mother's station wagon. When he caught sight of me, our eyes locked for a moment, everything being communicated silently and immediately. Warren's eyes moved down the street to the soft glow of Rick DeSesso's, to its steady thrum of music and laughter and voices, and watched it with a guarded interest. But he never asked me what had happened. He never asked me about my date with Bobby Vanni. Instead, we glided over the smooth, black suburban streets with the windows down and the early summer air on my bare arms, and I rested my head on the seat back, thinking about how much I wanted to get out of Harwick and my mother's house. Thinking about how much I wanted to become someone new. Maybe when I went to college, I'd dye my red hair jet-black and pierce my nose. Maybe I'd major in art and smoke cigarettes and have sex with someone without telling him first that I was a virgin. Maybe I'd get a tattoo. And as I tried on all these rebellions in my mind, Warren was silent until he finally said to me, his stare focused on the manicured world beyond the windshield but acutely aware of my reaction, "Grandpa's been coughing a lot lately."

"He's probably just got a cold, War," I said dismissively.

In the end, I did get my nose pierced, having taken the train into New York and finding a little West Village storefront. I stood in front of their window display, running my eyes up and down the rows of savage-looking hoops and bars, breathing New York's distinct smell in and out. I remember the popping sensation as the small stud I'd selected punctured my skin. I remember how it made my eyes water, and how the world went blurry for a moment as I blinked the tears away. That nose ring

was in for two months before my grandfather died. I took it out
for the funeral and never put it back in.

When Rose and I left Maggie's house that night, with Rose's
tired, sugar-racked body slung over my hip, I thanked Lance
for dinner. "It was so nice of you to make your mom's meatballs," I said.

"Remember last year?" said Maggie. "How we tried to
order pizza?"

I did remember. We waited for over two hours for it to be
delivered, and when it finally arrived, it was stiff and cold.
"Warren says Halloween is the busiest night of the year." I
thought about my brother, as he was surely racing around
Harwick in his thick, gray Pizzeria Brava sweatshirt, rushing
from house to house carrying his square red insulated bag. His
brow would be furrowed; his still battered-looking face would be
turned downward toward a ticket as he asked, the words coming
out slowly, *Three Meat Maniac Pizzas?* Then he'd slide the boxes
out, his thin shoulders slumped, watching as wallets were pulled
from pockets and purses, as bills were taken out. His body would
remain still but his gaze would move around the room, taking in
the behavior and habitat of these normal families the way a sci-
entist would observe a species of interest. "He'll probably have to
hit half of Harwick tonight."

It wasn't until Mom called the next day that I learned the
number of houses Warren visited on Halloween: fifty. He

delivered pizzas to fifty Harwick families. Seven of them called to complain. It was the way he looked, with his stitches, his bruises. It was the way he acted, with his watching, his stillness. It was everything about him. *We hate to make a stink, but . . .*

At noon on November 1, his boss, Fung Huang, phoned Warren and asked him to come in. He told him that he could no longer keep him employed as a driver for Pizzeria Brava due to customer complaints. Warren stood there for a moment, as if the information Fung had relayed took a long and circuitous path to his understanding. Then, when Warren seemed to fully comprehend that he had just been fired, he brought his hand to the top of his head and pressed down, saying only, "I'm sorry about this, Fung."

"I'm just so worried about him." Mom's anxiety was reverberating through the phone line.

She explained that Fung had called her after Warren left, warning her about what had happened. He was apologetic but said that he couldn't afford to lose business, not since Dino's had expanded its delivery area. And these complaints weren't the first Fung had had about Warren. *He makes some of the customers uncomfortable.*

I pressed the black receiver to my ear, feeling Maggie's eyes on me from across the office. "Where is he now?" I asked.

I heard Mom's rush of breath. "He didn't tell me anything. He just took his fishing pole and tackle box and left." I pictured Warren driving toward the black water of a river. He would stand at its edge, surrounded by silence. He'd cast in his line and finally there would be a tug. He'd pull a fish from the cold, its body a solid length of muscle, its gills splayed and searching. He'd gently pull the hook from its mouth and admire it for a moment, appreciate the singularity of its existence, the imperative of which was to simply survive. Then he'd set the fish back into the water, waiting for its tail to begin undulating again—just like our grandfather had taught him—before releasing it. *There you go,* he'd say. *There you go.* That's what I imagined anyway; Warren never kept them anymore.

"I'll come home," I said.

"No, Jenna," said Mom, as if this was a burden she needed to bear alone. "It's all right."

Warren didn't get home until nearly one in the morning. Mom called me when he arrived. My head jerked away from the computer where I was working on a new package for Apothecary and I answered the phone. Whispering, my mother said that she had just seen his car pull into the driveway. "Thank goodness," she said. "Thank goodness." So relieved was she that she forgot to mention the red and blue police lights that churned the darkness as they traveled down Royal Court, preceding Warren's return home by half an hour. As soon as he walked in the door, the fact of them seemed a secondary concern, a false alarm. It wasn't until the next day that she heard about the robbery.

. . .

Thirst

1965

Perhaps she heard footsteps or breathing. Perhaps she saw some movement in her eye's periphery. Or perhaps it was instinctual, the knowledge that Hattie was behind her. With her hip propping open the refrigerator door, with the milk jug already in her hand, Priscilla did it anyway. She poured a glass, then brought it to her lips, tipping it back and drinking it down. And when the last drops slid into her mouth, she wiped her lips with the back of her wrist and pushed the door shut. But now that her defiance was complete, she no longer felt quite so brave. Now that her defiance was complete, she didn't want to turn around.

Hattie took her time before she spoke. "You already had your eight ounces this morning."

"I was thirsty," answered Silla, sounding more confident than she felt. Her head was hinged forward, her fingers still gripping the handle of the refrigerator.

"You think that milk is free?" asked Hattie.

"*No*," responded Silla, with all the sass of the teenager that she was.

"Your daddy is out there working hard," said Hattie, the words meandering out, "and you're just going to stand there and guzzle down his money."

"I don't think Daddy would mind."

"Oh, you don't?" asked Hattie, her voice rising with false innocence.

Silla wheeled around, her cheeks a furious red. "He drives a Cadillac and you get your hair done twice a week." What she said next was unplanned. "Besides, it's my mama's money anyhow."

Hattie's face curved into a reptilian smile and an observation that lodged almost out of Silla's reach was just how empty those eyes looked. Just how black.

"Oh, your mama's money," said Hattie. "Your wonderful *mama's* money." Hattie reached into the pocket of her dress and pulled out her cigarettes, tapping one out and bringing it to her lips. Her head bowed as the lighter sparked and when she lifted her chin again, the tip of the cigarette brightened at the inhalation. "Tell me something," she said, the smoke lazily leaving her mouth. "Do you know where your mama *is*?"

Silla drew back, silent. Speaking of her dead mother with Hattie felt heretical, the worst sort of sin. Again, Hattie smiled. "Well, then. By all means, don't let me stop you from drinking down your dear departed *mama's* money." Then Hattie started out of the kitchen, crossing slowly in front of Silla, her hips moving with their usual pendulum-like rhythm, her cigarette burning between her fingers.

As soon as Hattie had left the kitchen, Silla turned and burst out the screen door, not slowing as she took the steps and marched down the driveway. She imagined herself leaving. She imagined never coming back. And as she walked, escape seemed possible. Her steps were fueled by the image of Hattie having to explain to her father that she was gone. She pictured her father slamming his fist down, screaming at Hattie; she pictured him shaking her. And Silla kept walking. *He'll be so angry with her,* she told herself. She wanted so much to believe it. And so she kept walking.

If she had a plan, it was to go to the bus station. To board a coach to California. Never mind that she didn't have the fare. Never mind that she didn't know a soul outside Texas. It was a warm evening but comfortably so. The sort that brought people onto their porches, letting the humid air surround their work-weary limbs. It was gradual, Silla's realization that she was walking to nothing and to no one. That she was just a girl. That she could be devoured by this world. *Hey, baby girl!* she heard a man in a tank top call from a passing car.

When dark had settled in, she finally turned around. She walked even more quickly home, her heart lurching and skittish in her chest. And when she rounded the curve of Beechnut Street, her shirt was as damp as her skin, and she was both re-lieved and terrified to catch a glimpse of her house. She saw that Hattie's car was gone. The only light left on in the house was in the attic. No one ever went in the attic except Silla. That's where they kept her mama's things—her pictures, her clothes. After Hattie and her father had married, her mother's possessions had made their way slowly up, until there was nothing left of Martha Briggs anywhere in the house except for the attic and Silla's room. And though Silla's legs were bone-tired, she began to run. Up the driveway, onto the porch. She ran into the house faster than she had burst out of it.

Hattie had left it open for her, the entrance to the attic. Its old wooden ladder extended down to the floor; its yellow light spilled out into the darkness. Silla wasn't higher than two rungs when she could already see what had been done. Her breath turned panicked until it ripped out as a sob. Reaching the top, she threw herself on the landing as if onto a grave. Nothing had prepared her for this tidal wave of loss. Nothing had prepared her for seeing the room empty, completely devoid of its contents. Finally and fully, she understood the consequences of crossing Hattie.

Then, suddenly and urgently, Silla sat up. Still weeping, she scrambled back down the ladder and hurried to her room. There, with shaking hands, she gathered up the four photos of her mother that remained. She hid two under her dresser, and two in the back of her closet. Still in the clothes that she had been walking in, she shut off her light and pulled up her covers. And with her back to the door, she stared at the wall until she heard Hattie's car on the drive, until she heard the clack of her heels through the house, her steps slow and stalking.

The next morning she would get up, she would dress for school, and she would keep her eyes down at breakfast. She would drink her eight ounces of milk. And not one drop more.

. . .

CHAPTER NINETEEN

Mrs. Castro

Bobby ran his hand over his chin and I noticed the thin lines that shot out like rays from the corners of his eyes as he squinted against both the cold air and the bright light of the park. "Yeah, I guess they got something like eight hundred dollars in cash, a laptop, and Dean's coin collection." With his characteristic calm, he was filling me in on the theft that had King's Knoll atwitter.

I pressed my hands deeper into the pockets of my jacket. "But the Doogans were out when it happened?"

He nodded. "They were in the city. And obviously they locked the doors before they left," he said with a shrug, "but there was no sign of forced entry."

"That's pretty creepy." I heard laughter and squeals from

Gabby and Rose. They were going down the slide on top of each other, their limbs as twisted and tangled as their voices. Gordo circled below, thinking that he was part of the fun, looking elated and insane as he struggled to lift his disproportioned body into playful half leaps.

My mother and I had been painting the house columns when Bobby's car had driven past; Rose was inside watching Warren finish one of his planes, listening as he narrated his every move while Gordo lay next to him. *You want to balance the wing at thirty percent back from the leading edge,* he'd said while Rose rested her cheek against his desk. When Warren was around, Rose and Gordo both preferred him to all other life-forms.

Bobby had given his horn a short, friendly beep and waved in greeting. I had waved back, then looked over to see my mother almost smiling as her brush moved up and down the tall column, her hair again pulled away from her face by a kerchief, her thick maroon parka covering her body from shoulder to knee. "You enjoy yourself around him," she'd observed.

"Yeah," I'd said lightly, looking only at the patch that I was painting. "Rose and Gabby have fun together."

My mother had nodded and continued painting. A few minutes later, my phone had rung and I'd pulled it from my back pocket. *Bobby Vanni.* Again, I glanced at my mother, then answered.

"Hey," he said. His voice was deep and warm as he asked me if I wanted to take the girls to the park.

"Uhhh, well, right now I'm helping my mom. . . ." I wondered if any other excuse would have sounded quite so girlish.

But my mother interrupted me. "Go on, honey," she said,

her eyes on another car making its way down the street. It was Beth Castro, Zack's mother. Mom watched her intently, her mouth a tight line as Mrs. Castro turned smoothly into her driveway. "It's getting late for this. I was just thinking of calling it a day, anyhow."

Twenty minutes later, I was standing next to Bobby, watching as Gabby leapt up to grab the monkey bars, swinging her legs after her and hooking them over the metal rod so that she was hanging upside down. Gordo found this thrilling, and tried to lick her face while his tail thumped against the ladder, causing it to ring the hollow sound of a broken bell. "Gordo!" I said, clapping my hands sharply. "Hey!" I didn't want his affection to make her fall, but Gabby just reached her arms around Gordo's neck as she continued to hang. "Oh, my gosh," I said, marveling at her dexterity. "Look at her!" Her coat was submitting to gravity, exposing her tiny belly to the cold air, and she had Gordo bathing her face in saliva, but still she hung elegantly, her long brown hair brushing the ground.

"I know," said Bobby, with a small chuckle. "She's a total monkey." He paused, giving what he said next unintended weight. "Her mother's like that, too. She used to be a dancer."

It seemed to be a door, an invitation to ask more, so I did. "Does Gabby still see her mom often?"

Bobby took a breath, and held it in his lungs. It was the way a man might cover up pain from a punch. "No," he finally said. "She lives out in California. She has a yoga studio out there, so she doesn't come back east much." He looked at his beautiful little girl, who had righted herself, her feet once again upon the earth. "And Gabs only goes out a couple of times a year." He chuckled at Gordo, who was now lying on his back and pawing the air, his tongue hanging out the side of his mouth in a state of spastic bliss.

"Rose doesn't see her dad much either," I said. "He lives in Japan."

Bobby took another breath and nodded, the rush of air over the back of his throat a quiet lament.

"I wish Gabby could see Mia more often. But you know how it is."

"Yeah. I do." That was all I needed to say. And though I still hadn't heard from Duncan, hadn't received confirmation of his return to New York, I thought about him coming back to the area. About what it would be like to have him blow more frequently and with greater force into Rose's life. To have him blow back out again.

"I don't think Mia was ready to have kids," said Bobby. His voice was deep and low; his eyes remained on Gabby. "At the time anyway . . ." Gordo ran a circle around the girls and came bounding toward us as fast as he could, which wasn't all that fast, and I saw one side of Bobby's face lift into a smile at the sight of him.

I stared at Bobby's profile, the lines of it cutting against dusk's deepening sky. And without thinking I leaned closer to him and hooked my arm through one of his. Feeling the heft of his shoulder, the strength that was there, I let my head tilt to rest against it. Maybe it was that I'd known him my whole life. Maybe that was why I did it. Maybe it was the sound of our daughters' voices, like the chatter of birds. Maybe it was the deep kinship I felt for him because he was raising a daughter on his own. But I wasn't thinking about any of that. I was thinking only that it was nice to have a place to rest my head. I held my body very still, the way I did when I was cold, as if the energy required to tense my muscles would warm them by some infinitesimal degree. "I can't believe they're not freezing," I said, nodding toward the girls. "The temperature is really starting to drop."

Bobby's chest rose and fell with a breath. "Yeah, it's getting late," he said. And in his voice was the regret I also felt, that we had to move from this spot. Then he angled his head down toward me, his lips at my forehead, so close that I could feel the warmth of his breath, his mouth slightly open in advance of words he had yet to speak. "I should get going," he said. "I have to be at the hospital."

I let go of his arm and smiled. "This was fun."

His brow tensed in thought and his gaze turned inward. "Maybe," he began tentatively, "we can get together for dinner sometime?"

"Sure," I said, lightly. "Rosie would love that."

He looked at me, pausing before he said, "Or we could do something with just you and me."

"Yeah," I replied, "we could do that."

His smile broadened and we remained eye to eye for a moment, until he turned toward the girls. "Gabs! We gotta get going!"

Gabby and Rose both froze and looked at us.

"Come on, Rosie! Gabby's daddy has to get to work!" I tried to whistle, but it sounded only like the wind. "Gordo!" I called.

Rose ignored me, but Gordo came bounding obediently in my direction. "He's a great dog," said Bobby, as he watched him.

"He is a great dog."

"Where'd you get him?"

"Well . . . ," I started, and as Bobby and Gabby walked Rose and me back to the house, I told him about how we came to acquire Gordo, about how when I went to one of those big-box pet stores to get a goldfish for Rose, a local shelter was there holding an adoption drive. They were set up in the center of the huge space, with a temporary fence around a green Astroturf carpet. There were several dogs and cats in cages around the perimeter. While we perused the store, collecting fish food and colored stones, I watched as families walked by, pointing at the cages. Every so often, a dog would be taken onto the green for playtime with a potential new owner. Gordo sat there, watching every person who approached with his goofy, cross-eyed eagerness, his tail going like it had a motor on it. Five dogs were there that day. Gordo was the only one that nobody wanted to play with. "Hey, Rosie," I had said. "Let's go meet that doggy."

As we approached his cage, Gordo had tried his very best to be still, but his seated haunches quivered with anticipation. Once the door was open, he bounded out, his whole body wagging with the force of a salmon trying to leap upstream. Rose wasn't yet two and could barely speak, but she laughed at Gordo, the fat insides of her cheeks showing through the enormity of her smile. I scratched his head, and he looked at me like I was Jesus.

"Why hasn't this guy been adopted?" I asked.

The woman from the shelter joined in by petting Gordo's fur, which was a dull brown with gray patches. "It's kind of a beauty contest with adoptions," she said sadly. I grinned hard to fight the tears that were rimming my eyes as I jostled his ears. And instead of a goldfish, we left with Gordo.

"Gabby would love to have a dog," said Bobby.

"She can play with Gordo anytime she wants," I offered, as we approached my mother's back deck. We took only a few more paces before I became aware of the shouting, the bursts of unintelligible words echoing through the neighborhood. My pace quickened as I heard them, and Bobby's sped up to keep time with mine. We glanced at each other, silently communicating our confusion and concern as the girls trailed behind us. There were two voices. As I drew closer to Royal Court, I heard that—even in anger—my mother's long, slow lapping vowels couldn't be mistaken. I turned to Bobby. "Can you keep an eye on Rosie for a minute?" I asked. Then I broke into a jog, Gordo running next to me.

I hurried through the side yard, between Mom's house and the Fitzpatricks', past Warren's car in the driveway, and my car in the street. Past the Dietzes' and the Rignarellis'. Past a lawn sign with Lydia's smiling face. The words were clearer as they rolled in from somewhere down the street, but I still couldn't see my mother. Then I heard Warren's name and wanted to reel back. The sound of it was like walking forcefully into a glass door. But I kept going, filling my lungs as the chilly air and anxiety brought cold heat to my cheeks. As soon as Squire Lane was in view, I saw Mom standing on the Castros' front porch, illuminated by the floodlights overhead as if she were on a stage.

Mrs. Castro loomed in the doorway, her arms crossed over her chest, her face pressing forward as her shrill voice delivered its barbs. "He's seventeen!" she yelled. "Of course he's going to be upset that his crazy neighbor stole his mountain bike!"

"Warren did *not* steal his *mountain bike!*" shouted my mother. "He's never stolen anything in his life!"

"Go tell that to the Doogans! They're out eight hundred dollars!"

I stopped at the curb. Gordo continued down the street before realizing that I wasn't next to him, then circled back around. Bounding toward me, he thought it was all a game, that we were going for a run.

"Mom!" I said desperately. She startled and looked back at me. Beth Castro straightened up, almost regally, and stood firmly in the entrance to her house. Looking at me for just a moment, she turned her attention back to my mother. "I just think that before you come over here, lobbing accusations at *my* son—"

"*Accusations?*" interrupted my mother. "You admitted that Zack beat up—"

But Beth Castro's voice overrode Mom's, her eyes bugging out as she spoke. "Priscilla," she said, holding up one finger of warning, "you had better look at the whole picture."

"*Mom,*" I called again. "*Please.*"

My mother let her head drop. "This cost my son his job," she muttered back at Mrs. Castro, as she started for the steps.

"Delivering *pizza*," said Mrs. Castro—her final blow.

Gordo trotted up the driveway to meet her, but I waited on the curb before I laid my hand on her back and walked silently with her toward her house, Gordo's claws tapping on the pavement.

"Zack Castro was the one who beat up your brother, Jenna," said my mother, her emotions too wild and unhinged for any particular one to dominate. She wasn't just mad or sad or hurt or scared. She was all of them. "He thinks Warren stole his mountain bike." She released a sputter that was somewhere between a laugh and a cry.

We walked silently back through the neighborhood, which seemed alert in its stillness, a village of murmurs and stares. Since I'd left the park, the sun had nearly sunk below the trees, leaving the sky an inky blue against which the houses glowed with an electric daylight. I held my arms tight across my chest as I watched my feet move over the black asphalt.

"Mom," I said, picturing her standing on the Castros' front porch, making her emotional, impulsive defense. "You shouldn't have gone over there like that. It didn't help Warren." *Those Parsonses*, the neighbors were probably saying. *Tut-tut*. And though Mom didn't respond, her body seemed to slow a bit, as if another weight had been added. We walked back through the side yard and from across the park, I saw Bobby holding the back door of his mother's house open for Rose and Gabby.

"I'm just gonna . . . ," I said, gesturing toward the Vannis' house. "Can you take Gordo?"

Mom nodded. "Go ahead," she said.

I jogged through the park, aware that Bobby needed to get to work. Through the glass back door, I could see that he was peeling off Rose's jacket, while his mother tended to Gabby's. Mr. Vanni was standing at the counter, his arm propped on its edge for support. I hurried up the steps and rapped lightly on the door.

Immediately, I had all the Vannis' attention. Bobby reached for the knob. "Is everything okay?" he whispered as I entered the bright warmth of their kitchen. I could hear the TV blaring from the next room; Linda and Sal must have been watching the evening news.

I bit my lower lip and planted my hand on my hip, not knowing how to answer. Bobby's eyes didn't leave me even as I couldn't find a spot for my own to settle. I glanced around the room. Sal was looking at me expectantly. "Hi, Mr. Vanni," I said. I had always loved Bobby's father.

"Jenna," he said with a smile, leaning shakily forward to kiss my cheek. His movements were slow and pained. "Good to see you, hon." I hadn't seen Mr. Vanni in years, having left the block party before he was able to make his way out.

Rose leaned in front of me, her face turned up. "Why was Nana yelling?" she asked.

Like a fish on a hook, Mrs. Vanni, who had been squatting to remove Gabby's shoes, lifted her head, a worried expression on her face.

"Oh, don't worry, Rosie," I said, bending down. "Everything's okay." I glanced at Mrs. Vanni and tried to smile. She would hate to hear about my mother and Mrs. Castro shouting at each other in the street.

Taking the jacket that Bobby had just placed on the chairback, I held it open for Rose. "We need to go home and check on Nana, okay? I'm sorry for barging in like this," I told the Vannis. Then I turned to Bobby. "I know you're trying to get to work."

He paused for a moment, his face somber and concerned. "Will you call me later?" he asked.

"Of course."

With Rose on my hip, I again walked through the park. The hill and the pond below it were beside us when Rose let her head sink against my shoulder. "I'm hungry," she said.

"I know, Rosie," I said, laboring to carry her. It used to be so easy; she used to be so light. "We'll get you something to eat at Nana's."

Gordo's nose was pressed against the back door as he awaited our return, and he looked as though he wanted to break right through the glass.

Mom sat at the kitchen table and our eyes met. I opened the door. "Hey, Nana," I said as casually as possible, while Gordo wound himself around my legs. "Rosie is getting pretty hungry." I set Rose down on the floor and again peeled off her jacket. "You want to watch a show while I fix you something?" I asked.

She did. And while my mother settled her in front of the TV, I began making her a grilled cheese sandwich. I had just turned on the stove when Mom came to stand next to me. "Is Warren upstairs?" I asked, as I added a pat of butter and watched it slide across the hot pan.

Mom rubbed her hands over her face, then clasped them in front of her, nodding. "Yeah," she said. "He's working on a plane."

We stood in silence while the sandwich browned, each submerged with our own thoughts. After I cut the grilled cheese into four triangles, I brought it, along with a bowl of apple slices and a glass of water, into the family room. Pulling one of the TV trays from its holder, I set it down in front of Rose, who leaned her head past me so as not to miss a second of her show. Without moving her eyes from the screen, she picked up a piece of apple and began eating. I ran my hands over her wild red curls. "You're a funny girl, Rosie," I said softly, before turning and walking back through the kitchen. My mother was still standing by the stove, her face angled toward the window above the sink. I needed to talk to Warren.

. . .

"Hey, War," I said, rapping lightly on his door. "It's me."

I waited a moment for him to answer. When he didn't, I pushed the door open and peeked inside. He was at his desk, the bright halogen lamp bowed over his slender fingers as they gently twisted together two wires that protruded from the belly of a plane. Walking across the cornflower blue carpet, I sat on the edge of his bed, his plaid comforter pulled smoothly over the mattress, and watched him.

Warren spoke first. "Mom shouldn't have gone over there," he said, not looking up, his hands illuminated as he worked.

"No," I said. "Probably not. But she was only trying to look out for you, you know?" There were a few more beats of silence before I asked, "How much did you hear?"

His brow tensed slightly, but he didn't look up. Nor did he answer. I imagined he'd heard the start of the argument, then begun working on his plane. That's what he used to do toward the end of our parents' marriage, when their fights would rock the house, when Lydia's name was lobbed about like a grenade. He would go up and work on his planes and I swear that he wouldn't hear another word.

"I guess Zack Castro thinks you're the one who stole his mountain bike." At this, Warren's hands stopped. I paused, not knowing how much more to tell him. But then, seeing the side of his face, the line of neat stitches above his eyebrow, I said, "Mrs. Castro says that's why he did what he did."

Slowly, Warren raised his head, and though he remained still, his eyes moved back and forth, as if scanning the lines of some cryptic text. He seemed to be reliving some event, replaying it in his head, and he smoothed his bangs down over his forehead.

"Warren, I'm sorry," I said, thinking that maybe it had been stupid to come up here to tell him what Beth Castro had said. "I didn't mean to . . ." I looked around, at a loss for a phrase to explain what I hadn't meant to do.

But Warren's head jerked around and he found my eyes. "No," he said, to stave off my apology, my remorse. Then his attention turned back down to his desk, his chin tucked to his chest. "It's good that you told me."

I steadied myself with a breath, preparing for the question that came next. "Warren, I'm sure you don't . . . but I have to ask. Do you know what happened to that kid's mountain bike?"

He let his head fall to the side. "No, Jenna," he said. "I don't."

And not for a moment did I doubt him. Rising from his bed, I wrapped my arms around him, hunching over him from behind in a tight, enveloping hug. I heard him let out a low and slightly uncomfortable chuckle before reluctantly patting my arm. "Oh, boy," he said, delivering another pat. "Okay."

On the way back down the stairs, I passed a framed photo of Warren and me with our grandfather. He had on his fishing hat with one arm extended around each of us. Warren and I were both smiling, looking skinny and gangly. Our grandfather looked exactly the way I would always remember him, in a plaid wool shirt tucked neatly into his trousers.

When Grandpa was diagnosed with lung cancer, my parents hadn't spoken to each other in over a year. Now they had to get on the phone because someone needed to take Grandpa for radiation. Dad had just been promoted and was traveling almost constantly. And Lydia had our half sister, Alexandra, who was a toddler at the time, to look after. *You'd think you or your* wife *could get your father to the hospital,* my mother would say, the word "wife" particularly sharp. But my father was across the country. And Lydia said that she'd really like to, *but . . .* So it fell to my mother. Or more accurately, it fell to my mother and Warren.

Really, my mother adored Grandpa and was grateful that it was she who cared for him during his final months. He'd lie in bed and close his eyes and ask her to sing. He had always loved music, loved singing. He used to take Warren and me to see a Broadway show every year at Christmastime. So Mom would sing and he'd hum along as best he could, his blanket-shrouded toes tapping the air. And Warren was there as well, sitting just out of view on the floor beside the couch, or in the narrow foyer. Every bit present, but safely out of reach.

That was in the fall of our senior year of high school and I was on the varsity soccer team. *Go to your game,* Grandpa would say. *I'm not much fun right now anyhow.* And the emphasis he put on the present always made me believe that there would be a future. Or maybe that's what I told myself. Because while I was on some bus traveling to some field to play in some game, Warren would be standing in my grandfather's kitchen with a large oven mitt on one hand, frying him catfish and trying to tempt him to eat. Grandpa would always take a small bite for Warren. *Mmmm. Tastes fresh,* he'd say. *Did you catch it yourself?* And Warren would swell with pride.

When the day of the funeral arrived and it was time to walk

into the nave that held my grandfather's casket, Warren wouldn't go. My mother and I both begged him, whispering hushed pleas as we stood before the heavy wooden doors, splayed open to reveal the flower-laden altar, the pews full of people. Lydia was there, wearing formfitting black and sobbing in the front row. But Warren just shook his head, refusing to look down the aisle, his feet planted on the floor. He could take care of our grandfather during his final months, could pretend not to hear as he vomited into an emesis basin, but he couldn't quite manage the spectacle of the funeral. And when it was over and we walked outside, red-eyed and hollowed out, we found Warren sitting cross-legged on the lawn outside the church. Dad saw him and his jaw hardened. He marched across the lawn and stopped right in front of him, looking down at his son, who was running his fingers over a blade of grass. "I have *never* been so ashamed of you," he said, his voice shaking with fury and regret. "After everything your grandfather did for you, you couldn't even pay your respects."

Back in the kitchen, my mother was still standing at the stove, and Rose still watching TV. Gordo was lying on the floor by her feet. He lifted his head and when he saw it was me, he grunted and lay back down.

"Warren's doing fine, Mom," I said, preempting her question as I sidled up next to her. "We're going to fix this, I promise. I'll go talk to Beth Castro. I'll explain the situation." Because wasn't it fixable? Wouldn't she understand that Warren hadn't stolen anything? Couldn't that be made clear?

Mom looked at me the way I sometimes looked at Rose,

when her innocence made my heart break. "Jenna, honey," she said. A cartoon crash sounded from the television and Rose's laughter bubbled through the air. "This is bigger than you think."

"What do you mean?"

She looked thoughtfully down, and I noticed how thick and black her eyelashes still were. "I mean that some of the neighbors have been saying things."

I was suddenly angry, already knowing the answer to the question I was about to ask. "What have they been saying?" Though I didn't let myself look around, I thought of the house, of its contents cluttered and piled and filling every available space. I thought of the exterior, chipped and faded; the lawn that had spent all those years littered with this and that. I thought of all the FOR SALE signs up and down the neighborhood. And then I thought of Warren walking the streets, his gaze extended heavenward, toward his flying machines as they swooped through the sky.

Mom and I stood eye to eye for a moment before she got down on her hands and knees and pulled loose the wood facing beneath one of the cabinets, letting it echo hollowly as it hit the tile floor. It was her hiding spot, where she used to keep cigarettes before she quit. She reached carefully into the tight space and pulled out a small stack of papers.

"Here," she said, handing them to me. "They've been coming in the mail."

I scanned them quickly, passing from one to the other, trying to make sense of what I was seeing. They were letters, written anonymously. And though each consisted of only a single sentence, the words occupied the entirety of the page.

"They're in order," said my mother.

The first ones were cryptic, with lines like, *Neighborhoods are built house by house—we all need to do our share!* But they became increasingly direct. *The condition of your home is impacting the value of ours!* Then it seemed that once the thefts began, so did the attacks on Warren. *Your son cannot use this neighborhood as his ATM!* And finally, *Warren has become a burden that this neighborhood can no longer bear!*

"Oh, my God," I said, looking up at my mother, the papers held loosely in my hands. "Who are these from?"

Mom remained still, but her eyes shifted to the letter at the top of the stack. It was printed on paper that was bordered with illustrations of little martini glasses—the sort that Beth Castro might use to send out invitations to Bunco night.

"Mom, who's sending—"

"I don't know, Jenna," she interrupted. Then her face changed, her expression indicating that she hadn't meant to direct her frustration at me. "It could be one person. It could be a whole group."

"You need to go to the police, Mom."

"Absolutely not! How would that help anything? Getting the authorities involved?"

I thought about it, about whether calling the police would further escalate a situation that my mother had probably already escalated tonight. "We need to do something."

"We *are* doing something," she said. "We're doing exactly what they want. We're fixing up this house."

· · ·

CHAPTER TWENTY

Cal Harper

1968

Cal Harper's face drew into a smile and he leaned back onto the heels of his feet, his hands stuck in the pockets of his slacks. "I'm a *judge*," he said, the words oozing out like syrup, his accent thick and slow.

"How are *you* going to judge a beauty contest?" teased Priscilla's father as he hauled his golf clubs into the back of his car.

"It's a problem, I know," said Mr. Harper. "I'll want 'em all to win." He pulled out a handkerchief and blotted the sweat from his forehead. "But I must do my civic duty, Lee."

Silla's father let out one of his laughs—a pulsing of air through his nose. Silla, who had been standing by the passenger door, saw Mr. Harper glance at her. "You know, Silla could enter this year." As Lee turned to close the trunk, Mr. Harper gave Silla a wink that was so fast she thought she might have been seeing things. "She's old enough now."

Lee scratched the back of his head and studied the pavement. "Well . . . ," he began, intending for that to be his only answer.

But Cal Harper knew Lee's sweet spot. "There's good money in it," he said, folding the handkerchief back up, square into square, putting it back into his pocket. "If she wins." When he looked back at Lee, he could see that he now had his attention.

"How good?" asked Lee.

Mr. Harper just smiled. "Priscilla," he said, taking his time to turn to her. "How'd you like to be in a beauty contest?" His gaze moved quickly and casually from her feet up to her face, taking it all in, but not lingering on any one part. There'd be time for that.

Silla had worn her white tennis dress to the club, and though she loved how it felt on the court, loved how she could look down and see the muscles in her legs, loved how freely she could move in it, she suddenly regretted that it was so very short. "Well, I . . . ," she started. "I never thought about it, I guess." In truth, once she had become aware of her looks, she viewed them as a liability, the opposite of camouflage. Especially while living with Hattie.

Mr. Harper turned back to Lee. "It's good for 'em, I think," he said. "Teaches 'em poise." From the rolling green golf course, there came the hollow crack of a club meeting the ball, and Mr. Harper's eyes were drawn toward the sound. "And the higher up they go in these things, the bigger the pageants they compete in, the better the prizes." He followed the arc of the ball until it began its descent. "They can really turn it into a nice little career."

"Is it too late to register?" asked Lee, feigning disinterest.

Though Mr. Harper was still facing the course, Silla saw his face form a victorious grin. "I'm sure we can pull some strings," he said, just as Hattie was walking out from the clubhouse. Sunglasses covered her eyes and her solid sheet of blond hair had been teased and then smoothed into a chin-length helmet. As soon as she was within earshot, Cal said, "There she is," as if he had been waiting all this time just to catch a glimpse of her. "You're surrounded by beautiful women, Lee."

Hattie's raspberry lips curved into a closed-lipped smile. "Cal Harper," she said, leaning in, letting him kiss her cheek. "Your wife just gave me the most delicious-sounding recipe for steak Diane."

"Oh, Lord," he said. "I hope she's not telling you to ruin a perfectly good steak by covering it in black pepper and mushrooms."

Hattie swatted him playfully. "You are just terrible, Cal," she said.

"Well," he said with his sly smile, "guilty as charged, I suppose." He began sauntering back toward the clubhouse, his hands back in his pockets. "Call me about that contest, Lee." As he passed Silla, he gave her another wink. "I think you could have a winner on your hands."

It would be years later, while reading his obituary, that Priscilla would learn that Cal Harper had made all his money in horses, that he had advised wealthy owners on new purchases, on what animals he thought had potential. It may not seem lucrative, but Cal Harper always got paid, one way or another.

Hattie made for the passenger door without acknowledging Silla, and Silla instinctively stepped aside. As the car glided away from the country club, Hattie lifted her sunglasses and pulled out a compact to check her face. "What was that about a contest?" she asked her husband.

"Cal thinks Silla's got a chance in that Miss Harris County contest," he said.

Hattie froze, and Silla watched as the gaze reflected in the compact mirror moved from her own face to Silla's.

That night, after they got home, after Lee slipped into the den and a Tom Collins, Silla was waiting for the ham loaf to finish heating and was thinking about what Mr. Harper had said. *They can really turn it into a nice little career.* A nice little career was more than she had hoped for, but now she thought about it. About what it might be like to have some money of her own. Maybe she could get her own apartment. Maybe she could have a bedroom with white lace curtains and a vanity with a little vase of yellow flowers. That's what she was thinking when Hattie came into the room. Silla's head snapped up, as if she had been awakened from a dream. She turned to see a small but steady stream of smoke piping from the vent of the oven.

"Oh!" she gasped as Hattie pulled on oven mitts with the stern look of a military medic. As smoke billowed out of the open oven door, Hattie lifted out the baking sheet and dropped it on the cooktop with a clatter.

"Silla, what were you doing?" she demanded, her face sharp and hard as she inspected the burned ham loaf, a ring of char circling it in the pan.

"I . . . ," started Silla. "I didn't realize."

Hattie's beautiful jaw shut tight and she looked at Silla, letting the weight of the silence achieve its full impact before she spoke. "I swear," she said, the words coming out slowly, as if they had a flavor she wanted to savor. "Sometimes I think you're going to end up just like your mama."

. . .

CHAPTER TWENTY-ONE

Oysters

As I dressed, I could hear Rose in the family room, showing the babysitter her toy collection, explaining that her Barbie dresses actually fit on her barn animals and that sometimes the cows liked to pretend that green Legos were grass. I had asked the sitter to come early so that she and Rose could spend some time getting acquainted, since Rose had only rarely been left with someone.

"A girl named Kimmy is coming over to play with you tonight," I'd said.

Rose had looked at me, her chin raised inquisitively. "A big girl or a little girl?" she'd asked.

Kimmy was a senior in high school. "A medium-sized girl," I'd said.

Taking one last look at myself in the full-length mirror in my room, I flipped off the lights.

"Hey, Kimmy," I called, as I stepped into the bright warmth of the family room. She looked up, already smiling. "Does this look okay?" I asked tentatively, gesturing to my outfit. From his dog bed, Gordo lifted his head, looked at me, then groaned and rolled over on his side.

Kimmy nodded with a teenager's cool enthusiasm. "Totally," she said. "It looks awesome. I *love* that dress with those boots."

"Yeah," said Rose, positioning herself next to Kimmy and adopting her assessing posture. "You look *really* pretty."

"Thank you, guys," I said. I perched on the edge of the couch beside Gordo's bed. Watching Kimmy and Rose play, I slowly rubbed one of Gordo's velvety ears, my thoughts drifting back to Royal Court, as they had more and more often recently.

I think Warren likes that Mehta girl down the street, my mother used to say hopefully. Paru Mehta had moved onto Royal Court when we were in high school, and Warren had seemed intrigued by her. With her melodic voice and elegant nose, we were all intrigued by her. *The Mehtas' house smells like curry!* kids used to whisper on the bus, as if that were somehow salacious and shameful. I remembered the way Warren would look at them as they snickered, his head cocked to the side as it so often was, as if he had to look at the world from a different angle in order to see it properly. I didn't know what had happened to Paru Mehta or her family, only that they had moved out of Royal Court about seven years ago, having sold their home to Beth and Rob Castro.

Headlights turned from the main road into our driveway. I waited to see if they would veer in the direction of the Pritchards', but they held steady, and I hooked my hands around my knees. The doorbell rang and Gordo barked, lumbering back to his feet.

"I'll get it," I said, smiling at Kimmy as I stood.

I put my hand on the cold brass knob and turned. Bobby smiled as he stood on the cracked concrete of my front step, my brass porch light valiantly trying to illuminate the night.

"Hey," he said, before his balance was nearly disturbed by Gordo's greeting. He chuckled and bent slightly forward to attend to Gordo, finding the sweet spot behind his ears. "Oh, there you go, buddy."

Stepping aside, I waved Bobby into the house. "Come," I said. "Come on in."

Rose, suddenly interested in our visitor, piped right up. "Hey, Gabby's daddy," she began, "where's Gabby?"

Bobby squatted down so that he and Rose were eye to eye. "She's home with her nonna," said Bobby, his forearm resting on his knee. "Is it okay if I take your mom out tonight?"

Rose thought about it for a moment. "Yeah," she said with a shrug. "I'll just play with Kimmy."

I kissed Rose on her cheek, and quickly ran over the bedtime routine again for Kimmy. "There's a sheet in the kitchen with everything you need to know," I said, referring to the page I had typed up with cell phone and doctors' numbers and a list of Rose's favorite stories. Then I waved good-bye and stepped out the door for my evening that was not a date with a man whom I knew very well yet not at all.

Freedom, I mouthed to Bobby as the door clicked shut behind us.

The gravel crunched under our feet as we walked side by side down the path to the driveway, the cold night feeling bright and electric around us. As we approached his car, Bobby stepped ahead of me and reached to open my door, the hinges of his old Jeep groaning with effort.

I thanked him as I slid in, then watched him hurry across the front of the car, his keys in hand. He got in and closed the door, and we looked at each other for a moment before both laughing quietly, simultaneously, and without any clear reason. "I'm glad we're doing this," he said, as he turned the key in the ignition.

"Me, too," I said, recalling the last time I'd been out with a man, how different it had felt. When I had tried to date after Rose was born, I had always felt the weight of the past, of all the explanations it required. I would have to tell a new man about Duncan, and about Rose, of course. Eventually, I'd have to tell him about Warren and my mother, about my father and Lydia. Bobby already knew it all.

"I was thinking," he said, as he cranked the stubborn old gearshift into reverse and glanced over his shoulder, "that we could go to Orto. Have you ever been?"

"No," I said. "That sounds great." Orto was known as an eccentric little gem of a restaurant with a garden tended by the chef's first-generation Italian mother. Duncan always used to speak highly of it, though we had never eaten there together.

As we drove, we wove out of West Hills, where Rose and I lived, into one of the more elegant neighboring areas, talking about Bobby's work at the hospital, about why he had decided to become a doctor. "I had always wanted to go into medicine but had talked myself out of it," he said. "After a few years doing the corporate thing, none of my reasons—the debt, the hours—seemed good enough anymore." And I talked about Wonderlux, about how I got to go to work with my best friend and pick my daughter up from school and design beautiful things.

"And what made you leave New York?" he asked. Duncan and I had lived in the city together for eight years. I'd tried to stay after he left, but the financial reality was too daunting.

"Money," I said with a sad chuckle. "Maggie and I were both new moms starting a business and we couldn't afford the city. Her uncle owns the building that our office is in and he gave us a great deal on rent. So coming back to Jersey was sort of a no-brainer."

"Yeah," he said, lifting his chin as we approached what looked like an old white farmhouse. "I went to med school at NYU. But to raise kids in the city is *brutally* expensive."

He turned the wheel. "This is it," he said, as we pulled into Orto. It was located on a dark stretch of road and identified with a simple but elegant sign, flooded with light. Navigating around to the back, we came to a parking lot and he slid into a spot.

"I used to live out here," he said, as we walked through the cold night toward the sanctuary of the restaurant. "Before Gabby and I moved back with my parents." It was a subtle reference to his life with Mia.

Bobby opened the glossy black door into what felt like someone's home. The hostess stand was set up next to the staircase and from it, you could see into four dining rooms, each of which held five or six tables. The walls were nearly bare, the lights very low, and they were playing the sort of jazz that nearly everyone I knew had "discovered" in some smoky dorm room. It was an unassuming little restaurant that didn't seem to pay much attention to trends, but found itself on the right side of many of them.

We were brought to a small table near a window and ordered drinks that I'd never had before. They came in thick lowball glasses and smelled like herbs. I took a sip and felt the liquid slide down my throat, settling snugly in my stomach and warming me from the inside out. A beautiful older woman with caramel-colored skin and Sophia Loren glasses came out, and without a word, she set down a single plate. "Some pickled beets from the kitchen," she said in a heavy Italian accent; then she winked at me. "For sharing."

Bobby and I smiled at each other, and with his fork, he cut one of the beet slices in half. Stabbing it with the tines, he swirled it in the little puddle of magenta brine at the bottom of the plate, and then handed the fork to me, watching me as I took a bite. Mr. Vanni used to be like that, a man who loved to indulge people, loved to watch them enjoy themselves. I smiled and covered my mouth with my hand. "Delicious," I said, handing Bobby back his fork.

"Gabby loves beets," he said, a bite about to enter his lips. "We planted some this summer, but the rabbits got 'em."

Our waiter returned, prompting us to pick up our menus, which we hadn't yet given so much as a glance. "Do you like oysters?" asked Bobby. I did.

They came, carefully laid in a circle on a bed of pristine ice, still wet with seawater. I brought one to my lips and breathed in the ocean, tipping the shell back and rolling the flavor back and forth on my tongue. Looking at the empty shell, a small opalescent cup, I turned it over and ran my fingers over the oyster's rough, plain exterior. And I decided I liked things like that: things that kept their beauty hidden. When I looked up, Bobby's gaze was on me. "Sorry," I said, laughing at myself for fondling an oyster shell. I set it back down on the ice. "It's just kind of gorgeous . . . don't you think?"

Without hesitation, he answered, "I do." And for a moment, neither of us looked away, until our waiter came back to fill our water glasses.

"Thank you," I said, as I shifted in my chair, my ankle brushing against Bobby's. Reflexively, I went to move it. Then I stopped myself, settling into the feeling of a small patch of my body touching a small patch of his. And Bobby smiled.

"How's your family doing?" he asked, as he took a sip of his drink.

"Can I tell you something?"

Bobby straightened up, became alert and attentive, like the Dr. Vanni who rushed around the beds in the ER. And so I told him about the Castros. I told him about the notes.

"So she's been sending these for a while?" asked Bobby, his head inclined, his forearms resting on the table.

"We don't *know* it was Beth Castro. But yeah. For a few months, at least."

Bobby was silent for a moment. "I'm sorry," he said.

"I'm hoping it can all get sorted out." I spread my hand over the smooth white tablecloth. "I'm going to go try to talk to the Castros."

"Do you want me to come with you?"

And though I insisted that no, it was fine, that I didn't want to involve any more residents of King's Knoll than were absolutely necessary, I took solace in his offer, and in the readiness with which he made it. "I just feel really bad for my mom," I said. "I know her house isn't in the best condition." It was an admission that I found difficult to make, if only for its obviousness. "But she's been living in that neighborhood for almost thirty years. You'd think this all could have been handled differently." Taking a sip of my drink, I spoke through its afterburn. "And she's trying to clean things up. We're painting the columns. And she got some quotes on painting the exterior in the spring."

We each ordered another drink, the mood turning again toward the jovial as we exchanged stories about Gabby and Rose. "Gabby is pissed because she doesn't have a flower name," Bobby said, his affection for his daughter deep and clear. "She says she wants to change her name to Hydrangea." I let my head fall back in laughter. By the time our entrées arrived, we had moved on to talk again about our families, about growing up on Royal Court. "Do you remember Howard Li?" asked Bobby.

"Of course I remember Howard!" I said. "He used to be friends with Warren."

"Did you hear that he won the Nobel Prize in chemistry?"

"What?" I asked, shocked. "The *Nobel Prize*?" I was astounded that I hadn't read about it in the papers. Though Howard's family had moved away soon after he finished high school, I would have thought that the human-interest-story-starved *Star-Ledger* might have picked it up. "Oh my God," I said, picturing Warren and Howard, shirtless and skinny and wonderfully weird. "Howard and Warren used to spend hours together in our backyard."

"I remember that," said Bobby, smiling fondly, his hand on his chin. "They'd be whipping those..." He snapped his fingers, searching for the name.

"Forsythia branches," I said, my eyes on the rim of my glass as I pictured the yellow flowers bursting from the bark. When I was Rose's age, I wove a single one of those pliant branches around and around until I had a small hoop, looped with gold. *Mom, look!* I had said. *It's a crown!* And she took my chin in her hand and tried to smile. But she didn't speak a word. "It's funny," I said, looking at Bobby as I took a sip of my water, "what stays with you from growing up." It seemed it was the small moments that made us who we were, the moments that were supposed to be insignificant, the ones that we didn't know quite why we remembered. They were the ones that mattered, those that were like messages in a language we didn't yet speak.

CHAPTER TWENTY-TWO

. . .

Surprises

"How was it?" Maggie's voice was sleepy; she had been waiting up for my call.

"It was good," I said, watching the taillights from Kimmy's car retreat back down the driveway. "Really good."

I heard rustling on the phone line, as if Maggie were moving to a more discreet location. "Did you guys kiss?" she asked.

I smiled, knowing my answer would madden her. "Not really," I said.

"Not really?" asked Maggie impatiently. "What is that? What is 'not really'?"

Not really was the honest answer. Bobby had walked me to

the door and we could see the bluish flashes from the TV through the transom above. Kimmy was just inside, watching a show full of beautiful young kids with dramatic and tortured relationships, a contemporary version of the sort of thing I used to watch when I was her age. And Bobby and I both just stood there, not wanting to break the seal of the night, not wanting to open the door.

"I had a good time," I said to him. But he didn't answer. Instead, he reached for my hand and rested it on his lower back, pulling me into him. I looked up at him, our faces inches apart, our hips angled toward each other. But when he leaned in, his lips landed lightly on my forehead, resting there until I closed my eyes and felt my heart become still.

"He kissed me on the forehead," I said to Maggie.

"Your forehead?" asked Maggie, with disbelief and worry, afraid that all my protests about my evening with Bobby *not being a date* were well-founded. *You kiss your sister on the forehead,* I imagined her thinking. But it was actually that moment, standing on my doorstep with his hand gently holding mine in place on his back, when I knew that I was, in fact, on a date with Bobby Vanni.

"It was actually really . . . nice."

Maggie asked me a few more questions, but I found myself volunteering the answers, glad to talk about the evening I had spent with a man I liked very much. "What did you guys talk about?" she asked.

"Oh, God," I said. "Lots of stuff." I thought about the way my laughter had seemed magnified by his, my concerns diminished by sharing them. In fact, the only subject we avoided was Mia. And Duncan.

. . .

The phone rang just after six thirty the next morning. I sat up with a sudden breath and fumbled for the receiver, wanting to silence it but fearing what I was about to hear; good news never came this early.

"Hello?" I said.

There was a brief delay.

"Jenna!" It was Duncan's voice.

I closed my eyes and sank back in bed. "Hi, Duncan," I said unenthusiastically.

"What time is it there?" he asked.

I lifted my hand and let it fall back down on the bed in exasperation, letting it make a muffled thump on my soft, white comforter. "It's not even seven, Dunc."

"Hey, listen," he said, without an apology. "I wanted to talk to you about some stuff." I remained silent, knowing that the "stuff" he wanted to talk to me about was his move back to the States. The one Miriam had mentioned weeks ago. The one that he had been planning for who knew how long. "Jenna," he said. "Are you there?"

I took a breath, letting my head sink into my pillow. "Yup," I said. "I'm here." *I've been here all along.*

"Hey, Rosie," I said as I stirred brown sugar into her oatmeal. "Would you like it if you got to see your daddy more often?"

I kept my eyes on my task as I waited for her response. "Yeah," she said lightly, as if I'd just offered her something moderately tasty. Something like oatmeal. "I'd like it."

I nodded and set her big red bowl down in front of her. My conversation with Duncan had become strained rather quickly. As I had anticipated, he'd announced that he was moving back to New York.

"When?" I'd asked.

"In about a week. I'm going to spend a couple of days in L.A. on my way back."

"That'll be nice," I said, and I wondered if he detected the resentment in my voice.

"So anyway," he began, "I was thinking that it would be cool to spend Christmas with Rose. Up at my parents' place."

"You were thinking that would be cool," I said flatly.

"Yeah, I mean, she's my *daughter*." It was clear that he intended to hit the tricky spot between indignant and contrite.

Oh, now she's your daughter?

Sensing the trajectory our call was taking, I ended it quickly after that. I told him that I had to go, but that I'd think about it. Then I congratulated him on his move. I had promised myself that when it came to Rose's relationship with Duncan, I would always put her interests before my own. But as I stared at her now, as she lifted her nose and looked down into her bowl to search for the very best bite, the one that promised to hold a treasure trove of barely dissolved brown sugar, I realized that her best interests might not always be so easy to determine.

"Hey, can we go see Uncle Warren later?" asked Rose suddenly, her legs starting to kick under the table, the spoon erect in her hand.

I chuckled. "We actually *do* need to go out there today."

Rose's eyes widened gleefully. I watched her for a moment. "You like your uncle Warren, don't you?"

"Yeah," said Rose, with a cool shrug, an affectation she may have gotten from Kimmy. "Uncle Warren is awesome."

I smiled and took a sip of my coffee. During our recent visits to Royal Court, I had seen the affection Rose and Warren were developing for each other. And I often heard them engaged in the sort of animated conversations that I used to have with him when I was younger, when I used to sneak into his room at night and lie next to him on his bed. He'd tell me wonderful, fantastical things. Talking and talking, he would move his hands with his words, and his mind would skip from thought to thought, following a fluid path that made me feel as though I were on a ride. *Did you know that the Milky Way is spinning?* he'd ask me, not waiting for my answer. *It's moving at something like*—he'd lift his hand, as if he were about to make a random guess, as if he were about to estimate the number of candy corns in a jar—*two hundred twenty-five kilometers per second.* I'd ask him if that was fast. He'd think about it and tell me that depended on what you meant by fast. Then he'd tell me that not only is the galaxy spinning, but it's also traveling through space as it spins. *And then, if you factor in the rotation of the earth.* He'd rest his hands under his head and laugh softly, having officially blown his own mind.

"I'm surprised we're not all dizzy all the time," I'd say.

Warren would look up at his ceiling, as if he could see the cosmos through it, spinning and rotating and orbiting in a most miraculous dance. "We're all moving even when we're standing still."

And I would close my eyes and almost feel it: the universe's teacup ride.

But such conversations had grown more infrequent as I had

aged and become less and less able to see the things that Warren did. As I became less and less able to let myself.

Rose was about to dig into her breakfast, her spoon cocked, when she looked up at me. "Hey, did you know that I'm an Aurotite?" she asked.

I looked at her with mock skepticism. "Says who?" as if I didn't know.

"Uncle Warren. He says you can tell by my spot." She pointed at her birthmark. "I told him that Tucker said it was ugly, but Uncle *Warren* says it shows that I'm an Aurotite and that only Aurotite *princesses* have spots." Her eyes grew wide with delight as she declared her royalty.

And at that moment, I couldn't have loved my brother more.

I felt Rose's feet kicking the back of my seat as we sped down the highway toward Harwick. Maggie and I had had a rare unproductive day at Wonderlux, one in which we each kept our respective files open, but would constantly call over our shoulders to each other with confessions and observations and questions. She had asked me more about my date with Bobby. "You really like him," she said.

I do. Whatever was between Bobby and me was too vulnerable and new to speak about freely. Like something beautiful and wild, something I might spook and send running. I cleared my throat, acquiescing in my silence. I did it again now as I looked back at Gordo, who was panting and taking in the view.

"Did you know that Uncle Warren is making me a plane?"

asked Rose. She had been talking nonstop during the drive, and I had been enjoying a lull in the conversation.

"He is?" I said casually, unsure of the veracity of the claim.

"Yeah," she said. "He asked me what color I wanted and I told him *red*."

"Red looks nice on planes."

"Me and Uncle Warren are on the same team," she said. Rose had just learned about the concept of teams in her weeklong soccer peewee day camp this summer.

"What team is that?"

"The *Good* Team," she said. "You can be on it, too."

Glancing at her in the rearview mirror, I smiled. "Thanks, Rose."

"Uncle Warren is the leader, though," she said, as if breaking difficult news.

"Okay."

"But that means if you need him, all you have to do is rub your ear and say his name and he'll come."

Again I looked in the rearview mirror, more alert this time. "Did he tell you that?" I asked, remembering all the times I had needed him. All the times he had come running.

As I turned into King's Knoll, I glanced at the sky through the windshield. The clouds looked as though they had been raked across the faded blue, leaving long wisps as they hurried to some great meteorological disturbance, some churning of air hundreds and hundreds of miles away. The high tomorrow was supposed to be only in the low forties, and it was going to get progressively colder after that. *It never used to get this cold this early,* I thought. And I wondered how much of adulthood was spent benchmarking the present against the past. Thinking about how things were so very different from what you remembered, so very different from what you'd expected.

I let my eyes flitter only briefly to Lydia's lawn signs. When I was a child, I never ever imagined that Lydia Stroppe would be my stepmother. And yet she was. I never imagined that my parents would be divorced or that I would be a single mother or that Warren would come home one night, his nose broken and face cut. But I had also never imagined that I would have Rose. Or Gordo. Or that one day, I'd turn onto Royal Court and see Bobby Vanni standing on a stepladder on my mother's front porch with a paintbrush in his hand.

And yet he was.

I felt a sudden surge in my chest, an overflowing.

"Who's that?" asked Rose, aware of my attention. He wasn't dressed as usual, in his jacket and jeans. Instead, he was wearing a pair of battered khakis and a sweatshirt, the hood of which was pulled over the thin wool cap on his head. He had a paint bucket at his feet, and his arm was lifted above his head, the brush concentrated on a spot on the column.

I swallowed and then opened my mouth to speak, my smile shaky and unsure, like something just born. "That's Gabby's daddy," I said.

CHAPTER TWENTY-THREE

· · ·

A Conversation

My eyes didn't leave Bobby as I pulled into the driveway. One side of his face lifted into a warm smile as he saw me. Wiping his paint-covered hands on his pants, he stepped off the ladder. I shifted the car into park and opened my door. "Hey," I said, as I stood, crossing my arms over my chest.

We walked toward each other, and met on the dry grass of my mother's front yard. "I hope you don't mind," he said, jerking his thumb back at one of the columns. "Your mom's at work, but Warren said he thought it would be all right."

"I don't mind," I said, shaking my head, my words soft with gratitude.

We stood looking at each other for a moment until I heard

Rose's muffled voice coming from the confines of the car. "Hi, Gabby's daddy!" she called, waving.

He lifted his hand. "Hi, Rose!" he said back.

"Why are you painting my nana's house?"

Bobby looked at me, as if that was his answer. As if I was. We stood there for a moment, something silent but clear passing between us. Then I tilted my head back toward the car. "I'm just gonna get her out," I said, and Bobby nodded in affirmation.

I unstrapped Rose and set her feet on the pavement, then rounded the back of the car, lifting the gate to free Gordo. He lumbered down, exerting great effort and grunting as his front paws made contact with the ground, letting his hind legs follow. His tail spun with joy as he rubbed the side of his face against Bobby's leg in greeting.

I lifted the two additional gallons of paint that I had bought from the trunk. "I got some more," I said, raising them for Bobby to see as I crossed back toward him.

"I was wondering about that," he said, running the wrist of his paint-covered hand back and forth against his chin.

Gordo plodded up the steps and sat on the welcome mat, staring at the front door. As if on cue, it opened, and there was Warren in his gray sweatshirt and his pleated khaki pants. Gordo stood and wagged wildly, his whole body curving from one side to the other and back again as his tail thumped against my brother's leg. Warren said something in Dog and patted Gordo's head, chuckling as he did so.

"Jenna got some more paint," said Bobby casually, as he stepped back up onto the ladder. It was the way he might tell a buddy that there was another six-pack in the fridge. Then he pointed to the farthest column. "You could start giving that one its second coat."

I was ready for Warren to turn on his heels and head inside without a word. Instead he looked at me. And with his wounds nearly healed, his stitches gone, our eyes met just long enough for me to see them flicker with something familiar, something I had longed for. Then Warren walked slowly toward the far end of the porch, poking me lightly on the stomach as he passed, and picking up one of the new cans of paint by its thin metal handle.

I watched him as he popped off the lid and submerged the stirrer into the opaque white, watched him carefully dip his brush into the paint. With slow up-and-down strokes, he let his eyes follow the brush, watching as the column became pristine and new, almost magically so.

"Is there an extra paintbrush?" I asked.

"We got this, Jenna," said Bobby. "Right, War?"

"Yeah," said Warren, sounding both pleased and surprised by his answer. Then he let out his quiet chuckle. "We got this."

For the next half hour, Rose and I sat inside coloring while Warren and Bobby painted my mother's front columns, with Gordo supervising. From the dining room where I had set us up, I could hear Bobby and Warren make bits of conversation that was sparse but comfortable sounding. They talked about the gas mileage of Warren's Civic and the battery life on his AC planes. They talked about D'Antonio's bakery closing and how the town was supposedly paving that small stretch of dirt road that ran between Harwick and Montborough.

Then I heard my mother's car go over the dip in the beginning of the driveway. Gordo let out a few high-pitched, clipped barks. I drew a big smiley face on the yellow construction paper. "Nana's going to be happy," I told Rose.

"Why?" she asked.

"Because you and me and Uncle Warren are all here. And because Gabby's nice daddy is helping her paint her house." I stood and peered out the window, wanting to see the look on her face when she saw Bobby and Warren. And I didn't understand at first why it wasn't her white Camry that was in the driveway. Why it was a car I had never seen before. I felt my whole body seize as a man in a blue shirt, tan pants, and a green jacket got out of the car. I realized that even without any of the dressing, the car parked in our driveway still looked a whole lot like a police car, in the same way that a cop, even without the uniform, still looked a whole lot like a cop.

"You stay right here and color for a sec," I said to Rose, trying to keep the panic from my voice. The man was walking up toward the house, slowly but with intention. "Mommy has to go talk to someone." I went quickly to the front door, forcing a soothing smile to my lips and winking at Rose just before I stepped outside.

As the screen door clattered behind me, I exchanged a look with Bobby before stopping at the top of the steps. Bobby and Warren were on ladders on either side of me, though Warren's body was half-hidden behind a column. "Hi there," I called. "Is there something I can help you with?"

The man took a few more steps, then reached into his pocket and pulled out what looked like a small leather wallet onto which was mounted a badge. "I'm Detective Dunn," he said. "From the Somerton County Sheriff's Department." He had a ruddy complexion and round features that gave him an almost childlike appearance, though his thinning blond hair and creased forehead suggested that he was at least middle-aged. He looked like a family man, a guy who was the youngest of twelve in a big Irish family and spent weekends tailgating in the parking lots of Giants Stadium. "Do you live here, miss?" he asked.

"I do," I volunteered quickly, before realizing that that wasn't true. My hands turned in front of me, as if unspooling the truth. "I mean, my mother does."

Detective Dunn's expression didn't change as he glanced briefly up toward the house, then down to the yard, his trained eyes not lingering for long, but seeing everything they needed to. "Your mother is Priscilla Parsons?" he asked, his face still impassive.

"She is."

"Is she home?"

I heard Bobby descend the stepladder and felt him come up next to me, his hands on his hips, his stance wide. I shifted, resting my hand on top of the railing. "She's at work. But we expect her back any minute now." Though I didn't look away from the detective, I knew that Warren was frozen, his gaze focused on the ground, as if directing all his sensory power on the auditory. "Can I ask what this is about?" I asked politely.

"There've been several burglaries in the neighborhood." Again, his eyes moved to the house, then to Warren, while his head remained still. "And does your mother live here alone?" It was a question to which he knew the answer, a question designed to flush out the true reason for his visit.

We looked at each other for a moment, the detective and I. "No," I said. "My brother, Warren, lives here, too."

"And is this Warren?" asked Detective Dunn, still looking at me as he tilted his head in the direction of my brother, his hands in his pockets.

I hesitated, though there was only one answer I could give. "Yes," I said.

Detective Dunn's focus shifted immediately. "Warren," he said, taking a few plodding steps closer to the porch. "You used to deliver pizza in the area." He stopped, angling his head up. "Is that right?"

Warren paused, then almost indiscernibly nodded.

Detective Dunn rested his hands on his haunches and glanced around at the neighborhood. "You must have delivered to most of these houses," he said. "Been inside of 'em. Is that correct?" Detective Dunn nodded once, instructively.

Warren remained still.

"Bet you saw a lot of nice things in those houses," he said. He waited for a reaction from Warren. When it didn't come, Detective Dunn jerked his head toward the road behind him. "How about you come in and have a conversation with me," he said.

Immediately, Warren's face changed and he stared down at the concrete steps, as if deciding something profound and final.

Detective Dunn stood there, looking at Warren, unmoved as he waited. Then Warren smoothed his bangs down on his head, his face like a soldier's in preparation for battle, and reached to pick up the navy warm-up jacket that he had peeled off for painting.

"Warren," said Bobby, "you don't have to go anywhere."

But Warren pulled his jacket on and zipped it to his chest. It bloused at the bottom and in the sleeves. He paused for a moment, his fingers still on the zipper pull; then he looked at me.

"I'm going with you," I said, as I instinctively patted my back pocket for my phone and scanned about for my purse, which was inside.

"It's okay," said Warren, his lips barely moving as he spoke. *I'll be all right.* Then he slowly made for the steps.

Bobby reached out to stop him, resting his hand on his shoulder. "You should talk to a lawyer," he whispered.

But Warren shook his head. "No," he said. "It's better this way."

Sliding past us down the steps, he took them one at a time, keeping his gaze on his feet.

And as I watched my brother walk away from me and toward the detective, I felt the urge to throw myself between them, to spread my arms and block my brother from the man with the watchful eyes and gold badge. Warren didn't know what he was doing. He couldn't protect himself. "No," I said, starting down the stairs after him. "I'm coming."

Warren halted, his head hung forward. But he didn't turn around. "Jenna," he said just before I reached him. And the anger in his voice stopped me short. We had always run to his defense, rushed to his aid, my mother and I. It hadn't occurred to either of us that that might not be his preference.

"We're just going to have a conversation, Sis," said Detective Dunn, drawing my stare from the back of Warren's figure. Then the detective looked at Warren. "You take your car and I'll take mine," he said calmly, as if he were talking to a man out on a ledge. *Nice and easy.*

I glanced at Bobby and he at me, but we were silent as we watched Warren get into his car, and pull away after the detective. We were silent as we saw Mr. Kotch on his bicycle, pedaling steadily but unhurriedly after them. He trailed Warren's car until Warren made a right out of the development and was no longer in the jurisdiction of the King's Knoll neighborhood watch.

"Hey, Mom." Rose was peeking out through a crack in the front door, a bored pout on her lips. "I'm tired of coloring."

"Oh, I'm sorry, Rosie!" I said, bending to bring us eye to eye. "There was a man that . . . we needed to talk to." Reaching for her hand, I turned to face Bobby.

"I can stay, Jenna," he said, his voice low but emphatic. "I don't have to be at the hospital for an hour and a half. I can stay until Warren gets back."

"It's okay," I said, shaking my head, feeling the threat of tears as Rose tugged on my arm. "You should go."

"Jenna—"

"Really," I said. "Thank you so much for all of this," I said, nodding toward the almost finished columns. "But I know how busy you are. We'll be fine."

"Are you still up for tomorrow night?" he asked. We had made plans to have dinner together—the four of us, at my house.

"Of course," I said. As much as I wanted him near me, I was now eager for him to go. Because soon my mother would be home. She'd walk in the house, holding the strap of her purse, her eyes cautious. And before she even said the words,

I'd know the question that was on her lips because her face would look as it always did whenever she had to ask it. I'd tell her that Warren had left and why. *What did they want to talk to him for?* she'd say. Then I'd see her eyes being pulled in the direction of the Castros' house, as if drawn by some distant, building clamor. And with her face in profile, her skin marble white, she would have the look of a cameo, of a woman long-forgotten but immortalized nonetheless.

CHAPTER TWENTY-FOUR

· · ·

The Crown

1972

The two women stood side by side, their bodies angled toward each other, their gowns encircling their feet. And as they held hands, sweaty palm to sweaty palm, they looked like the two halves of a shell, splayed open and emptied.

The announcement of the winner was only moments away, but Silla could think only about the weight of everything. The weight of her dress and her makeup. The weight of her jewelry. The weight of all the hair on her head. A small bead of sweat sprang from her hairline and trickled down her forehead. It was so hot up there. So hot that she felt dizzy and all she wanted to do was close her eyes and concentrate on standing up.

The MC's voice echoed through the auditorium, at once distant and right next to her. "We're just moments away, folks," he said, as if the information he was about to reveal could heal the sick. "From crowning *Miss Texas 1972*." Silla felt her eyelids grow heavy and her legs loosen, as if she might start to sway. "But first I'd like to take a moment to acknowledge the lovely ladies who gave it their all this evening. Weren't they terrific, folks?" There was a burst of applause that faded, as if on cue, for the commencement of the drumroll.

"And now," the MC declared, his words like claps of thunder, "the first runner-up . . ." Silla took a breath in and out. She felt Miss Hunt County squeeze her hand. And then the MC's voice boomed out, as if from a cannon, "Miss Hunt County, Jeanette Wylie!" The noise in the room sounded like an explosion. *"Miss Houston, Priscilla Harris, is our new Miss Texas!"*

Priscilla covered her mouth with her shaking hand, almost overcome by a mixture of disbelief, terror, and, yes, elation. Miss Hunt County gripped her shoulders and kissed her cheek and looked at her with the bravest smile she had ever seen. Beauty queens were supposed to be icons of femininity—the ultimate women. And what else did being a woman mean but standing still and smiling? Looking happy when you weren't? What did being a woman mean but letting someone else decide your fate?

Loud, tinny music began to blare over the loudspeakers, joining the cacophony of the crowd and the MC. Silla gazed out toward the audience. The lights were so bright that she couldn't make out the faces. They looked like phosphorescent flashes in the night sea, shimmering and indiscernible. *Thank you!* she mouthed, waving. *Thank you so much!* She knew her father was there. And Hattie. She knew that Cal was sitting at the judges' table, though she tried not to look at him. *Just smile,* she thought. Cal always said that her smile alone could win a pageant. *Makes you look wholesome,* he said, biting his cigar. *Judges love it when the girls look wholesome.*

From behind her, she felt someone putting what must be a crown on her head, fastening it with pins that pressed into her scalp. Then there was someone in front of her, someone whose face she did not recognize, putting a bouquet of yellow flowers in her arms. "Our new Texas rose!" boomed the MC. Silla waved and waved with her shaking hand. *Thank you! Thank you!* She blew a kiss to the audience. *Thank you!*

She saw the runway in front of her. She knew what came next. She was supposed to put one foot in front of the other and walk down it. So she took a tentative first step with the flowers and crown, like a beast of burden getting accustomed to a new load. She kept the smile on her face, tilting her head to change its angle as she made her way down the long, narrow peninsula. She used to keep her head still, but she had fixed that. *You look like a damn robot up there, Silla!* her father had said. And so she had learned to smile and pretend to see something other than a dark, shimmering sea of faces.

She paused at the end of the runway, then turned toward the other finalists, who were clapping politely, smiling for her, as if this were the happiest moment of their lives.

"Priscilla will go on to represent Texas at the Miss America pageant in Atlantic City!" came the voice of the MC. The applause rose again and Silla glided to her mark, then turned to face the crowd, the MC next to her.

"How does it feel, Priscilla? To be the new Miss Texas!"

The microphone was suddenly in front of her lips. Silla looked out, willing herself to smile, not to move or shift even though the thorns from the yellow roses were pricking her arm. She leaned in toward the microphone. "I'm speechless," she said.

The MC's body swiveled to the crowd. "Well, it's a good thing you weren't songless, sweetheart!" he said, bringing a chuckle from the audience. "Tell us a little more about your platform, Priscilla. What do you hope to accomplish as Miss Texas?"

"I hope to go on and win Miss America so that I can join the USO tour and entertain our troops in Vietnam," she said, with just the right blend of humility and pluck.

"What a heart of gold!" said the MC, his handsome face tanned and glowing in the spotlight. "And I'm sure that this isn't the last we'll hear from Miss Texas 1972! This little lady's got a bright future in front of her, folks!"

• • •

CHAPTER TWENTY-FIVE

Coffee with Nondairy Creamer

Warren and Rose sat beside each other at the island in the kitchen, each with a glass of milk in front of them. Warren had returned home at five thirty—an hour and a half after he left with Detective Dunn. I was making them dinner.

"I still don't understand what information they thought you'd be able to give them about all this," said my mother, as she paced, then hovered, hovered, then paced in the space behind them. She couldn't bring herself to refer to the "thefts" by name.

Warren looked into his milk cup, silent to all our attempts to find out more about his time with Detective Dunn. He had come home with a strange, resigned calm about him, as if events had been set in motion that he was now powerless to stop.

I squatted down to stare through the door of the oven, seeing my reflection in its tinted glass. "They're probably talking to everyone," I said, not managing to convince even myself. "War, do you want ketchup with your chicken nuggets?"

Warren looked at me as if I had suggested something perverse. "No," he said. "No ketchup."

"You should try it," said Rose with both elbows resting on the counter. "It's really good." Warren looked at her, his expression amused and skeptical. "How do you know if you don't like things unless you try them?" demanded Rose, her already high voice reaching an even higher note.

Rose looked at me for corroboration. "That's right," I said, my lips twisting in a smile. "You've got to try things."

The timer sounded and I pulled the baking sheet from the oven, setting it on the stove top. Loosening the nuggets with a spatula, I divided them between two plates, giving Rose a third of them, then adding a healthy squirt of Heinz. "It's hot, Rose," I said as I set her meal down in front of her. "Blow, okay?"

Sticking the tip of her finger in the ketchup, she licked it off, then turned to Uncle Warren. "Did they give you food in jail?" she asked, leaning onto the counter.

I felt my mother tense. "Uncle Warren wasn't in jail," I said quickly. "He was just helping the policeman do his job."

But Warren was looking at Rose as if hers was the most delightful company he could keep. "They gave me coffee with nondairy creamer," he said.

Again, she dipped her finger into the ketchup and sucked on its tip, her legs kicking under the table, her eyes casting about the room until another question came—urgent and sudden. "Did you see Maglons?" she asked.

He dropped his gaze and his eyebrows drew together, but he kept his small smile, letting out a low chuckle that sounded like an old piece of groaning machinery. Rose took this as an affirmative. "Why didn't you call me?" she demanded, her open palm inviting explanation. Warren's head shot up, like a teacher finally being rewarded with a worthy student. Rose reached up and rubbed her earlobe. "Like this," she said. "I would have come to get you."

With my hands on my hips, I stared at the printout of the recipe that lay on the counter. *Turn the potatoes halfway through roasting.* Then I pulled the roasting pan from the oven and set the spatula to work. "Shit," I whispered as a potato sprang from the pan onto the floor. "Man overboard." Gordo immediately lapped it up, his eyes staring at me with an addict's urgency as his body remained tense in anticipation of more salty starches raining down from the sky.

"Hey, Mom!" called Rose from the family room, where she was watching a *Sesame Street* DVD; it was the segment in which Elmo talks to babies. "Tucker said that his brother eats from his mom's *boobies.*" She giggled, thinking she was being bold and naughty.

"Lots of babies do that," I said, as I opened the fridge door and pulled out a small wedge of a very nice cheese, the sort I only ever bought for company. "You did."

Following a silence that hummed with her thoughts, Rose asked, "What about babies who don't have moms?"

"Well," I said, my hands resting on the countertop, "those babies drink from bottles."

"Is that what Gabby did?"

I looked at Rose, trying to gauge whether this question marked some sort of defining moment. Rose glanced back at me, her eyes shifting from me to the TV and back again. "Gabby has a mom, honey," I said. "She just lives far away now. Like your dad."

"Oh," she said, as her focus moved more permanently back to her show. I watched her for a moment, wondering if these explanations would eventually become more difficult. If they would someday involve more than a recitation of facts.

Unwrapping the beautiful bit of cheese, I set it on a plate with some nuts and dried apricots. Then with her full capacity for wonder and elation, Rose declared, "They're here!" Barking, Gordo began circling the space in front of the door.

I grabbed the dish towel and wiped my hands, bending down to check my face in the door of the microwave, then stepped into the family room to see the headlights of Bobby's Jeep suddenly drop to black. Car doors were opened and shut. Gabby's chatter and the crunch of feet on gravel drew closer.

I slid my fingers up the back of my head near my scalp, letting them run through the length of my hair while Rose stood bouncing in front of the door. "Hi!" she boomed, waving as Gabby and Bobby passed in front of the big window. It was only a little before six, but the sky had already sunk into darkness. The nearest homes lined up neatly across the street, their windows forming distant, trim yellow rectangles.

Bobby knocked once, sending Gordo spinning. "Go lie down, buddy," I said, my hand on the doorknob. As I turned it, I felt a sensation that was almost like free fall, almost like that blissful millisecond after you step off the diving board but before you land in the warm, calm waters of the pool. Gabby and Rose scampered immediately inside, a rush of cold air following them as Gabby flopped down on the floor and Rose helped her pull off her boots. I stood in front of Bobby just long enough for the warmth from our house to collide with the frigid night beyond. Then I reached for his arm and gently pulled him inside. "Come in," I said.

"They weren't kidding," he said. "It's gotta only be like thirty degrees out there." Meteorologists with stern expressions had been discussing the unseasonably cold temperatures for several days now.

"Those damn Canadians with their Arctic blasts," I said, as I pushed the door shut behind him.

In Bobby's hands were a bottle of wine and a slender brown paper bag containing a beautiful baguette, the emerging end coming to a slim point. I thanked him as he handed them to me. Then he slipped off his coat, turning to hang it on the hook by the door. And as he stood with his back to me, I noticed the solidity of his form. And I imagined putting my hands on him, running them under his sweater and up his back, my fingertips lingering on each knot of his spine. When he again faced me, he smiled, nodding toward the kitchen, from which wafted the scent of roasting chicken and potatoes. "Smells great in here," he said, his voice low and intimate.

I rested my hand on my chin as I leaned over the table, my eyes flickering to Bobby's and his to mine as we listened to Rose and Gabby chatter and giggle. Dinner's dirty plates had been mostly cleared and piled by the sink, and the wine Bobby had brought had left me loose and warm, with pink cheeks and a content smile.

"Do you guys want some dessert?" I asked the girls as I glanced at the clock. It had been a long meal, one spent luxuriating over the conversation and the company.

"Yeah!" they both said at once.

"Have you ever heard a no to that question?" asked Bobby as I rose to pull out the brownies I had bought at the high-end bakery near Wonderlux, where hip-looking women with red lipstick wore retro aprons and baked from scratch.

I snapped the twine off the box and set the brownies on a plate, then shuffled happily back over to the table, setting the plate down in front of Rose and Gabby. Rose immediately grabbed two, and handed one to her friend.

Bobby and I watched them eat with easy bemusement. When they had finished, I suggested that they go to Rose's room to play. Bobby and I followed, hovered in the doorway as they pulled plastic horses and Barbie dolls from baskets, indifferent to our presence. Then we returned to the kitchen.

"So, I'm glad there were no issues with that cop yesterday," said Bobby, bringing the last of the plates to the sink.

"Yeah," I said, sweeping crumbs off the table and into my open hand. "I'm still a little uneasy about it."

Alerted to my lingering concern, Bobby grew serious. "Has Warren told you anything about what was discussed?"

I gave him a look as I took a seat. Although Warren hadn't told me a thing, I wanted to move away from the weightier topics of the present, if only for another hour or so. For another hour or so, I wanted to forget that my brother had been questioned by the police, that I couldn't afford cable much less the fancy brownies I had just fed to two four-year-olds. Bobby turned on the water to begin the dishes, but I patted the table. "I'll do that later," I said. "Come sit."

Bobby poured himself another inch or so of wine, then walked across our tiny kitchen and pulled out the chair next to mine. We stared at each other in a way that felt like a confession, his knee touching mine, our hands inches apart on the table. "Do you remember," I began, "that party you took me to at Rick DeSesso's?" The memory had risen up unbidden.

Bobby chuckled and tilted his head, as if trying to get a better view into my mind. His pinkie finger rose off the table to stroke mine. "I do," he said.

I slid my leg under his beneath the table. "Why did you ask me to that party anyway?" I said.

Bobby smiled and looked down. "Uh . . . ," he said. Our eyes connected for a moment before he looked back down, chuckling.

"Oh, no," I said with mock dread, leaning back in my chair, but keeping my hand where it was. It was suddenly clear, like one of those secret-image pictures that you stared at for hours before shifting your head to find that the image was obvious, so obvious you didn't know how you had missed it before. "Your mom. Your mom made you take me."

His hand curled around mine and he pulled it closer to him. "I think she thought that you needed to have some fun," he said, his gaze falling away.

"I used to have fun," I protested, though as I said it, my

surety slipped away, undermined by the memories of my mother's face when I would ask her if I could go to this or that party, to this or that dance. *What about Warren?*

Bobby held my hand tight and tugged it close to his chest. "You always seemed to have a lot of responsibility."

When Bobby left that night, we hugged good-bye. Our legs had touched, our hands had touched, but our lips still hadn't. "I'm at the hospital all day tomorrow, but on Friday, I finish at seven," he said. "I'd love to see you."

I glanced down at Gabby. Her eyelids had begun to look weighted and her hands disappeared inside the too-long sleeves of her quilted purple down jacket. "Well, actually . . . ," I stuttered. "Rosie is going to spend the night with my friend Maggie's boys for Sam's birthday, so . . ."

"It could just be me," he said. And as I looked back at him, I felt the deep, churning thrill of wanting someone. Of having him want you back. "If that's all right."

I nodded. "That's all right," I said.

He picked up Gabby and pulled open the door. "Say thank you to Rose's mom," he prompted.

Gabby rested her little chin on his shoulder. "Thank you," she said sleepily.

When I shut the door behind them, I smiled at Rose and scratched her head. "Let's get you to bed, monkey." Gordo rubbed his eyes against my thigh. "You, too, Gord."

I changed Rose into her flannel nightgown, the one my mother had gotten her for Christmas because it looked like the ones that I used to wear and "was on a big sale." Then I propped Rose up on the vanity in the bathroom, helped her brush her teeth, and carried her to bed.

"Did you have fun tonight?" I asked, as I pulled the covers up to her chin.

"Yeah," she said, rubbing her eyes with her small fist. "I like Gabby."

I kissed her forehead and said good night, leaving the door cracked open.

Walking out to the kitchen to begin cleaning up in earnest, I saw the baby doll Gabby had come with. I picked up the phone. "Gabby forgot her baby," I said when Bobby answered.

"Shit," he whispered. I chuckled, familiar with the decision he was making, the inconvenience of turning around weighed against the inconvenience of time spent without a favorite toy. "I'll come back and grab it."

"If she can live without it tonight, I can drop it off tomorrow after work."

"Really?" he said. "That would be great."

• • •

CHAPTER TWENTY-SIX

Of Great Use

As I drove from the office to Royal Court the next day, I tried to use the trip to shed the tension from what had turned out to be a terrible day at work. A vendor slipup on a project already fraught with an unrealistic timeline and unreasonable client demands had resulted in hours spent on the phone trying to remedy an issue that wasn't our fault but was most certainly our problem. There was little quite as frustrating as having to bite your tongue through an unwarranted and gleeful reprimand. Maggie, being particularly unsuited to such tongue-biting, had gone down to the corner store at three o'clock, returned with a long, rectangular brown paper bag, and poured herself a glass of wine.

"Want one?" she'd asked, as the wine sloshed into the floral paper watercooler cup.

I'd shaken my head. "I have to go pick up Rose," I'd said, thinking about the evening that lay ahead of me. "And there are some things I have to do later."

I hadn't told my mother that I was coming to Royal Court that day, hadn't told her what I planned to do. I had called Beth Castro that morning and asked if we could speak.

"What about?" she had said, her tone already confrontational.

"Please," I said. "It won't take long. I just think a conversation would help clarify some of the issues there've been"—my tongue had moved through my dry mouth—"between your family and mine."

But the day had turned my mood dark and it remained so as I pulled into King's Knoll. I found myself wondering why I was in this position. Why was I the one who had to smooth things over with the Castros? Hadn't I moved away from Royal Court? Didn't I have my own problems, my own concerns?

So when I opened the door to my mother's house, and she said, "Hey, honey. What are you doing here?" I didn't look at her. I didn't look at her when I said that I needed to drop something off at Bobby's and could she watch Rose for a few minutes. Rushing back out the door, I stopped short, hearing a clatter behind me. Rose's backpack had snagged on the lace runner that ran the length of the table in front of the stairs, and when she'd turned, the runner had pulled, sending a vase full of dusty, faded fake flowers toppling into a pile of magazines and boxes in front of it. My mother caught the vase, pinning it against a box, her foot rumpling the side of a shopping bag. "It's all right," she said, to both Rose and me. "It's fine. We're fine." My eyes met Rose's and I paused for a moment before continuing out the door.

It was cold out, so I took my car rather than walking, cutting the wheel fast and heading first toward the Vannis'.

I'd put Gabby's baby in the nicest shopping bag I had on hand, and when I arrived, I grabbed its handles and hurried up to the house, keeping my chin tucked to my chest to ward off the chill.

As I rang the doorbell, I glanced behind me. Bobby's car wasn't in the driveway, but I hadn't expected it to be. Lights were on inside, but it was taking an unusually long time for someone to come to the door. I was about to try ringing once more when I heard the front door unlock. A few seconds later, the door slowly opened.

"Hi, Mr. Vanni," I said, softening at the sight of him. He was still a formidable-looking man, with the large frame and broad shoulders that gave him the appearance of a retired football player. But he had diminished, his skin hanging from his bones without the benefit of his once-dense musculature and his joints twisting like roots.

"Jenna," he said, giving me a smile, his eyes as reflective as a pond. "Sorry about the wait. It takes me a little while to get around now." He extended his hand toward the foyer, the motion much less fluid than it once had been. "Come on in."

"Oh," I said, lifting the bag with Gabby's baby, "I can't. I just wanted to drop this off for Gabby. It's her doll."

"Oh, good," he said, his eyes brightening. "She's been missing that thing all day."

"She left it at our house last night. Bobby wanted to come back for it, but I told him I'd just drop it off."

Mr. Vanni nodded. "He's a good boy. He works hard. I'm glad he's enjoying his free time a little more these days." Though his gaze had been on the neighborhood beyond me as he spoke, he gave me a sidelong glance. "Anyhow," he said, "I'm not going to keep you standing out there in the cold. It's crazy, this weather."

"Yeah," I agreed, taking a small step back. "Take care, Mr. Vanni."

He began to shut the door. "You, too, Jenna," he said. "Give your family my regards."

Burying my face in the collar of my coat, I took the stone steps quickly as I made my way back to the car. There was another stop I needed to make before returning to my mother's.

The bell sounded through the house, its ring long and drawn-out. A set of heavy plodding footsteps approached, and with a teenager's lack of urgency the door was pulled open. I remained still as I took him in. Zack Castro was several inches taller than me with a smattering of acne. He had pale blue eyes that looked as vacant as air. His baseball hat was turned backward and he wore a pair of long, shiny basketball shorts and a thick hooded sweatshirt. Though he was only seventeen, his physical presence, if nothing else, was impressive, with a sports-honed physique that lent him strength if not maturity.

"Hi, Zack," I said, his name coming out as if weighted. He set his head back a bit at the sound of it, as if looking to gain even an inch of distance between us.

"Who are you?" he asked, with an arrogant lift of his chin and calm disinterest.

I paused for a moment. "I'm Warren Parsons's sister." His eyes registered only the slightest bit of alarm before fading back into apathy.

From the bright kitchen behind him I saw Beth Castro drying her hands on a dish towel. "Zack," she said, as she hurried toward us. "Go watch your game."

Zack released the door with a push, letting it swing wider as he turned on his heels, passing his mother without saying a word as he returned to the couch. He fell onto it and hoisted his legs up onto the coffee table. Beth immediately replaced him in the front doorway, gripping its frame with her hand.

She looked at me expectantly, as if I should announce myself. "Hi, Beth," I said. "Thanks for seeing me."

I waited for her to invite me in, but she simply stood there, her body blocking my way into her home. "So what is all this about?"

"I'd like to talk to you about what happened between Zack and Warren."

She let out an exasperated gasp. "I just don't understand why you people keep coming over here," she muttered, looking everywhere but at me.

"I'm *coming over here*," I said, keeping my voice level, "because my brother came home last week with injuries that sent him to the emergency room." She snorted into the air—all rolling eyes and shaking head. "And my mother has been receiving some very upsetting notes. And I can't help but think that the two are related."

"So what? It's a crime to write your mother *some letters*? About that *house* she lives in? About what it's doing to property values in the neighborhood?!"

"No," I said, with a concessionary nod. "But I'd say what she's been getting borders on harassment."

"*Harassment?!*" Beth gave a manic laugh. "Well, you know what's a *bigger* crime?" she said, as if she was in a position to know, in a position to weigh and measure wrongs. "Stealing someone's eight-hundred-dollar mountain bike!"

I felt my jaw tighten, felt the advantage of poise begin to slip away. "I can assure you that Warren did not steal Zack's mountain bike."

"Then what's he *doing*?" she demanded, her shrill voice nearly making me wince. "Walking around the neighborhood with those damn airplanes! He ends up in people's yards! Poking around near their windows!" I drew back, only slightly, but Beth could see she had me now, that I was on the defensive. "Dina Margolis said he ended up in her *garage* a few weeks ago!"

From my memory came Seth Werlock's face as he tripped Warren on the playground. Almost three decades later and I still remembered his name. And I supposed it was those incidents—the ones from your youth—that found their way into your layers of self, and remained there, like fossils, the deep and undeniable truths of your past. "Warren would have no *use* for a mountain bike," I declared.

Beth Castro's lips now slid into a grin. I had given her just what she wanted. She glanced down and, smoothing the creases of her pants, said, "Well, a mountain bike can quickly be turned into cash. And I think you'll agree that cash is something that *everyone* has use for." She would probably repeat that line again and again, over meat loaf with her family, on walks with the neighbors. *So I said to her, I think you'll agree that cash is something that everyone has use for.* She savored the words that came next. "Especially a woman with an adult son living at home, a broken-down house, and a mountain of bills to pay."

"Beth," I said, my voice quiet now.

"The authorities have the information. It's in their hands now." And with that, she shut the door.

· · ·

CHAPTER TWENTY-SEVEN

Bewitched

1972

The television was set on a metal stand against the wall, in front of which were arranged two avocado-colored armchairs occupied by Hattie and Lee Harris. Priscilla sat on the floor between the chair that held her father and the wall. Her legs were stretched out in front of her, and her arms were at her sides, propping her up. She flinched slightly at the sound of Hattie's laugh. It was a jarring noise, sudden and drawn-out; it consisted of a single "ha" followed by a sustained, nasal "haaaaaaaaaaaaa." *Ha-haaaaaaaaaaa. Bewitched* was on and it was Hattie's favorite show, so there would be lots of *ha-haaaaaaaaaaaa*s.

Hattie tapped her cigarette on the ashtray at the end of the armrest, her heavy cocktail ring sliding off center as she did so.

Silla's father rattled the remaining ice cubes around his otherwise empty glass.

Hattie looked at Priscilla, her eyes heavy and lidded, before she took another drag of her cigarette and turned back to the TV. "Priscilla," she said, "your daddy needs a drink."

Priscilla got up without speaking and took her father's glass. "Thank you, sugar," he said, peering around her at the television.

Priscilla padded softly across the thick carpet, pausing to glance back at the TV as Hattie released another long *hahaaaaaaaaaaaaaaaaa*. Then she turned back and made her way to the bar cart at the end of the living room. *Miss Texas,* she thought, *sitting around on a Friday night making drinks for her daddy and watching the television.* She had just set down his tumbler when the phone rang.

Lee Harris glanced at his watch. "Goddammit," he said, as he stood with what appeared to be at least a modest effort. "It's after nine." He was a few drinks into his evening and when he turned toward his daughter, she noticed his tie was loosened and the top button of his shirt was undone.

Hattie watched him stand, her gray eyes following him until doing so would have required an effort, at which point she turned back to the TV, her helmet of blond hair visible over the chairback.

Swaying a bit, Lee brushed past Priscilla as he hurried to the kitchen to silence that intrusive ringing. Silla lifted the lid of the ice bucket. On the other side of that wall was the phone.

She heard her father answer it. "Hello," he said abruptly, effectively communicating the magnitude of the disturbance.

He was silent for a moment. "Speaking," he said.

When Silla heard his voice again, it was only a whisper. "An aneurysm?" he said. "And that was . . . yeah. Yes, sir. No, I'm glad you did." He made a noise, a quick rush of air that popped from his lips. He was silent again as he listened. "I'm assuming that that can all be handled . . . by mail," he said. There was another pause. "In terms of arrangements, should I speak with someone . . . ? Good, fine. I'll call tomorrow."

He was on the phone for no more than two minutes.

Priscilla heard the receiver being set back into its cradle on the other side of the wall and quickly placed three new cubes of ice in her father's cup. Then she poured in enough whiskey to cover them. She was cracking open a new can of club soda when her father returned to the living room.

"You got that drink, sugar?" he asked, almost sheepishly. Priscilla quickly poured in a glug of the club soda, threw in a piece of lemon, and handed the glass to her father without looking at him.

Priscilla saw Hattie eye him with curiosity as he made his way back to his armchair.

He sat down and leaned back, gazing heavenward for just a moment. Then he hunched forward, resting his forearm on his knee, his hand cupped around his drink, and angled himself toward Hattie. "Martha," was all he said. He said it so silently that he practically mouthed it. And maybe that's what he had intended. But after a few drinks, Lee Harris was always a bit louder than he should be. "They said it was an aneurysm. Just a couple of hours ago."

Hattie's hand slid onto his knee, her thin fingers looking stiff and petrified, her nails a slick pink. "Least it's over now," she said. "Least it's over."

Priscilla backed slowly out of the room. She lay on her bed that night, but she didn't sleep. No one came in. No one explained a thing. That was the first of many nights when she lay in bed, trying to remember what her daddy had told her about her mother. What they had told people when they'd moved from Corpus Christi to Houston. What her mother's parents had said, the few times they had conceded to a visit. In short, Silla tried to remember when "she's gone" had become "she's dead."

. . .

Once

I was in the bathroom zipping Rose's toothbrush into a Baggie when my phone buzzed in the back pocket of my jeans. Slipping it out, I looked at the smooth black screen. It was my father's home number. With a mixture of gratitude and dread, I answered it.

"Dad," I said, pressing the phone to my face.

"Jenna, it's *Lydia*." Her name was an admonishment. "What's all this I'm hearing about Warren being a *suspect* in the *burglaries*?"

My eyes shut. "Lydia," I started, trying to sound calm and unemotional. "Warren isn't a suspect." Those words had a repellent flavor in my mouth, like something rancid. "The police just talked to him."

"Well," she huffed, "I think that means he's a suspect!" I felt my own panic rising to meet hers, rendering me mute. Lydia waited for me to respond, but all I could do was grip the phone. "And I had to find out about all this when meeting with a client! They wanted to know if Priscilla was somehow involved!"

"Lydia, that's *crazy*!" I said, losing my very flimsy grip on my cool. "Could you honestly imagine my mother and Warren masterminding some suburban burglary ring?"

Her silence answered for her.

From the family room, I heard Rose call my name. "Listen, I'm so sorry, Lydia, but I really do have to go. I have to bring Rose to a sleepover."

"I'm sure I don't have to explain to you how terrible this could be for my business," she said.

"No, Lydia," I said. "You really don't."

"Can you *please* keep me posted on all of this?" she asked sternly.

"I will," I said.

"All right," she breathed, in preparation for a brisk good-bye. But I preempted her.

"Hey, when does Dad get back?" I asked. I had left my father a few voice mails on his cell phone, but hadn't heard back from him.

"Tomorrow," she said. "I'm picking him up at the airport and we're heading right to Russell's party at the Hyland Inn."

I sat down on the closed lid of the toilet. *I'm so sorry, Warren*, I thought, as I pictured our grandfather's watch, elegantly wrapped in a box with a thick cream satin bow. Again Rose's voice sounded. *Hey, Mom!* "I really need to speak with my dad," I said, "before you go to the party. . . ." And then Lydia and I hung up. I sat there for just a second before I called back to Rose. "Hold on, Rose! I'm just getting your stuff together!" I glanced over at her slippers, which lay underneath her fuzzy pink robe that hung from the hook on the back of the door. "Do you want to bring your slippers to Sam's?"

Rose reached up to ring Maggie's doorbell, her mouth opened in a wide smile, her tiny white teeth all visible. I heard Sam and Henry roar to the door, the lock sliding. "Sammy!" called Maggie from inside. "Don't push your brother!"

The door opened and Henry's face appeared below Sam's. "Happy birthday, big man!" I said. Sammy roared in response, then charged back inside the house, flinging himself on the couch headfirst. Henry copied his older brother and followed suit. Maggie walked briskly across the family room and pulled the door open wider. "Come on in, Rosie," she said.

Rose took Maggie's hand, but I saw her hesitate slightly. "It's okay, Rosie," I said, laying my hand gently on her back. Rose had been to Maggie's house scores of times. And she and Sammy had been raised like brother and sister, even sleeping in the same bed when we all went to Maggie's family's cottage on Cape Cod. But Rose looked up at me with concerned eyes. "Is Gabby coming?" she asked.

"You know," I said, picking her up into my arms and closing the door behind me, "I think that's a really good idea. We should introduce Gabby to Sammy and Henry. But Gabby is at her grandmother's house tonight, right near Nana's."

Rose glanced over at the boys, who were attacking each

other with light sabers. I realized that the age when boys and girls naturally started to segregate themselves came earlier than I had remembered.

"Sammy! Henry!" commanded Maggie. "Knock it off!" Then Maggie reached out to take Rose. "They're just showing off for you, Rosie. All boys do it." Rose slid into Maggie's arms. "We're going to have an awesome night. We got *movies*. We got *popcorn*. We got *cake*."

"*Cake!*" screamed Sammy from the couch, and this time it sent a giggle through Rose. She wiggled down from Maggie's arms and went to join the fray.

"So this is sort of spectacular timing," Maggie said to me, with a saucy lift of her eyebrows. A wink-wink, nudge-nudge.

I let my gaze fall. I had always wanted to be the sort of woman who was unflappable when it came to dating, who would scoot a man out of her bed and call him a cab when she was finished with him. But it wasn't in me. To my detriment, it wasn't in me. "I'm freaking out a little," I admitted.

"Why?" she asked.

I thought about my body, how it had changed since I'd had Rose. "It's been a while."

"Oh, stop," she said. "It's just like riding a bike!"

Leaning against the wall, I felt Maggie's almost maternal watchfulness. "I'm happy for you," she finally said. She had googled Bobby and found his picture on the hospital's Web site. *Oh, I totally get it now,* she'd said, staring at his image, and assuming his proximity was the reason for my visits to Royal Court. *I'd paint your mom's columns, too. I'd mow the lawn and power wash the deck and seal the driveway.*

"Thanks, Mags."

"So go, go," she said, pushing me toward the door. "You need to get ready. You can't entertain gentlemen callers looking like you're chaperoning a field trip to the pumpkin patch." A reference, I was sure, to my L.L. Bean boots and fleece jacket. "I'll call you if there are any issues."

Later that evening I was sitting on my couch with my hands hidden beneath my thighs, waiting for Bobby to arrive. He was late, but not so much so that it warranted a phone call or undue concern. Playing softly on the stereo was the Velvet Underground. I brought my wrist to my nose, breathing in the perfume I rarely wore. The scent was deep and soft. Gardenia maybe. In front of me was a glass of red wine, the bottle from which it came, and another glass, an empty one, for Bobby. Taking its stem, I turned it, watching the light move through its bowl, waiting for the man whose profession was healing to arrive at my home.

A set of headlights turned into my driveway. As they beamed through the shades, I took a sip of wine, letting it mute—just a bit—the anticipation. Then I stood, walked over to the door, and smiled into the glass of its small window. As Bobby's car came to a stop, the outside light was tripped, illuminating the darkness. And as quickly as I saw him, I could tell that something was wrong, that he'd had the type of day that empties you. He opened the car door and stepped out. Gordo, now alerted to company, stood from his bed and spun in a few tail-chasing circles, then joined me at the door. Together we watched Bobby attempt a smile in our direction, then make his way up the gravel path, his shoulders sagging, his hands sunk in his pockets. I opened the door as he approached, feeling the sharpness of the air. "Hey," I said, with concern in my voice.

"Hey, Jenna. Sorry I'm late," he said. "I couldn't get out of there tonight."

"It's all right," I said, beckoning him toward me. "Come in."

I shut the door behind him and he seemed to slacken with relief, as if he was finally outside of the world's grasp. Reaching for my wrist, he closed his eyes and pulled me into him. His hand slid under my hair, bringing my head to his chest, and I wrapped my arms around his back, feeling its breadth. For a few moments, we stayed like that, silent and entwined. "What's wrong?" I finally asked.

"It was just . . . a hard night."

"Are you okay?"

With his hand still holding my head, I felt his breath pull deeply in, then rush out. "Yeah," he finally said. "I'm just trying to shake it off." His words were a whisper, their warmth in my hair. "And I can't."

I thought about the sights and stories that would make for a difficult night in the emergency room. The lives changed. The lives ended. "Are you supposed to?" I asked. "Be able to shake it off?"

He let out a small, sad laugh. "I don't know," he said. "I think so."

I waited for a moment, thinking perhaps he would continue. "What happened?" I asked.

Another stretch of silence came. "There was this little kid," he said. "Seven years old." I could feel his body tighten. And at that, he took a hard breath—a substitute for events he wouldn't repeat.

I raised my head. "I'm sorry, Bobby," I said, meeting his eyes. But he pulled me back to his chest. And there, with his hand in my hair, with my body pressed against his, I felt something inside me shift. Running my fingers up his spine, I lifted my mouth to his neck.

Maybe it was meant to be only a comfort, the kiss, but he gave a soft groan, and his hand slipped down past my back. "Jenna," he whispered, and it sounded like a plea. Because what could take the loss away more entirely than my skin on his? What did either of us want more than that?

I hooked the tips of my fingers into the waistband of his jeans, pulling him in just as he backed me against the wall, the weight of him against me. We were eye to eye for a moment, and then our mouths met—all breath and hunger.

Lifting my hands above my head, he cupped my breast and I felt myself shudder. Then he pulled my shirt over my head and slid down one strap of my bra, so that it hung off my shoulder, his hand skating over my bare, uninterrupted skin. Without a word, I wove my fingers through his, and led him to the bedroom.

As soon as we stepped over the threshold, he found the clasp of my bra and unfastened it, letting it drop to the floor in front of me. I leaned back against him as his hands moved over my body. I turned around and his shirt was off, then my pants. I reached for his belt buckle and his hand dipped into his back pocket, discreetly removing a condom. We shifted to the bed; there was the tearing of paper. And then we were together.

With each movement, I felt something inside me slacken and fall away, like bindings loosening. I closed my eyes and lifted my chin and opened my mouth. And when it was over, he lay on top of me, our hearts thumping, calling and answering in a disorganized rhythm. Then Bobby rolled onto his side and I onto mine, so that we were facing each other on the yielding white plane of my bed.

We stayed that way, in reflected contentment, until Bobby spoke. "Hi, Jenna Parsons," he whispered.

And red-faced, my chin kissed raw, I beamed. "Hi, Bobby Vanni." Bobby let out a quiet but glowing laugh and I reached for his hand. Pulling it up to my chest, I curved around it. "Who would have thought, right?" I asked.

Bobby rolled me onto my back, and moved his body on top of mine. Propping himself up so that he could see my face, we stared at each other until I felt a low churning grumble in his stomach; he probably hadn't eaten all night.

"All right, Dr. Vanni," I said, sitting up. "You stay here." I groped for my underwear and slid them on. Then I sat up and opened my dresser drawer, which I could reach from the bed, and pulled out the first top I laid my hands on. "I'll be right back," I said, as my head emerged from the neckhole of an old gray NYU shirt.

I padded over the avocado-colored carpet of the family room and into the kitchen, finding my house, even its flaws, more charming than I ever had before.

Bending down into the fridge, I pushed aside a milk container to assess what I had on hand. Having assumed that we would order Chinese after he arrived, I had very few grown-up-friendly options with which to feed Bobby, but I figured he was too ravenous to wait for delivery. Finally, I pulled out the melamine Santa tray that my mother had given me, loaded it up with cheese, crackers, smoked turkey, pickle slices, and some mustard, then headed back to the bedroom, grabbing the bottle of wine on my way.

Bobby was sitting up in bed, the white covers pulled over his lap. "This is going to be the very worst dinner you've ever had," I said as I set the tray down on my dresser.

Bobby laughed. "I doubt that," he said. "I eat in a hospital six nights a week."

"No, seriously," I said, as I began crafting him a triple-decker cracker sandwich. "This is the kind of thing you eat when you're stoned." I handed him my creation.

Smiling as he took it, I had a fleeting thought, almost unnoticed: that my terrible postcoital meal would become one of our stories. That every year, we would eat turkey and Triscuits and pickles and cheese. And we would remember tonight.

Bobby tried to take a bite of my unruly sandwich, cupping his hand under his chin and seeming to contemplate the combination of flavors and textures. "I think you could have a future with Hewn Memorial dining services," he teased.

I let out a quiet laugh while my eyes remained focused on assembling a sandwich of my own. "So is it definite that you're going to stay on there? After your residency is done?" I asked, taking a bite of my sandwich.

Bobby moved his head as if he had a sudden and painful twinge in his neck. "I don't know," he said. "I don't know if it's going to work out there."

"Why not?" I asked, covering my mouth with the back of my hand. "I'm sure they want to keep you."

"They do," he said. "They want me to work the same schedule." He looked at his sandwich. "But I need better hours. I need to see Gabby more."

"Well, there are other hospitals, right?"

"Yeah," he said. "There are other hospitals."

And then I knew. I felt a clenching in my chest, as if it was in the grip of something outside of my influence. "Where else are you looking?" I asked, trying to remain light, impassive.

"There's Overlook," he said. Overlook was about forty minutes away. "And there are a couple of other hospitals that I'm considering. Out in California. Near Mia." He looked at me, gauging my response. "I've only started talking to them. But I think they might come up with the best package."

I made myself smile. "That's great!" I said. So convincingly. So cheerfully.

"Yeah?" he asked.

"Of course!" I said, adopting my mother's pageant smile. Then I looked down at my sandwich, pretending to contemplate the placement of another bite. "So, do you think your parents would stay in Harwick?" He had mentioned that they had wanted to leave, to flee to warmer climes. Bobby was all that was stopping them.

"I don't know," he said. "I haven't really discussed it with them yet. But I think they'd consider moving out there."

"That's really perfect, then," I said again, perhaps less convincingly this time. Because as we talked about the process doctors went through to find a job, I noticed Bobby's observant glances, his lingering stare. He would start his new position, wherever it might be, in July.

And when I had heard enough, when my lips could no longer manage my smile, I nestled my head back against his chest and let my eyes slip shut. I felt his fingertips move slowly up and down my back. Lying as still as I could, I let my body become limp and heavy, as if with sleep. After several minutes, he whispered quietly, "Jenna?" I said nothing, but took a rustling breath. "Jenna?" he asked again. When I didn't respond, he carefully slid his arm out from underneath me and lifted himself out of my bed. Though I kept my eyes closed, I heard the clink of his belt as he pulled on his jeans. Then he left the room. I waited to hear the front door open and shut, but the sound of his footsteps traveled to the kitchen, where there was the distant rumbling of our old drawers opening, then shutting again. Then the floorboard creaked as he came back to the bedroom.

I lay there when he stepped in, like I used to when my parents' marriage was in the process of imploding. Warren would go to his planes, becoming lost in their wires, in their wings. I would go to my room and close my eyes and to all the world, I'd look like a girl asleep. Then next to me, I felt the weight of Bobby's hand on the bed, and the warmth of his lips on my forehead. He moved quickly then, out of the room and the house.

I heard his car start, its old engine awakening grumpily. I sat up, opened my eyes, and next to me on the bed was a piece of orange paper folded in half. It was a xeroxed copy of a note from Rose's preschool that I had left on the counter, announcing a family potluck in honor of Thanksgiving. I had gone last year; dozens of families had made awkward small talk with plates full of six different kinds of pasta salad teetering on their laps. On the back side of the note, Bobby had written:

I didn't want to wake you, but I have to be at the hospital early.

And don't go to this potluck. It sounds terrible.
Let me take you and Rose out to dinner instead.
I'll call you tomorrow.
 Love,
 Bobby

I laid it on the pillow next to me, sliding my hand under my cheek as I stared at it. I would save it, of course, as a memento of the one and only night I would spend with Bobby Vanni.

CHAPTER TWENTY-NINE

· · ·

Break-O-Lean

1972

"Sing for them, Silla," urged her father, as he sat with the executives from Millhouse. They were shooting the advertising campaign for their new instant meal-replacement shake. As the corporate sponsors for the Miss Texas pageant, Millhouse had awarded Priscilla Harris with a contract, which meant that today she was sitting on a cold, windy beach in a red bikini, surrounded by men who looked like they were dressed for the golf course. "That's how she won," said Lee Harris, speaking to the executives. "Go ahead," he urged. "Do 'Snowbird.'"

Priscilla, whose hair was being sprayed into a windproof helmet by the only other woman in the vicinity, didn't sing. "Daddy," she pleaded quietly. But Lee Harris had already moved on, enjoying the company of the men. When he met the

Millhouse executives, he shook their hands and patted their backs like they were old college pals. Lee Harris liked men. He liked sitting at dinner tables full of men, smoking cigarettes and making excuses to call over pretty young waitresses. He liked that he was still handsome enough to make them blush.

"You said the packaging was going to be red and white?" he asked the youngest of the Millhouse executives. He was the one who seemed responsible for more than sitting in a folding chair and smoking cigarettes.

"Yes," the young man answered, his eyes moving toward the stack of Break-O-Lean cans arranged on a small table. "She'll be holding one in the shot."

"That'll look nice with her hair and bathing suit," Lee offered, his index finger tracing Silla's form, several yards away.

The young man didn't bother telling him that, yes, that's why they had chosen a red bathing suit. That's why the foreground of the photograph would have the red and white life preserver. That the tagline for the campaign was "How Miss Texas Saves Calories." The young man also didn't tell Lee that he thought the concept was all wrong, suggesting that the drink would retain calories rather than help eliminate them. And he didn't tell him that his daughter made a poor spokeswoman for a diet drink. That though she was sexy as hell, they needed more of a Twiggy than a Marilyn. Instead, he said, "Can I get you something to drink?" as he sidestepped over to a cooler and pulled out a Coca-Cola.

Lee thanked him as he took the bottle, damp and slick.

The young man's gaze flickered back to Priscilla in her red bikini. "Would she like a drink?" he asked quietly.

Lee's chin lifted as he called out, "Silla, you thirsty, honey?"

Priscilla looked across the line of seated men, then back at her father. She nodded. The young man handed Lee another bottle and Lee walked as quickly as the shifting sand would allow toward his daughter. She took the bottle and with his hand now free, Lee grabbed hold of the flesh of her stomach. "You're going to need that Break-O-Lean," he said loudly, giving her stomach a shake. "I'll bet you can talk these fellas here into a year's supply." Smiling, Lee glanced back at his audience; the men emitted a few amused chuckles.

But Silla shrank forward, as if her body was caving in on itself. She tried to turn her back to the men. The hairdresser, who was now circling her with a bristle brush, gave her a sympathetic look, but Priscilla stared purposefully at the sand. *Just get through it,* she told herself. *Just get through it.*

Lee, making his way back to his seat, quipped, "The blue skies will be nice for the photo, but Lord, it's cold!"

And Priscilla sat in her bikini, her pale skin rough with goose bumps from the brisk air. *Just get through it,* she told herself, steeling her body against the wind and the stares. *Just get through it,* she repeated over and over as she stared down at the sand.

So when the photographer was ready, Priscilla stood and gave her most winning smile, channeling warmth and youth and radiance as she held up the red and white can. And when it was over, when the photographer announced that he was all set, Priscilla finally exhaled and let the smile slip off her face. When she looked up, the young executive—the one who she would learn was named Stewart Parsons—stood in front of her, holding his jacket open. She smiled at him, then lightly bit her lower lip, just the way Cal had always liked. "Thank you," she said, as she turned to let him wrap the jacket around her.

After the men all shook hands, Silla slid back into her father's car and turned the heat on high, holding her fingers in front of the vents as she leaned back in the seat, feeling emptier than she ever had. The road traveled along the gulf for a ways and she looked out at it. She had been born near here, near that gentle expanse of water. Looking at it, you'd never believe that it played host to some of the most violent storms anyone had ever seen: monstrous meetings of wind and water. The hurricane of 1900 took eight thousand lives in Galveston alone. And as they flew over the bumpy, windswept road, Silla let her head rest on the back of the leather seat, feeling it rock gently from side to side as the road dipped and swayed. As she saw a sign with the name of a town she hadn't been back to in seventeen years, she no longer had the will to keep herself from thinking about what she had tried so hard not to know.

"Daddy," she said slowly, the dare in her voice only just hidden by her easy, languid words, "why don't I remember Mama's funeral?"

As she turned her head to look at him, the expression on his face was one she'd never forget. She wouldn't have been able to describe it at the time, but later, once she was a mother, she would be able to place it. It was the look of a child who had been caught. Caught doing something just awful.

. . .

CHAPTER THIRTY

Search and Rescue

Maggie and I sat at the table, our elbows splaying apart the printouts that lay scattered across it. I flexed my toes, which were covered by Gordo's warm, soft belly. "You know you can't just blow him off," said Maggie. Our meeting about work had become a conversation about why I hadn't spoken to Bobby since our night together.

When he'd called on Saturday morning, I had let it go to voice mail. I did the same when he called that evening. On Sunday, I answered. I told him I wasn't feeling well.

He paused for a moment. "Do you want me to come over?" he asked.

"It's okay," I said quickly, realizing that I was playing sick with a doctor. "I think I'm just run-down."

"Are you sure?"

"Yeah," I'd said. "I'm going to take it easy today."

Now I pushed up and leaned back in my chair, though my eyes were focused on nothing. "I know," I said to Maggie.

"I mean, if you don't want to get involved with someone who's probably going to be moving across the country, I guess I get it. But you owe him an explanation."

"I know. I just needed to think it through. Before I talked to him about it." I had spent the last couple of nights trying to convince myself that I could keep on seeing Bobby when I knew the next several months would be a countdown. But I kept coming to the same conclusion.

"Is he definitely going to move?"

"No. But he should," I said. "Gabby could be closer to her mom and his parents have been wanting to move somewhere warmer for his dad's arthritis. They could all go out there. It makes sense."

My thoughts occupied the pause until Maggie spoke again. "Is Duncan back in New York yet?" And I knew the path her thoughts had taken in the silence. But it was too easy to blame Duncan—too neat. I thought of my mother. How my father's leaving seemed to be a manifestation of her worst fear rather than the source of it, as if she had suffered from an emotional mutation. *Mutations are caused by two things*, Warren might say. *Natural chance or external influence*. The lottery or a lightning bolt.

"Would you ever . . . ?" began Maggie.

"No," I answered quickly, before she could ask if I'd ever move with Bobby. "Not with my mom and Warren here." *Not anymore.*

I reached down and slid my fingers over one of Gordo's velvet ears. He moaned in appreciation. I was about to ask him if he needed to go out, about to tell Maggie that I was going for a quick walk, when my cell phone rang. My mother's name was crisp white on the black screen.

"Hey, Mom," I said, answering it.

"Jenna," she said. And at once I could hear her panic, the tempo of her words like a heartbeat. "Linda Vanni just called me at work. She said there are two police cars in front of our house." Her breath seemed to catch. "She says they're taking things out in *boxes*."

"*What?*"

"Jenna." My name was spoken like a plea. "Warren's there by himself."

"I'll go right now," I said, standing suddenly, the action providing some small relief. "I'll be there as soon as I can." And I hung up the phone.

Maggie half rose from her chair, her face alert. "What's going on?"

"I gotta go," I said. "The police are at my mom's house. I have to get over there right now. Warren's alone."

Without another word, I slid my computer into my bag. "Can I do anything?" Maggie asked.

"No," I said, shaking my head. "I'll call you later." Tapping my thigh and giving a brisk whistle, I called Gordo.

Gordo kept time with me as we rushed down the stairs. I snapped on his leash and walked him quickly to the back lot, where he hopped without prompting into my wagon.

As I lowered myself into the driver's seat, I pulled out my cell phone, scrolling for my father's cell number. Though I hadn't yet heard from him, I knew he was back in the country; he wouldn't have missed Russell's party.

My knee bounced through the first, second, and third rings until there was a voice. My father's voice. "Hey, kiddo!" he said. "How've you been?"

"Dad," I said, as I threw the car into reverse and pulled efficiently from the parking space, "Warren might be in trouble."

"What do you mean?" he said, his voice sobering immediately. "What's going on?"

I stared down a length of the street, waiting for a break in the traffic. "The police are at Mom's right now," I said.

"The *police*?" he asked, confused and shocked.

"I've been trying to get hold of you for *weeks*," I said. "There've been *these thefts* in King's Knoll and everyone in the neighborhood thinks Warren had something to do with it." I zipped onto the street, cutting off a minivan and eliciting a loud honk. "Didn't Lydia tell you any of this?"

I heard a voice in the background, the tone insistent though the words were indiscernible. My father made a shushing sound.

"Are you at work?" I asked, though I was sure that he wasn't. He would never shush a colleague.

"No," he said. "We're coming back from driving Alexandra to school. She was down for the weekend." His tone was a reluctant confession before he returned with urgency to the matter at hand. "But, Jenna, what are the police doing at your mother's?"

I stared up at a red light. "I don't know," I said. "Mrs. Vanni told Mom that they were carrying out boxes."

"Did they have a *warrant*?!"

"I don't know, Dad!" I snapped, not understanding how this had happened, how we had become a family that had to make sense of a police search. "When are you going to be home?"

"Wednesday," he said. Then he paused. "We're going to spend a couple of nights in Newport." Stewart Parsons was not a man who readily revealed guilt, a characteristic not bred in the boardroom but almost certainly nurtured there.

I watched the steady stream of cars cross the intersection in front of me. "Mom can't do this by herself, Dad."

There was a hard breath. "All right," he said. "I'll make some calls. It's time to get a lawyer."

I heard rumbles from Lydia in the background. *Stewart, this was supposed to be our vacation!* I, however, felt a modest amount of relief. Much could be accomplished via my father's phone calls. "Thanks, Dad," I said, hanging up just as I merged onto the highway that would take me back to Harwick.

I drove unaware of the act of driving, relying on the muscle memory of returning home to bring me there. When I approached the KING'S KNOLL sign at the entrance to the development, I turned in and craned my neck over the steering wheel, anxious and terrified to glimpse the house. But it sat there, as it always had, proud and battered. The police cars were gone, the driveway empty save for Warren's Civic. Pulling in next to it, I stepped quickly from the car and opened the gate. Gordo hopped out, his claws hitting the pavement, and he looked up at me, seeming to sense my gravity. We walked side by side into the house.

Warren was sitting at the kitchen island with his back to me. His only movement came from the strumming of his fingers on the counter in front of him. Gordo rushed him, his body wagging wildly, his tail clanging as it glanced off the objects around him.

He nudged Warren's leg with his snout and Warren chuckled softly, patting Gordo on the head. *Hey, boy. Hey.* Gordo looked at me, as if to say, *See? Everything's okay!* Reaching for the stool next to Warren, I pulled it out, its feet bucking against the linoleum. I sat down and looked at my brother.

"War," I finally said. "What happened?"

His face tensed a bit. "Detective Dunn came," he said, his lips barely moving as he spoke.

I glanced around the room, which appeared largely untouched—my mother's baubles and knickknacks undisturbed, the drawers and cabinets shut. I had imagined upturned tables and slit couches. "Mom said they left with boxes."

Warren's brows drew together and he almost smiled. With the most minute of movements he was able to express volumes. "One box," he said, his fingers galloping over the counter.

I had visualized flashing lights and police tape, camera flashes and sirens and detectives on their hands and knees. But in truth, it had been a quiet affair, with Detective Dunn carrying off a single box. "What was in it?" I asked.

Warren's pointer finger lifted millimeters off the counter, in the direction of a piece of white paper next to the sink. Sliding from my seat, I took three steps, just enough so that I could reach it, so that I could take it by its edges. It was a plain document with black type and crisp boxes. Detective Dunn's name appeared on it. In the largest box was written: *picture frame.*

"A picture frame?" I asked, confused. "What kind of a picture frame?"

Without looking up, Warren's head shook slowly from side to side, like the pendulum of a clock. "I hadn't seen it before."

My heart started pumping as my mind turned from path to path, searching for an explanation. There were very few. Only two people lived in this house. "War, you're not . . ." I remembered how when we were little, and would find our way into mischief, Warren would always try to assume all the blame. Who drew on the floor? Who broke the lamp? Who spilled the juice? *Sorry,* he would whisper, while his lithe fingers tinkered with a plane. *I'm sorry.*

"You're not trying to protect anyone, are you?" I asked now.

His head lifted suddenly and he looked at me, as if reading my mind front to back. And I suddenly felt ashamed of my question. Then his gaze shifted from my own, to the park behind me, the angle of his eyes moving in tiny increments as he scanned the sky. His lids narrowed slightly as he seemed to see something. Or sense it. I glanced over my shoulder, but all I saw was the faded, familiar landscape—the dry hill, its green leached by the cold nights; the leafless maple beyond it that cast its shadow on the pond during late-summer sunsets, when the sky burned with color. "It's going to get windy tonight," Warren said.

I planted my hand on my hip. "Oh, yeah?" I said, hearing my voice shake.

"No rain, though."

"Warren?" I waited until he looked at me. "Do you know where the picture frame came from?"

Again, his gaze moved past me, back to the park. "There's a large area of high pressure over Greenland."

I dropped my head forward, letting it hang there, Warren seeming as incomprehensible and foreign to me as he ever had.

• • •

Meeting Martin

1973

Silla hadn't quite gotten used to driving Stewart's Cutlass. Even though it was smaller than the cars her daddy always had, she checked her blind spot three times prior to switching lanes, then glided slowly over the pavement until she found a vacant spot at the curb and pulled up.

She heard the high roar of a plane taking off as she turned around and craned her neck over the seat back, running her eyes over the people that were standing there on the concrete, their suitcases at their feet. A tall, upright-looking pilot in a pressed uniform walked out of the terminal. He caught her eye and gave her a smile, which she returned tightly before looking away, wondering if she had any idea what it meant to be someone's wife.

Two months. That's it. That's how long she and Stewart had known each other before going to city hall one day and getting married. They had talked about it the night before, made their plans amid whispers and giddy giggles. And as Silla had packed her bag that evening, in the bedroom of her father's home, she'd wondered if she needed to bring her own toothpaste. *Or will I use Stewart's now?*

It was out of character for Stewart to run off and marry a girl from Texas who hadn't even met his parents, but she was only just beginning to understand that. When they had stood next to each other and said their vows, she hadn't even known that he liked his steak rare. Later, she would once again see Stewart behave impetuously when it came to love, but then it would lead to the end of their marriage rather than to the beginning.

Seeing someone she thought might be her father-in-law, she raised her hand in a tentative wave, but he kept walking, so she lowered it again. She had seen pictures of Stewart's parents, but sometimes men just looked like men to Silla. *He'll find you,* Stewart had said. And when she had asked him how, he'd only wrapped his hand around her waist and said, *How many gorgeous redheads do you think there'll be driving an orange Cutlass at the airport this Thursday at two o'clock?* She sometimes laughed hearing him talk like that; he didn't realize that he still sounded like a Yankee trying on Southern charm. She wished he were here now. She wished he weren't working. She didn't want to meet Martin on her own.

Her eyes were on the glass doors, on the periodic bursts of bodies coming through them, when she heard her name.

"Priscilla?"

She startled slightly and saw a man standing next to the passenger side of the car, his posture straight, his sport coat draped over his forearm. He was looking at her with an amused, dignified curiosity. It took her a moment to process the fact that this must be Martin. "Oh!" she exclaimed. Quickly opening the door and stepping out of the car, she pulled up the neckline of her thin maroon polyester dress, wishing she had worn something a little more modest. Her heels clacked on the blacktop as she hurried over to her father-in-law.

She brushed her hair off her shoulder and extended a hand. Martin smiled and took it. "I'm so happy to meet you," she said, pumping her arm vigorously up and down.

"Likewise," he said. "Likewise." They stood like that, shaking hands, until Martin brought his other hand up to steady Silla's. "Oh," she said, embarrassed. "Sorry."

His short hair was almost entirely gray, with only hints of the former sandy brown he'd once shared with Stewart. His eyes were watery and gentle, like small blue puddles. And perhaps it was her youth, but she thought that there was something almost grandfatherly about him, something wise and safe.

"Well, I suppose we can get going," she said, fidgeting, not knowing where exactly to stand or what exactly to do with her hands. She eyed his suitcase.

Again, he smiled gently and nodded down to his suitcase. "I'll just put this in the trunk."

If Silla was uncomfortable behind the wheel of Stewart's car when she was alone, she was doubly so with Martin next to her. He drove a car for a living, serving as the chauffeur for Harold

Barnes, the son of the founder of Millhouse Incorporated. He'd done so for the past thirty years. Silla knew that it was Martin's relationship with Harold that had helped Stewart get his job.

"So how was your flight?" she asked, her eyes on the rearview mirror as she waited for an opportunity to pull away from the curb. For a moment she thought she could make it, stepped on the gas, then changed her mind and hit the brakes.

"Just take your time," said Martin calmly. "I'm not in any rush." Martin had a way of carrying himself in the car—relaxed and alert and always watching the road, as if he were the one driving.

Once the airport was behind them, Silla started to feel more at ease "I'm so sorry that Eleanor couldn't join you," she said. Eleanor was Stewart's mother. He had only said that she wasn't well enough to travel. Eleanor would later die of complications associated with alcoholism. Silla would know her to be a kind drunk. *Did you know I grew up in an orphanage?* Eleanor used to ask nearly every day at the end of her life.

Martin just smiled. "I'm sorry, too," he said. "I know she's very eager to meet her *daughter-in-law*." He ended the sentence with a jovial formality.

Silla smiled and blushed. "I hope you and Eleanor weren't upset by the way we did things," she said, referring, of course, to the elopement.

"I suppose you had your reasons," Martin said thoughtfully. And Silla's smile faded as she pictured Hattie's triumphant face. *You know they call it* Miss *America for a reason.* "How did your folks take the news?"

She hesitated as she always did now when talking about her

mother's death. Clearing her throat, she said, "Well, my mother passed away some time ago."

Martin's brow furrowed in confusion. Perhaps Stewart hadn't told him. Perhaps he had forgotten. "I'm sorry to hear that," he said.

"And my father . . ." Silla tried to make her voice lighter, tried to build up to her punch line. "I think he was just happy that he got out of paying for a wedding." It was her standard bit, one that usually played well, but Martin just gave her a polite chuckle and adjusted the jacket that he had draped over his lap, pulling out a packet of cigarettes. "May I?" he said, angling them toward Silla.

She nodded. "Of course."

He gave the bottom of the pack a tap and pulled out a cigarette, settling it between his lips as he retrieved his matches. Silla heard the strike, then smelled the burn of tobacco. Had she been more courageous, she would have asked him for one.

They rode in silence for a while, watching Houston's faded-looking buildings spread out against the dusty earth, before Martin said, his eyes still on the road, "Stewart tells me that you're a singer."

Silla let out a shy gasp, but inside she was beaming. She loved being described as a singer. "I'm not a professional or anything," she conceded. "But I do love to sing."

"What sort of songs do you like?" he asked.

Again, she blushed. "Jazz," she blurted out before she could stop herself. "I like singing old jazz standards." It was a strange thing for a Texas beauty queen to admit during the 1970s.

Martin's eyebrows lifted—he was surprised, it seemed, but

pleasantly so. Without warning, as if it were the most natural thing in the world, he began to sing. "I'm gonna love you like nobody's loved you, come rain or come shine." His voice was deep and unhurried.

Silla felt her heart shudder and jump. "Come Rain or Come Shine" was one of her favorites. "High as a mountain," she began, relishing the feeling of the words coming from somewhere deep within her, somewhere secret and safe, "and deep as a river, come rain or come shine."

They sang the whole song that way, trading lines back and forth. And when they finished, they both laughed, squeezing each other's hands as Silla kept one on the wheel, a mutual and spontaneous congratulations for their impromptu performance.

Martin smiled. "I think we're going to get along just fine," he said.

And Silla pressed against the seat back, her face young and glorious. She was Priscilla Parsons now. Nothing could touch her anymore.

. . .

CHAPTER THIRTY-TWO

Windstorm

The storm arrived that night. The relentless wind made our cottage feel like a boulder facing the steady rush of a river. The walls creaked as they withstood its force and I listened to the whistle of the trees as the gusts swept through their branches. But except for a few errant drops that whipped against the windows, there was no rain.

The gale built steadily all evening, so that by the time the power went off, Rose was already asleep, wrapped in her covers as the moonlight made shadow branches wave across her bedroom walls. Storms never scared Rose, though. She would have loved to see the trees dancing for her.

Gordo deposited himself on his bed, his head jerking up suddenly with the louder whips of wind, only to settle back down again with a satisfied groan a few seconds later. I watched him from the couch, my feet tucked beneath me, until I slid down and sat next to him on the floor, my arm resting over the long curve of his back. Reaching for my cell phone, I picked it up and called my mother.

"How is everything?" I asked. The family room was lit by a handful of lopsided white candles, the hardened wax that dripped from their sides looking like the wet sand with which Warren and I had decorated our castles on the beach when we were little.

"Okay," said my mother. We had already talked twice that afternoon. There was nothing more to say about the box, about the frame. She had gone through the house to try to locate all of her frames in an attempt to explain the origin of the one that the police confiscated, but that was a bit like looking for an absent sapling in a forest. We had gone through the possibilities and the maybes—the convoluted, desperate explanations—and now all we could do was wait. It felt as if we were holding vigil, anticipating a great event without knowing what it would be. But it seemed as though when the police carry a box from your house, even just one, the story isn't yet finished.

"We lost power," I said. "About an hour ago."

"You can come here," said my mother hopefully.

And as I listened to the wind's empty scream, I wanted nothing more than to be at the house at 62 Royal Court, despite the notes and the thefts and the accusations. Despite how much I had run from it over the years. I realized that it was still, in a very real way, home. It was still where the collective memories of my family resided—the beautiful, the terrible, and the ones not yet spoken. "Rose is already sleeping," I said.

We sat in silence for a moment. "Your father called," said Mom. "He told me you two talked."

I paused for a moment. "Yeah," I admitted. "I called him."

Her breath came through the phone, and I waited for her reprimand. But when she spoke, her voice was small. "I'm glad you did, honey," she said. "There were some things we needed to discuss." I remained silent, waiting for her to say more. After a few moments of quiet that was louder than the wind, she did. "He's calling Lewis Marshall," she said.

I winced. Lewis Marshall had handled my father's end of my parents' divorce, but his firm's specialty was criminal defense. *He's got that damn shyster working for him!* I'd heard my mother say.

"No, it's good, honey," said my mother. "I think it's good."

Gordo shifted, kicking me with his back leg as he stretched out, exposing his warm, pink belly.

"So," she said, "what does Bobby have to say about all this?"

"Oh," I said lightly, trying to hide the crack in my voice, "I don't know. We haven't talked in a few days."

There was a pause. "Are you still spending time with each other?"

"Well, he's so busy with his residency. And I've got my hands full with Wonderlux. So, I don't know if the timing is really right."

From the pitch of the silence, I could picture the exact look on her face. Her head would be tilted to the side, her face soft and sad. "Jenna, you know," she said, starting slowly, "when you and Warren were babies, I felt like I had to . . . hold him more."

"It's okay, Mom," I said, sensing her regret and wanting to stanch it. "He probably needed it."

"It's just that he was so small. And you were happy just sitting in your little bouncer."

"Mom," I said, chuckling uncomfortably. "It's fine."

"I shouldn't have done that," she said, with remorseful resolve. "I shouldn't have always made you be the strong one."

I swallowed, then opened my mouth, waiting for the words to come.

After I said good-bye to my mother, I went into Rose's room and lay down next to her on her bed, relegating my body to the tiniest sliver of mattress, lying on my side and staring at her. In the blue-tinged light, her skin looked almost phosphorescent, so pale that it seemed to glow, like snow in a black night. With her red hair spilling out around her head and framing her face, she might have been a beauty from a fairy tale, an elfin princess under the spell of sleep. And I imagined my mother and Warren at home. I wondered if Mom would still lie next to her child in his bed, tracing figure eights on his back and singing. I imagined she would. I imagined the song would be low and mournful—an old spiritual, maybe, once sung by the enslaved and encoded with the path to freedom.

> *Wade in the water*
> *Wade in the water, children,*
> *Wade in the water*
> *God's a-going to trouble the water*

The shadows of trees waved on Rose's wall and the storm outside had become so loud, it almost swallowed my voice. So when I spoke, it sounded like a dream.

"Your uncle Warren named you," I told the sleeping Rose. "I didn't know what to call you." I didn't like to think back to

Rose's early days, to the emptiness of the hospital room. "I was all alone when I had you, Rosie. Your nana wanted to be there, but . . ." Feeling my eyes grow warm and wet, I let out a soaked-sounding laugh. "I don't know, I thought that would be weird." I swiped the back of my hand across my eyes and looked at Rose's face, at the lines of her profile, which was so much like my brother's. "You know your uncle Warren and I are twins. Kind of like those whirligig seeds I showed you," I explained. "And I don't know what makes him the way he is, but I was afraid that if you ended up that way, too"—I hooked one of her curls around the tip of my finger—"I wouldn't be able to love you like Nana loves Uncle Warren. Because she loves him so much, Rosie. She never wanted him to be any different than how he was." I paused, feeling the full weight of the past. "But I did," I whispered. "For a long time, I did."

I lay in Rose's bed that night, letting my mind enjoy a rare stillness. Gordo eventually lumbered in as well, climbing as discreetly as he could onto the foot of the bed and settling on my feet. I wiggled my toes against him and he grumbled in annoyance. I felt a chuckle come, private and fond, as I remembered how I used to drive Duncan crazy by doing that, back in our happier days. But thoughts of Duncan led to thoughts of Bobby, of his smiling face inches away from my own, the side of it pressed against my smooth white sheets. And in the dark of Rose's room, I thought of what I would say to him, how I would explain myself.

Rose, Gordo, and I slept together all night, and when we awoke the next morning, seemingly simultaneously, I felt the cold air rush into the warmth that had formed between our bodies.

Looking around the room, at the dead display on Rose's clock, at her dark butterfly night-light, I surmised that the power was still out and that meant we had no heat.

"I'm cold," groaned Rose, her eyes still closed as she wiggled deeper under the blanket.

"I know, Rosie," I said. "We'll get you warmed up."

I stood up and, tucking the blankets up under her chin, began to make phone calls. Rose's school was without power and canceled for the day, so I called Maggie to let her know I wouldn't be in to the office. She didn't answer, but I left a message, asking her to call me when she could. Then I dialed my mother. She answered after the first ring.

"Are you two all right?" she asked.

"We're fine," I said, snuggling back down with Rose. "Just freezing."

"Why don't you two come over here?" she said. "It's nice and warm."

Within five minutes, Rose, Gordo, and I were in the car on the way to Royal Court, the sound of the heat rushing from the vents muting the kids' music that was playing on the stereo. "My God," I said to myself as I drove toward the highway, seeing the evidence of the storm's full impact. Huge trees lay on their side, their roots reaching from the ground like great gnarled old hands, rocks and earth still clinging to their twisted fingers. "I can't believe how many trees are down."

CHAPTER THIRTY-THREE

. . .

Kept

1973

Silla brought the cigarette to her lips and pulled in the smoke, hearing the dim crackle of the tobacco as it burned. Holding her breath for a moment, she released the gray cloud into the wind, which took it instantly. The wind was wild that day, disappearing entirely only to return in a furious gust. She leaned against the hood of the car, the cigarette held erect between her pointer and center fingers. She had parked as far away from the building as she could. And now she just stood there staring at its unadorned facade. At the bars on the windows. At the peaks of its roof. It looked much as she had thought it would, which was perhaps why she couldn't bring herself to go inside. Instead she took another drag of her cigarette.

Stewart hated when she smoked. He told her it would ruin her voice and he was probably right. *How are you going to make it as a singer if you lose your voice?* he'd ask her. But she'd just smile and tell him she didn't know. That she didn't know and that she wouldn't smoke anymore. Then when he'd fall asleep, she'd crawl out of their bed and step out onto the balcony of their apartment, seeing the vast flat city of Houston that always looked like the bottom of the ocean to her. She'd slide her hands underneath the planter that held the green and purple-leaved coleus, pull out a hidden pack of cigarettes, and think about all the things she didn't let herself think about when she was with her husband.

He was away on one of his trips now, probably imagining her at home, drinking a Tab and practicing her scales. He was always on a trip—meeting the head of this region or that, talking to a supplier or a vendor.

She brought the cigarette to her lips again, then dropped it on the pavement in front of her, stomping it out with the ball of a high-heeled shoe. She lowered her head, crossed her arms around her body, and marched toward the concrete walk that led to the entrance, past the flags of Texas and the United States, past a cold-looking marble bench with an inscription that she could not bring herself to read. She pushed open the heavy metal door and walked up to the front desk, where three women in white uniforms sat in a fortified glass box.

Silla leaned down and spoke through a pocked plastic circle. "Good afternoon," she said. "I'm here to pick up Martha Harris's things." Her words sounded unrehearsed and fresh, though she had run through them over and over on the way down. "I'm her daughter." She nodded in introduction. "I called yesterday and spoke with Penny Ward."

The three women exchanged glances in a silent negotiation over who would tend to the redheaded girl in high heels and a tight sweater. Finally the middle one stood. Her body was shaped like a chicken's, with a full mound of breast and a short torso balanced atop long thin legs. Her hair had been set into tight, pert gray-brown curls and she had a sharp nose and jowls that hung past her jawbone. "This is one of the boxes from the basement," she said to her colleagues. "Penny told me about this." With a key ring in her hand, she shuffled to a side door. "I'll be back in a minute," she said as she opened it. Then she disappeared slowly down the hallway that was a tunnel of yellow. Yellow floors. Yellow walls. Yellow lights.

Silla tried not to look at the other two women as she waited, though she felt their gazes pass over her as they carried on their hushed, leisurely conversation. "I don't know why we keep 'em," she heard one of them say. "We're not a storage facility." Silla strained to hear more, to make out any sound but the women's murmurs, but silence filled the air like water. And she wondered if her father had ever been here.

Finally the woman came shuffling back up the hallway, a small brown box in her hands. It looked like a container in which you would store files, only smaller. On either side was a hole through which she hooked her fingers.

Silla took a few steps to meet her and relieve her of her load. "Thank you," she said. She was braced for the box to have some weight, some heft, but it was as light as a whim. The woman turned to walk back toward her coop. "Pardon me," Silla said.

The woman swiveled her head around. "Did you know my mother? Martha Harris?"

The chicken's face went from hard to soft. "I stay at the front desk, dear," she said, before turning back around.

"Thank you," Silla called after her.

She pressed the door open with her hip, taking care not to brush the box on the doorframe. It felt sacred. Holy. And she thought of Mrs. Lloyd, who used to quote Psalms to her. *Though I walk through the valley of the shadow of death, I will fear no evil: for thou art with me.* Silla never really knew what it meant; she still didn't. But the words ran through her head now as the bright midday sun drew the shape of the building on the balding earth below her feet.

All the way across the parking lot, she judged the contents, their slide, their volume. She tried to imagine what was inside, what her mother had kept with her. What still remained. Opening the driver's-side door, she scooted into her seat and slid it back, making room to hold the box on her lap. Through the windshield, she felt the sun warming her hands and the brown cardboard of the box. Then, quickly and efficiently, she lifted the lid. Inside were three things. Set in a slim wood frame was a black-and-white photograph of Silla as a toddler, colored so that her cheeks were rosy pink, her eyes hill green. Next was a yellow hat with a faux bird, its wings outstretched in frozen flight and pinned against a tiny veil of netting. But what Silla couldn't take her eyes off was the doll that she had given her mother all those years ago, the last time she saw her. Silla lifted it up, the memory of her mother suddenly thick and deep enough that she could have drowned in it. Stripped now of its green pinafore, the doll's cotton muslin torso was the color of dishwater, the smooth plastic of its limbs worn dull. She tilted the doll back, watching the thick fringe of its lashes draw down like a shade, then lift again as she brought it upright. They stared eye to eye for a moment, she and the doll, as tears ran from Silla's eyes without sob or sound.

. . .

Roots

We pulled into Royal Court, passing neighbors wearing fleece hats and carrying rakes as they righted overturned lawn furniture and cleared away broken branches, calling to one another from their respective yards and comparing the damage. It felt strange to be here now, as if the entire Parsons family had been implicated in everything that was wrong with Royal Court.

Under the guise of surveying the scene, I drove toward my mother's house, then turned, continuing to the Vannis'. Keeping my gaze ahead, I noted Bobby's Jeep in the driveway; then I looped around the cul-de-sac and headed back to number sixty-two. As I pulled into the driveway, I saw that the tarp that had protected the porch during the painting project had blown into the Fitzpatricks' bushes, so after unstrapping Rose and releasing Gordo, I hurried over to retrieve it, crossing over a distinct line where my mother's weed-addled yard met the Fitzpatricks' ChemLawn-bolstered turf.

As I folded the tarp haphazardly against my chest, Rose and Gordo bounced up the front steps, reaching the door just as my mother opened it. They bounded in, Rose giving my mother a quick *"Hi, Nana!"* as she scampered up the stairs to the second floor, Gordo trailing behind her. My mother watched her, looking as though she was smiling through the pain.

"Is Warren up there?" I asked, nodding toward his room.

Mom took a deep breath. "He is," she said.

"What's he doing?" I asked, setting the tarp on the floor just inside the door.

She shook her head. "He's just been staying up in his room," she said. "Working on his *planes*." It was the first time I'd ever heard her speak of Warren's hobby with anything even approaching derision. "He won't go outside."

She headed toward the kitchen and I followed, my voice dropping to a murmur as I asked, "And have you found out anything more about that frame the police took?"

We stepped onto the yellowing linoleum floor. "No, but . . ." She shook her head, her eyes finding the picture of her mother among the trinkets and treasures on her baker's rack. "All the neighbors are talking about it."

"But it was just a frame!"

"Linda Vanni called me this morning to tell me that Beth Castro's saying they found the Doogans' laptop here."

There was a calm defeat in Mom's voice, a sense that we were all hurtling toward some inevitability. I stood frozen in the face of her surrender. She had protected Warren all his life. Now it was possible that she no longer could. Finally she asked, "Has Rose eaten breakfast yet?"

"She had a little cereal," I said. "But I'm sure she'd love something warm."

Without a word, my mother shuffled toward the stove. "I've got some sausages in the freezer," she said. "Warren hasn't eaten yet either."

We began moving next to each other in the kitchen, communicating without words. She handed me the butter before I asked for it and I added a pat to the pan, watching it slide over the smooth black surface. "Does Warren still like his eggs—"

"Fried but not burnt," said my mother, finishing my sentence.

She put the bread in the toaster while I cracked the eggs into a skillet.

"This storm really was something," she said, looking out into the park through the window over the sink. Glancing back over my shoulder, I did the same. My gaze flickered to the Vannis' house before I made myself look away. Panning back over the sweep of dull green grass, still touched with frost from the cold night, my eyes snagged on a particular spot, at first registering only that something was different, then realizing what that something was.

"The maple!" I gasped. The old maple that had stood next to the pond was lying on its side, its roots reaching out of the ground and its trunk disappearing behind the curve of the hill.

"I know," she said, her voice a lament. "It fell in the storm." Her hand drew a line across the horizon. "It's lying right across the pond."

With my hands on my hips, I stared out from behind her at the void in the sky where just a few weeks ago the tree's leaves had blazed red. The maple was a monument on the map of my childhood, the one thing that had always seemed to grow more glorious and majestic with each passing year. I remembered how Warren used to scale its branches, fearless and light, as if his body were made to do so. Climbing trees was the one physical feat at which he had excelled, the one for which he was admired. He'd perch on the highest limbs and look out onto the world like some strange, wonderful bird as the rest of us groaned and grunted, trying to haul our clumsy bodies up after him. "I can't believe it," I said.

Smelling the eggs threatening to burn, I returned my attention to the stove. "Shit," I whispered, managing to grab a spatula and flip them before they browned. I gave them a moment or two more on the other side before plating them with toast and sausage. Then I set the plates on the island, each in front of a barstool.

"I'll go get Rose and Warren," I said.

Padding up the soft, thick carpet on the stairs, I passed the framed family photos in their jumbled and jammed arrangement. There were class pictures and snapshots, photos of Warren and me with our grandfather. There was a faded image of a redheaded siren in an evening gown holding a bouquet of yellow roses. And one of a middle-aged divorcée, her arms draped over her reluctant teenage children in front of the gray Sears portrait studio backdrop. If you didn't already know, you might never guess that the two photos were of the same woman.

As my eyes lingered, passing each picture, I heard Rose's and Warren's voices, growing clearer as I approached the landing.

With my foot already on the next step, I held the railing and listened.

"Can my plane be pink instead of red?" asked Rose.

"What plane?" asked Warren. His voice was distracted but unrushed and languid, the way it sounded when his hands were working under the bright light of his desk lamp.

"The one you're making me for Christmas," she said.

Warren chuckled. "Okay," he said. He had been teasing her. "Uncle Warren will make you a pink plane."

"And can it have my name on it?"

"Rosie the Riveter?"

"No, just *Rose*," she said.

I heard the sound of a wire being clipped. "Just Rose," he agreed.

A few beats of silence passed. "Uncle Warren?" asked Rose. From her tone, I imagined her little elbows resting on his desk, her fist tucked against her chin and her eyes deep and worried. "Do you have any brothers or sisters?"

I could almost see Warren's smile as his eyes remained fixed on some minuscule plane part. "Your mom is Uncle Warren's sister," he said.

"I don't," said Rose quickly. "I don't have any brothers or sisters. But Tucker at school has a brother *and* a sister."

"Well," said Uncle Warren, his tone leisurely and long, as if it had been trolling through deep water. "You have an uncle Warren. I'll bet Tucker doesn't have an uncle Warren."

Rose seemed to think about this. "Yeah," she said, more than satisfied with the logic. "He doesn't have an *uncle Warren*. That's *better* than a little brother."

"Uncle Warrens don't wear diapers."

Rose's giggles spilled over. "Yeah," she repeated. "Uncle Warrens don't wear *diapers*."

I heard the squeak of Warren's desk lamp being adjusted. "Not everyone likes Uncle Warrens, though," he said. It was the way you might caution a child that Santa was watching—a good-natured warning—but beneath it I sensed something more raw.

"Why not?" she asked, seeming to understand that they weren't being silly anymore.

Warren seemed to ponder the question. "I don't know," he finally said. "Nobody ever told me."

I shut my eyes as if to shield myself from the truth of it. In all his weirdness, with his odd little habits and strange manners of speech, Warren was just being Warren. He didn't know how to be anything else.

Then, perhaps alerted to the scent of sausages, Gordo's wagging body made its way out of Warren's room, his nose searching the air. My cover blown, I stomped loudly up the few remaining stairs. "Hey, you guys," I said, smiling as I crossed the threshold. "There's breakfast downstairs."

Rose sprang up from her seat and began bouncing toward the door. Still at his desk, Warren's thin body was turned to watch her, his shoulder blades visible through his long-sleeved T-shirt. She stopped and looked back at him. "Come on, Uncle Warren!" she said, scooping the air in front of her.

Taking a deep breath, Warren hauled his body up. "Okay," he said.

Satisfied that Warren was coming, Rose trotted ahead. I waited for my brother. "You know," I said as we followed Rose down the stairs, "you really should try to eat more." I squeezed his upper arm. "You're so thin, War."

Warren's brows drew together as his feet dragged over the carpet as if they were shackled. "I'm not hungry that much," he said.

Rose was already in her stool and eating a sausage with Gordo circling beneath her when Warren and I walked into the kitchen.

My mother looked at us and tried to smile. "My babies," she said through a breath. Warren slunk into the seat next to Rose and picked up a piece of toast.

I walked back over to the window above the sink. "I still can't believe the maple fell," I said. "The park looks so weird without it."

"It looks like the pond has started to freeze around it," said Mom.

"What's a maple?" asked Rose.

"A tree, honey," I said, without looking back. "It fell right across the pond. Like a bridge." I followed its line across to the Vannis' house. When I turned around, Warren was watching me. Our eyes met for a moment before he looked down and took another small bite of toast.

"They cut the surface roots," Warren said into his plate, referring to the great knotty roots that had extended a few inches above the grass, reaching out to grip the earth.

"Who did?" asked my mother.

"The landscapers," answered Warren. "The roots used to wreck the blades of their mowers. And they didn't like mowing around them."

"And that made the tree weaker. That's why it fell," I said,

Warren having drawn me toward a conclusion that felt profound in its own quiet way.

With his chin tucked to his chest, he looked at me from beneath his brows and nodded, his blue eyes appearing as they had for all of our thirty-six years.

"Rose, honey," said my mother, seeming eager to move away from this talk of fallen trees and butchered roots, "do you want Nana to put on a show for you?"

Rose leaned over the counter to better see the park. "No, I want to go see the tree," she said.

Before my mother could respond, the phone rang. Mom picked it up off its cradle. As she looked at the display, her face grew grave and she pressed the handset against her chest. "Excuse me," she said, as she hurried from the room. I heard the door to the office open, then shut behind her.

Warren and I looked at each other. *It's Dad,* I thought. *That's why she rushed out.* Whatever she and my father were going to be discussing, she wouldn't want to do it in front of Warren. Then, before I could change my mind, I reached for my coat. "Hey, War," I said. "Can you keep an eye on Rose for me?" Warren's eyes moved briefly across the park to the Vannis' house, and then back to me.

"Where are you going?" asked Rose.

One by one, I closed my toggle buttons. "I'm going to go see if Gabby's daddy is home," I said, avoiding Warren's gaze.

Rose tensed with excitement. "I want to come!" she said, making a move to hop down from her seat.

"How about you and Uncle Warren play Candy Land?" I suggested.

"No!!!" she protested. "I want to see Gabby!"

Laying my hand on her shoulder, I lowered my head so that we were face-to-face. "Baby," I said, "Mommy needs to go over there by herself, okay?"

"But I don't want to stay here!"

Suddenly Warren was down from his seat. "Come on," he said, already moving toward the doorway, his hand extending behind him—an invitation for Rose to take it. "You can help Uncle Warren with his plane."

Rose looked reluctantly at Warren's hand before she gripped it limply, as if it were a consolation prize.

I stepped out onto the back deck, then down the steps, squinting at the air, which was clear and bright and cold. The grass was hard beneath my feet, yielding little as I walked across it. Cresting the hill, I saw the maple that lay toppled on its side across the pond, regal and elegant even in repose, ice beginning to form in a thin layer around its submerged branches.

As step by step I drew closer to the Vannis' house, I felt a shaky uncertainty and dreaded delivering my canned speech to Bobby. *The timing. The job. Our responsibilities.*

Sunlight reflected off the kitchen windows, making them shine like mirrors against the sky. And as I stepped onto the back deck, I saw Mrs. Vanni through the window, sitting at her kitchen table. I waved and smiled as I approached. She looked out at me, but her face tightened a bit, as if she wasn't sure she recognized me, this girl clomping up onto her deck. As if she wasn't quite sure she wanted to.

My steps became less assured as I approached. I knocked on the glass of the back door. *Ba-bum.* Only then did Mrs. Vanni rise from her seat at the table. She walked over, the chair in which she had been sitting displaced behind her, her coffee mug resting where she had left it on the table.

"Hi, Mrs. Vanni," I said, smiling as she opened the door.

She returned my smile, but it was sad, full of regret. "Hi, Jenna," she said. "Come on in."

I stepped inside and shook off the chill. "I can't believe this storm!" I said, gesturing behind me toward the maple. But as Mrs. Vanni's face remained impassive, I felt a strange sinking, as if I were headed down a river in a raft, unaware of the falls that lay ahead. "Did you guys have any damage here?" I asked.

She seemed reluctant to meet my eyes. "No," she said with a slow shake of her head. "We were fine."

"Well, I actually just came over to speak with Bobby," I said, keeping my face and tone polite. "Is he home?"

"I'm afraid he's not," she said.

"Oh." Confused, I gestured toward the street. "I thought I saw his car out front."

"He went for a jog."

"Mrs. Vanni . . . ," I said, beginning slowly. "Is everything all right?"

She closed her eyes. "I'm sorry, honey," she said, shaking her head. "I know that everything that's been going on in the neighborhood has been hard on your family." Her eyes opened suddenly and she looked at me. "And I've been *defending* Warren," she said, needing me to believe her. "Whenever anyone has said anything, I've always said that Warren Parsons has lived in this neighborhood for over thirty years and never caused any trouble." Her gaze dropped away, as if she couldn't say what came next while looking me in the eyes. "But it's gotten hard to ignore what people are saying."

My instinct was to remain as still as possible. "What have people been saying?"

Her eyes met mine, and her face softened. "The police found a frame. At your mother's house."

My face must have begged for further explanation. *So? So what?*

"It was the frame the Doogans kept their coin collection in."

My eyes slipped shut as I tried to block out the information.

"And Lydia," Mrs. Vanni went on, referring to my stepmother, "told Shelley Ditchkiss that she thinks all of this is related to the problems that run in your mother's family." She looked at me, not wanting to continue but doing so anyway. "The *mental* problems."

"*Mental* problems?" *There are no mental problems,* I was about to say. Until I remembered my grandmother, the woman in the picture, with the eyes that could see through time. *Warren's more like a Briggs,* Mom had said.

"I'm just so sorry all of this happened," Mrs. Vanni said. Then her head began to nod, as if urging me toward a determination. "I think both your mother and your brother need help, sweetie."

I imagined Warren, moving softly and silently, his eyes searching and scanning the homes on Royal Court, seeing those things that were valued by the families that surrounded us, seeing those things that would ultimately go missing. It was as if he was collecting the relics of normal family life, perhaps to re-create it. You could see how Warren, growing up where we had, might think that things were the solution.

"I think I need to get back home," I said, my voice sounding faraway, even to my own ears.

"Let me know if I can help," she said.

"Okay," I said, making for the door. "Bye, Mrs. Vanni."

"Good-bye," I heard her reply as I slipped outside.

My breath came jagged and quick as I took small, efficient steps and hurried down the stairs, desperate to put my feet on the hard, cold earth beyond them. And I knew in that indefinable but undeniable way that the *mental problems* to which Mrs. Vanni had referred were real and secret and bigger than I knew. I imagined how Lydia had offered them up as a way to exonerate my father and by extension herself, to make Warren even more concretely my mother's problem.

Keeping my head down, I looked only at the grass beneath my feet as I walked, the sun beginning to melt the frost that had coated the blades. And I wished it were night. I wished that I didn't hear the buzz of chain saws in the distance, the murmur of voices calling to one another from porch to porch, deck to deck, saying again and again, *Can you believe this storm?* I wished the air around me were quiet and still and lit only by a round white moon. Because I didn't want any witness to my thoughts. It wasn't the first time that I had wondered if Warren had anything to do with the thefts, but it was the first time I meant it.

Passing the fallen maple, I tried to find that place, that spot deep in my core, that knew what Warren knew, that connected me to him, that tethered us always together. But it was as if the line had been cut. *Warren,* I whispered, as I remembered looking up to him as he sat in the tree's high branches, bringing my hand above my eyes to shield them from the sunlight that filtered down through its leaves.

I passed the wild-looking forsythia bush and its sprays of barren branches. The deck sounded hollow as I stepped onto it, and as I slid open the door to the kitchen, I saw that no one was there.

From upstairs, I could hear the unintelligible peaks of Rose's voice. She'd be telling Uncle Warren about how Gordo stole her pizza crust last night. Or that her plane shouldn't be pink or red but pink and red striped. And in the bright light of my childhood kitchen, I brought my hands to my face and I cried. It was a brief indulgence, a necessary one, before I followed the path to the office my mother had taken with the phone pressed against her chest.

When I opened the door, she was sitting in the corner, her head resting against the back of the old leather wingback chair. The office had been my father's. It was still painted forest green and the chair was embellished with nailhead trim. It was the sort of room in which a man was supposed to think big thoughts. The sort of room in which he was supposed to move the chess pieces of his life. It was intended to look collegiate and official, I supposed, but instead it looked like a stage set. As if you could push the walls gently and watch them fall to the ground with a thud and a cloud of dust. I imagined most of the homes in the neighborhood once had an office like this. I imagined that most had been turned into fitness areas or extra bedrooms.

Mom's stare didn't change as I entered. She looked out the window, in front of which the bayberry bush had grown tall. Hovering on the single step that led to the sunken room, I waited for her to acknowledge me.

"Mom," I finally said, "I just talked to Mrs. Vanni."

Mom's face was smooth and placid, though her head still relied on the support of the chairback. I took a breath and realized that my heart was racing; then I crossed my arms over my chest. When I spoke, the words came quickly. "Mom, the Doogans kept their coins in a picture frame."

Her stare dropped to an inconsequential spot in front of her, but she didn't say a word. I wanted her to come back to life, to acknowledge me. I wanted her to refute what I had heard from Linda Vanni. *I talked to Liz Doogan and she said they kept those coins in a leather box!* But my mother remained silent. I tried to keep the quaver from my voice when I spoke again. "I don't think this looks good for Warren, Mom." I studied the elegant line of her nose, the beautiful bones that you could still see beneath the soft pads of her cheeks. "And Lydia has been telling people things. About your side of the family."

Mom brought her hand to her forehead and stroked back her hair, closing her eyes and leaning against her own touch. "Hattie died," she said, looking back out the window. "The nursing home just called."

"Oh, Mom!" I gasped. I took careful steps, then sat on the edge of the ottoman in front of her chair, resting my elbows on my knees. "I'm so sorry."

"Don't be," she said. "Don't be sorry. She wasn't my mother."

Finally, Mom looked at me. The sadness in her eyes seemed ancient. "Jenna, honey," she said, "I need to tell you something." She waited, watching my face. And then it came out plainly. "Your grandmother didn't die when I was five. She was in an institution for seventeen years."

"What?" The word felt like an echo of a shout from somewhere in my chest.

"They had given her a lobotomy." I felt the muscles in my legs soften, as if a vial of chloroform had been passed underneath my nose. "And it didn't..." Again, she looked at the bayberry. "It ruined her." Her fingers almost drummed on the end of the chair's arms, but her voice remained steady. "And for all that time, I thought she was dead."

"My God, Mom," I said.

Again, my mother's head swiveled toward me, her face squared with mine. "They did things like that back then, Jenna," she said, reading my shock. "It was the fifties. You didn't talk about things like"—she shifted, as if channeling the era's discomfort—"*mental problems.*"

"Was she mentally ill?"

"Honestly, I don't know. I was so little when she went away." With her chin tipped back, she squinted at her memories. "I know everyone thought she was hard to handle. First her parents and then my daddy. I don't think she was the daughter or wife everyone wanted her to be." My mother inhaled. "I remember her being wonderful, though. Strange, but wonderful."

I pictured Warren walking through the neighborhood with his odd gait, his eyes on the sky, and on the plane gliding through it. I wondered what would have happened to him if he had been born a woman in Texas in the 1930s.

"Why did they do it?" I asked.

Mom shook her head. "It was supposedly voluntary." She glanced down at her legs, smoothing the black fabric that covered her thighs. "But the hospital where it was done closed down and she was moved. All the records are gone, so . . . there's a lot I don't know about it."

"When did you find out?"

My mother's shoulders dropped. And she looked at me as if it were *my* heart that was breaking. "The day she died."

CHAPTER THIRTY-FIVE

. . .

Hattie's Take

1973

Humming mosquitoes and fat moths thumped and bumped into the window screen in front of Silla, drawn to the light inside. Stewart and her father were in the Harrises' living room. They were leaning back in their chairs and discussing the types of things that fathers and sons-in-law discussed, while she and Hattie were supposed to be fixing appetizers in the kitchen.

"What do you want the franks to go in?" asked Silla, not looking up from the pot in which the contents of a package of cocktail wieners and a can of crushed pineapple were swimming around in a bottle's worth of chili sauce.

Hattie was leaning against the counter, her hand resting on the Formica with a cigarette between two fingers. She bent over to pull a silver bowl from one of the cabinets. "In here," she said, tapping it against Silla's back.

Silla took it from her, keeping her body angled toward the stove, her eyes on her hands. Hattie leaned back against the counter. Even without turning, Silla knew that Hattie was watching her. It was the first time they had been alone together since she had married Stewart. That was six months ago now.

Silla heard Hattie take a drag of her cigarette. Through her exhalation, Hattie said, "I know you think your father did some *horrible thing*." Her words wafted lazily up, like a twirling stream of smoke. "That's why you ran off with that boy." Silla heard her slide the amber glass ashtray across the counter. "But someday you'll realize that your daddy was actually doing you a big favor."

Silla was silent. She picked up the metal spoon and sank it into the pot, stirring. And even though she felt every muscle in her face tighten, even though she felt her jaw clench and her teeth press together, she remained silent. From the living room she heard her father slap his knee, heard him laugh. He was probably telling Stewart about the time they sent Silla to the store for a head of iceberg lettuce and she came home with a cabbage.

"Does Stewart know?" asked Hattie, her voice laced with false innocence. "About your mama?" At that, Silla's head whipped over her shoulder to look at Hattie. She couldn't help it. Hattie's eyes were heavy, her open mouth lifted at the corners. "He doesn't know, does he?"

Silla glanced at the long gray tip of her stepmother's cigarette, then quickly turned back to the stove.

"You think he would have *married* you if he knew?" asked

Hattie. And Silla prayed that she would stop talking, that she would just shut her damn mouth. But Hattie went on, her voice disinterestedly musing. "But you *had* to go diggin', didn't you?"

"I didn't go diggin'," shot Silla over her shoulder.

"Now you have to spend the rest of your life lying to your husband, when you could have just *not known*."

She heard her father's voice from the living room. "Hey, girls," he called, "where's that crab dip!"

Silla dropped the spoon on the counter with a deliberate clatter and jerked open the door to the fridge, pulling out the platter of crab dip and crackers. Without looking at Hattie, she walked out of the kitchen, forcing herself not to scurry, making herself move with defiant ease.

Her father and Stewart both turned toward her as she entered the living room. And so she smiled. "Mrs. Lloyd's famous crab dip," she said.

"Silla, honey," said her father, as she set the platter on the coffee table, "I was just telling Stewart about how it was Cal Harper who got you involved in the pageants."

"That's right," she said, humoring her father. "Mr. Harper had me sign up for Miss Harris County."

"You know, Cal said he really thought she had a chance," said her father, speaking to Stewart now, "at Miss America."

Stewart just smiled into his lap. He knew that the subject of Silla's abandoned career as a beauty queen was still a difficult subject for Lee. After all, he had been her manager. And married women were prohibited from competing in any of the high-stakes "Miss" pageants. They were allowed entry only into the dowdy old "Mrs." contests, where you might win a year's free dry cleaning and get your picture in the *PennySaver*.

Hattie slipped in, carrying the franks in a bowl and set them next to the crab dip. "Now, now," she said, sitting on Lee's lap and draping her arm across his neck. "You can't stop a girl from falling in love." Then with her hard jaw jutting out, she looked at Stewart. "So, Stewart, tell me," she said. "What's this about a job in New Jersey?"

The previous week Stewart had flown up to Morristown for an interview at Millhouse's headquarters. *They run cheese out of Jersey,* he had told Silla before he left. And she couldn't stop laughing. It just sounded so silly, these big giant companies having whole offices devoted to selling cheese.

"It would be a big promotion," she said, looking right at Hattie before Stewart could answer. "If he gets it."

"Imagine that," said Hattie. "Our little Priscilla, living up there in New Jersey. Wouldn't that be something?"

• • •

CHAPTER THIRTY-SIX

Tree Bridge

My mother and I sat in silence for a long time, my hand over hers as I watched her eyes. I saw relief there, a relief that rushed in after dread suddenly and with finality released its hold. My mother had never wanted anyone to know about what happened to my grandmother. To her, in a very real way, my grandmother *had* died when my mother was five.

"So Dad knew?" I finally asked, realizing that he was the likely source of Lydia's knowledge.

With the back of her head still resting against the leather chair, Mom looked at me. "Not for a long time," she said, before turning back to the bayberry. "He was the only person I ever told."

I imagined him driving back from Alexandra's college

yesterday with Lydia, his eyes fixed on the road. *What is it, Stewart?* Lydia would say. And he'd pause. *There's something I've never told you. About Priscilla's mother.*

"I'm so sorry, Mom," I said.

She turned her palm to meet mine and gave my hand a small squeeze. "It's all right," she said. "But if you don't mind, I'm just going to sit here for a little while."

I nodded. "Okay."

With my hands in my pockets, I walked from the room, my head hanging heavy as I thought about what had happened to my grandmother, about what might lie ahead for Warren. Hardly aware that I was in the foyer, I heard Rose's footsteps coming down the stairs and looked up. She was slumped forward, her arms hanging limply in front of her with her mouth sagging open like a trout's. "I'm *bored*," she said.

I smiled and tried to brighten my voice, the way mothers do. "Didn't you have fun building planes with Uncle Warren?"

"Yeah, but the new one isn't ready to fly yet," she said. I heard the jingle of Gordo's collar as he peered over the banister, then returned to Warren's room. Sensing that I wasn't entirely moved by her monumental boredom, Rose slumped even farther forward. "Where's Nana?"

As she finished her question, the phone in the pocket of the coat that I was still wearing began to chime loudly. Holding one finger up to Rose, I pulled it out and saw Maggie's husband's name on my screen. *Lance Dyer.*

I pressed it and brought it to my ear. Lance rarely called me, and never casually. "Hey, Lance," I said.

But it was Maggie's voice that replied. "Hey," she said. "Are you coming in today?"

"I don't think so."

"Why?" she asked. "What's going on?"

Bending down and pressing the phone against my chest, I found Rose's eyes. "Rosie," I said, "go back up to Uncle Warren's room. I need to talk to Maggie for a minute." She groaned and let her head drop back in protest. "*Please*, honey." From the phone, I heard Maggie's muffled voice calling my name. I saw Rose turn toward the stairs; then I opened the front door and stepped outside, clicking it shut behind me. My explanation was one I didn't want anyone to hear. Especially Rose.

"Maggie," I said, leaning against the hard brick facade, feeling its chill seep into my back, "I'm here."

"Is everything okay?"

"I left you a message this morning . . . ," I started.

"We lost power last night and my phone died. I'm on Lance's phone." Her voice was hurried and concerned.

"I'm at my mom's. Things aren't good here." I swallowed, feeling the cold prick my cheeks. "I think Warren might have had something to do with the thefts." I looked around at the neighborhood, at the peering windows of the homes across the street. "In King's Knoll."

"Why do you think that?" she asked, her voice grave, her words decelerating.

"There's some evidence. I think." Even saying the words felt like a betrayal. "And . . . there's a lot going on here, Maggie."

"Are you all right?"

I nodded, though I didn't respond. Then looking down the street, I saw Mr. Kotch pedaling on his bike, staring at our house as he always seemed to. "Listen. I'll call you later, okay?"

"Okay," she said.

Still watching Mr. Kotch, I hung up the phone. Without looking away, I slid my phone back into the wide pocket of my coat, and turned it round and around in my hand. Mr. Kotch's gloves gripped the handlebars and underneath his helmet, he was wearing a winter hat. I stared at him and he at me until he was right in front of my mother's house. His feet ceased pedaling and he glided with spinning tires and shimmering spokes over the cold, black pavement. I exhaled a white cloud of breath, and then he looked coolly ahead again, his front foot pumping forward as he took a curve and headed toward the beginning of Royal Court. I watched him grow smaller in the distance until he turned onto Prince Street, where his bike came to a stop in front of his beige house. I watched him long enough to see him open his back door and clap his shoes together over his deck railing. I watched him long enough to see him glance once again at my mother's house, then turn and head inside, where through the window I saw him switch on what looked like a brand-new, wide-screen television set.

I watched him until, next to me, the door pulled slowly back. In the thin gap appeared Warren's face. He scanned the front yard, then looked at me. "Where's Rose?" he asked.

From somewhere deep, I felt a mobilizing panic. "I thought she was with you?"

Warren shook his head. Immediately, I pushed the door open wide and stepped inside. "Rose!" I called, as Warren shut it behind me. "Rose, come out!" I marched toward the kitchen. "*Rose!*" I called again, sensing Warren at my heels. I spun around, looking suspiciously at the house, as if it had taken her. Then I saw Warren's stare, frozen on one of the chairs set around the kitchen table. For one, two, three seconds he stood there. And then the realization came to him, and it was like seeing rock meet the water of a deep, calm pool.

By the time I heard the back door open, he was beyond it, flying across the deck and heading for the stairs. My mind, which had always worked differently from his, offered me a picture of the chair that Warren had been looking at, the chair on which I had hung Rose's coat. The chair that was now empty.

"Rose!" I screamed, as I lurched through the door, following Warren through the yard and over the hill. I tried to catch him, tried to run like him, pumping my arms hard and fast, racing over the yellowed grass. *"Rose!"* I shouted again. My heart was rolling from fear and speed. I was far enough behind my brother that I saw him crest the hill, then disappear down the front of the slope. Sobbing and running as fast as I could, I pulled the freezing air into my lungs as I tried to get there, understanding by then that Rose hadn't gone back up to Warren's room when I went outside to speak to Maggie. Understanding by then that she had gone to see the tree. I imagined her pink tongue sticking out as she pulled herself onto it. She'd hold her arms straight out at her sides as she tried to balance, walking across its slick, frozen trunk. Over the deepest part of the pond.

I was at the top of the hill when Warren took his first step onto the water, breaking through a thin layer of ice that had begun to form at the edges. He took fast, steady strides until he was waist deep and had reached the felled maple. I was still running when he pulled Rose out, and I fell to my knees, sobbing, before I scrambled back up and stumbled to the edge of the pond, shaking my hands as if there were blood on them.

"Call nine-one-one!" I heard a voice behind me yell, close and distant all at once.

Warren held Rose, her body limp and white against his chest, her red hair like wet leaves plastered against her forehead. Her hair was dripping a steady stream of frigid water, as was her thick jacket. Warren was walking steadily, but more slowly now, his eyes focused one foot in front of him. He moved with quiet, supernatural determination until he reached me. I was up to my knees in the water when I took her from him, clutching her cold, wet body against me, the water brown and opaque around my legs.

Then Bobby was there, his breath coming fast from his run. Swift and efficient, he shifted her body to pull off her coat, which landed with a sodden thump. He slid off his sweatshirt and set it on the ground. Then he lifted her out of my arms and into his. "Take off your coat," he ordered, and with shaking hands I did, draping it around her body. "Get some blankets!" he yelled over his shoulder. Then he set her on the ground and in his thin white T-shirt, he began performing CPR. I was on my knees beside her, holding her hand, which was pale and small, like a little fish.

My chest shook when I saw the water gurgle out of her mouth, when I heard a gasping breath suck into her lungs and I pulled her up onto me so that her chin was resting on my shoulder. Bobby immediately followed, covering her with my coat. My mother was there now, and neighbors were milling around the perimeter of the scene, necks craning and eyes alert, muttering to one another about what had happened, about what they could do, while staying far enough away that they couldn't be considered involved. I saw Mr. Kotch on the periphery, looking haunted. Suspicious eyes fell on Warren, who had collapsed to his knees at the edge of the pond, trying to steady his jagged breathing.

"We need to get her inside," said Bobby, as his hands slid between her body and mine, pulling her into his arms.

I gripped her hard, not wanting to let go, wanting to feel the rising of her chest against mine, the vibration of her cries.

"Jenna," he said firmly. "We need to get her warm."

From somewhere, though I didn't know whether near or far, internal or external, I heard my mother's voice. And I let go of Rose.

I ran next to Bobby up the steep grade as he rushed her to the house. "Shhh, baby," I whispered, hearing her unfocused wails, tears still spilling from my eyes. "Shhhh."

We were halfway to the house when paramedics arrived. They rushed through the park carrying a stretcher and bright blue blankets. They took her from Bobby and he quickly and succinctly communicated critical information. *She was found in the water. The submersion time is unknown. I started CPR immediately.*

One of the paramedics, a young man with mahogany-colored skin and an exotic accent, placed a mask over her mouth. She twisted her face to the side, but he held her head to steady it. "It's all right, little girl," he said, his voice calm and cadenced. "You're going to be all right." And then they hoisted the stretcher up and we all hurried back over the rough earth to the open doors of the shiny ambulance.

Bobby climbed in ahead of me, his voice assured and strong, and began assisting the paramedics. They were wrapping blankets around Rose's head, around her torso and limbs.

The ambulance lurched into motion and glided in a smooth turn, its siren screaming as it headed back up Royal Court. And though I wanted to look nowhere but at Rose's face, at the blue crescents under her eyes, at the clear mask covering her pale mouth, I glanced behind me, through the high, wide rear window of the ambulance. And traveling swiftly down the street as we were traveling up it, I saw Detective Dunn's car, his once discreet lights flashing red and blue, cutting through the daylight.

CHAPTER THIRTY-SEVEN

. . .

Twins

1976

Silla's eyes opened and then slid shut again. She was still feeling the warm tingle of anesthetized sleep and might have let herself tumble back to unconsciousness but for the memory of what had brought her here, rising up through her mind like a single bubble to the water's surface. She felt a hand on her forehead, pushing back her hair.

Her tongue moved against the dry palate of her mouth and she tried to swallow. "Where are they?" she asked, her words a whisper. The last thing she could remember was a sweet-smelling mask slipping over her face while nurses and doctors had rushed around the room, their faces serious, their voices hard. Baby B, as it was called, was not coming out.

"They're fine," soothed Stewart. Silla forced her eyes to open, to look at her husband's face. "They're being cared for."

With relief, she let her lids close again. "Is the second baby—"

"A boy," said Stewart.

Without even seeing his face, she knew he was grinning and so she smiled, too. "A boy and a girl," she said, the words like a song.

Stewart released a grateful laugh as he took her hand. Feeling a tugging against her arm, she opened her eyes and saw a tube—red and thin—running into her skin. "You lost a lot of blood, honey," explained Stewart. "They needed to put some back in."

She made a sound of acknowledgment as her head slumped back. She was too exhausted to mind much about the blood, but she was slowly becoming aware of her body again, of the dull throbbing in her abdomen, its roar muted to a whisper by morphine. "But the babies are okay?"

Stewart nodded. "The little girl is in the nursery already," he said, and she could tell from the way the statement lingered that what came next would be worrisome. "But they brought the little guy up to the NICU. I guess they were concerned about his breathing."

"What's wrong with his breathing?" asked Silla, anxiety rising through her fatigue and the drugs.

Stewart held her hand between two of his. "They think he might have some fluid in his lungs," he said. "I guess it's not uncommon." He gave her hand a squeeze. "He's a tough little guy, though."

Again, Silla felt herself smile. "So what are we going to call them?" she asked. They had narrowed the names down to just a few for either sex, but hadn't wanted to choose any until the babies came. *It's bad luck,* Stewart had said.

"I like Warren," he said. "For the boy." He was silent for a moment. "It's a strong name. *Warren Parsons.*" Silla saw in his eyes that he was imagining who their son would become. What he would be with a name like Warren Parsons. "It sounds presidential."

She chuckled and moved her foot under the rough white sheet. "President Warren Parsons," she said.

"President Warren Parsons," repeated Stewart, his voice full of awe. Full of wonder.

CHAPTER THIRTY-EIGHT

· · ·

The Emergency Room

The driver pulled swiftly into the ambulance bay at Hewn Memorial, where Rose was rushed to a cold white room with bright lights. Another mask was placed over her mouth and nose, and patches were affixed as she wailed weakly. Nurses rushed past me, their arms full of warm packs and blankets. They wrapped them around her, having pulled away the sodden blue ones. Bobby and other doctors swirled about, using a language all their own. I heard their words, I heard them talking to the nurses, but it was as if I were underwater with Rose, and their conversations were happening somewhere above the surface. All I could do was watch the monitor above her head, and the lines pulsing rhythmically up and down, showing the beating of her heart.

Rose's eyes were still closed when they inserted the IV, but the volume of her cries spiked as they began to pump warm fluids into her body. I found Rose's hand and held it as color returned to her cheeks, as the tip of her nose turned pink. Though she was still crying, it had become a whine rather than a wail. And I stayed silent as I looked at her, as I sat beside her bed, resting my cheek against the mattress, feeling the rigid plastic underneath the sheet. Every minute or so, I'd turn my face and wipe my wet eyes against the stiff, rough, white cotton; black lines of mascara streaked my face, the bed. Then from down the hallway, I heard a nurse's voice. "Dr. Vanni wants her transferred to pediatrics to watch for respiratory distress."

Finally, Rose was silent, her body still. From beneath all the blankets she peered at me, the clear mask still covering her mouth. I reached up and adjusted it. It was warm to the touch. The nurses returned. They were walking more slowly now. Unearthing one of her feet, one of them repositioned the blood oxygen monitor on her big toe.

"So," said the nurse, as she watched the small red numbers flash ninety-seven, then ninety-eight. She was soft and well cushioned, like a grandmother from a cookie commercial. "She sneak out on you?"

A fresh wave of terror rose up my chest and burst through my eyes. I could only nod, pressing my lips tightly together.

After the nurses came in once and once again to take vital signs, after Rose sat up and drank some apple juice, after they picked up her chart and put it down, I was told that she would be admitted overnight for observation.

"Oh, thank you," I said, in awe of medicine and grateful that my daughter would be in its hands for at least a little while longer. "Thank you so much."

"They'll be down to bring her to Peds in just a minute."

I felt a sudden desperation. "Can I talk to Dr. Vanni?" I asked. "Before we go?"

She took a resigned breath. "I'll see if I can find him."

But when the orderly came, Bobby still hadn't returned.

"Wait," I told him. "I need to talk to her doctor."

Sticking my head from the doorway to Rose's room, I spotted the grandmotherly nurse and waved her down. She ambled over to me with no great urgency. "I was hoping to talk to Dr. Vanni?" I said hopefully. "Before we left?"

She crossed her arms loosely in front of her. "He's not available."

And from behind me, I heard the squeak of small, plastic wheels as Rose's bed was rolled out of the room.

Rose was brought up to the pediatric floor, into a bright wing with sunny murals and smiling nurses, and was placed in room 777. "Lucky number seven!" said a friendly young nurse with chin-length blond hair and apple-colored lips as she helped Rose into bed. She brought her graham crackers and a menu. "Everybody likes the chicken tenders," she said with a wink.

As I watched Rose nibble the crackers, I knew that I needed to call my mother and Warren, to tell them that Rose was all right. Just as urgently, I needed to know why Detective Dunn's car had been speeding down Royal Court as the ambulance was speeding up it. But my cell phone wasn't with me. It had been in the pocket of the coat that I had wrapped around Rose in the park, the one the paramedics had pulled off and replaced with dry blankets.

Lifting the receiver of the old beige phone in Rose's room, I dialed my mother's number. After seven rings, her machine picked up. I hung up and tried again. This time I left a message. "Mom," I said. "It's me. I'm here at the hospital. Rose is okay." I looked at my daughter, saw her legs begin to bounce under the blankets. "Just call me when you can," I said, then left the room number and hung up.

Rose is okay. The more I believed it, the more my mind allowed other thoughts to flood in. And as I sat next to my daughter's bed, with my shoulders hunched and my hand propping up my chin, I thought about my grandmother. I thought about my mother and how she had spent her entire life trying to replace the irreplaceable, trying to fill a starving void.

And then I thought of Warren.

I remembered the way he looked when he was running to Rose. Like a superhero. Like a warrior. I wondered how long it would have taken me to get to that pond, to have realized that's where I needed to go, if it weren't for Warren and his strange, brilliant mind. I wondered where he was now. Again, I pictured Detective Dunn's car.

Needing something to do with my hands, I straightened and picked up the menu. "Okay, Rosie," I said, a crack in my voice. "Let's see." I scanned the choices. "They have ravioli," I suggested. "And they have grilled cheese." I looked at Rose.

"Can you get a grilled cheese for me and chicken tenders for Uncle Warren?" she asked. "But with *no* ketchup."

"Oh, honey," I started, with a falling face. "I don't think Uncle Warren is going to be coming." I didn't know how I was going to tell her that Uncle Warren was in trouble. That he had done something bad and was caught.

Then from down the hall, I heard a sound, faint at first but distinct and unmistakable. And my heart gave a sudden thump of recognition as I waited, still and quiet, for the squeak of rubber-soled sneakers on the shiny hard floor to draw closer. I let out a single hopeful breath when I heard my mother's voice. "It's right in here," she said. "Number seven-seven-seven."

My mother burst into the room. She rushed over to Rose and pulled her against her warm chest. But my eyes stayed on the threshold, waiting, praying I hadn't been mistaken. *Warren*, I whispered. As if in response, there came a whistle just before his face leaned in past the doorframe. He looked directly at me, with his small, curious smile, as if we had planned to meet at this very spot, at this very moment. And he hadn't let me down.

Rose brought her hand over her mouth, her giggles spilling through her fingers like bubbles as she turned to me. "Told you," she said.

Warren's body followed his head into the room, where he planted his hands on his hips and looked at Rose. And though his intended expression was probably something close to stern, his innate gentleness belied his furrowed brow.

Standing, I strode over to him. "War," I said. He was in profile, still facing Rose, and though he didn't turn, he looked at me from the corner of his eye. Then tucking my head into the crook of his neck, I pulled him into me, feeling the slightness of his frame. "Thank you," I said.

He emitted his pained-sounding chuckle, the one he used whenever anyone forced him to submit to affection on their terms. "Oh boy," he said, reaching up and patting my arm. "Okay."

With my arms still around my brother, I heard my mother's voice. "They arrested that Zack Castro."

"What?!" I said, my head shooting up.

Mom was standing at the head of Rose's bed, her hand resting on its plastic railings. "For the burglaries."

"But his bike was stolen," I said, trying to recalibrate what I thought I knew.

Mom shook her head, her face heavy. "No," she said. "He didn't. He said it was stolen, but"—she swatted the air in front of her with the back of her hand, then let it drop to her thigh—"he sold it."

I glanced at Warren, who didn't move. "And everything else?" I asked my mother. "He took it all?"

"That's what it looks like."

I remembered the night Warren had come home with his face cut and bloodied. I remembered the way his hand had hung at his side, clutching his plane. *Sometimes after work at night, I fly it in the park.* I turned back to my brother. "War, did you see . . . ?"

Warren, still focused on the floor, lifted his chin and let it drop back down. It was his acknowledgment. His admission that the night Zack had beat him up, he'd seen him take something.

"I guess it was Zack and a *friend*," said my mother. "After they did what they did to your brother, they figured . . ." She stopped, tightening her lips. *They figured they could make it look like it was him.*

"Warren," I whispered. "Why didn't you *tell* us?"

With his head cocked to one side, my brother looked at me. We stared at each other until, without answering, he turned and walked slowly over to Rose's bed and stood beside her. Again, he planted his hand on his hip and tried to look displeased. "You were supposed to come find Uncle Warren," he said. "I would have taken you to the tree." Rose's green eyes looked chastened before she let her head dip down. Then suddenly, she reached up and wrapped her arms around his waist, the force of her embrace causing Warren to wobble a bit. Mechanically, he rubbed the top of her head.

"You know it was your uncle Warren that got you out of that pond, don't you, Rose?" asked my mother.

"Yeah," she said. "I called him." With her face still pressed to Warren's belly, her words muffled, she took her earlobe between her fingers and pulled. "Like this."

Warren emitted one of his laughs and sat on the edge of Rose's bed, his body barely making a depression on the mattress. He looked at Rose for a moment, his lips curved into a small, quizzical smile, then reached for a photocopied list of movies that were available. "Let's see," he said, as he scanned the titles. Warren, it seemed, was ready to move on from news of thefts and arrests, from talk of brave deeds and almost-magic rescues.

Over Warren's hunched frame, my eyes found my mother's. Mom only smiled before looking back at her son. "Do they have *Goonies*?" she asked. Warren's brow gathered as his fingertip ran back over the columns. "You used to love that movie," said my mother, leaning in to see the list better.

And when it came—the brisk knock-knock on the door—I

assumed it was the nurse with the apple-colored lips come to take Rose's temperature and blood pressure. But the polite smile that was ready on my lips dropped away as I turned to watch the door push open, and Detective Dunn emerged. My mother rose, her legs straightening as if they were being slowly inflated, and her gaze did not leave the detective's face. I looked at my mother. *Why is he here? Wasn't this supposed to be over?*

"I'm sorry to bother you all," he said, his already red face seeming to brighten slightly. "But I heard about what happened." He nodded toward Rose and Warren on the bed. "And I was in the neighborhood." He looked at my brother's back. "Hero of the day, huh, Warren?"

And though Warren tried to fight it, tried to hide it, I saw his chest fill, his lips curve into a smile. Detective Dunn stepped forward and gave him a locker-room slap on the back. "So, I wanted to thank you," he said. He paused for a moment and seemed to consider my brother's form, the bumps of vertebrae visible through his shirt, the way one shoulder rose higher than the other. "For your cooperation."

"Warren," I said. "You were helping the police?"

He nodded once, seeming pleased by my surprise. I turned toward the detective. "I thought Warren was a suspect."

From the look on Detective Dunn's face as his gaze dropped away, I realized that that was the whole idea. "With petty stuff like this," he said, "the Castro kid just needed to think he was in the clear long enough to get caught."

I looked at my mother for further explanation. "They found Gina Loost's watch in Zack's room," she said. "And there were a bunch of those coins in one of the basketball sneakers in his closet."

The detective allowed himself a chuckle. "I think next he was going to try for collectible spoons."

"But what about that frame?" I asked, not yet clear on how the thefts that had loomed so large over King's Knoll had deflated in importance to that of a precinct joke. "The one that you found in my mother's house?"

Mom answered for Detective Dunn. "Zack put it there," she said. "Bill Kotch saw him."

"Did you know about all this?" I asked, wondering if I was the only Parsons who hadn't been aware that Warren was working with the police and not against them. But Mom shook her head. Had Warren given her any information, she wouldn't have been able to contain it. She wouldn't have been able to resist riding it out, waving it like a flag, all in his defense.

"So Warren was bait?" I asked the detective. "Zack put him in the hospital a few weeks ago. Was that part of the plan, too?"

"No, no, no," said Detective Dunn, seeking to clarify. "We never put Warren in any danger. Warren and I only spoke after the assault. When I came to the house." He gestured toward me. "You remember."

I looked at Warren. Though his back was still turned toward us, he appeared to be entirely, though not altogether happily, attuned to our conversation. With his civic responsibility fulfilled, Warren seemed ready to be rid of Detective Dunn.

It was Rose who provided him with the opportunity. "Uncle Warren," she whined, "let's watch something."

Detective Dunn took that as his cue. "I'll leave you folks alone," he said, backing toward the hallway. To him, the investigation had been a nuisance, a trifling matter attended to between more serious cases. Attended to at all because of phone calls from the likes of Beth Castro. The detective had done his duty and done it well and was now ready to be finished with King's Knoll.

"Thank you," I said, not knowing what else to say.

He gave me a nod. "Take care," he said. Then he shut the door behind him.

Later, we would learn that Detective Dunn had it mostly all sorted out by the time he first spoke with Warren. After all, Zack mowed the lawns of many of the homes in the neighborhood. He had access to garages and, in the case of the Doogans, had found the house key that they kept under the fake rock near their deck. Really, he would have been the obvious suspect had Warren not been a more appealing one. But it was Bill Kotch's cooperation that helped the detective get his warrants.

Bill had trouble sleeping. *Fresh air and exercise!* his doctor had told him, so during the day, he would take to his bike, going round and round the neighborhood, hoping to tire both his mind and his body. It seldom worked. And Bill would find himself standing outside and breathing in the sharp night air, hoping not to wake Carol. That's what he was doing the night he saw Zack go into my mother's garage. When he saw him come out with less rather than more.

. . .

CHAPTER THIRTY-NINE

The Reckoning

After Warren and Mom left the hospital, after they gave me the bag that they had brought for Rose and me containing dry clothes and my wallet, after they promised that they would stop at the store and get Gordo his senior formula dog food, and that they would give him two cups at six o'clock, after Rose and I watched endless episodes of *SpongeBob SquarePants*, I sat in the chair in Rose's room, eating the hummus and carrots that had accompanied her dinner, and listening to the sounds of the family in the room next door. They were the happy, unintelligible murmurs of a father and a mother and two children. Every once in a while, there was laughter, clear and distinct. Every once in a while, the door would open and footsteps would pass in the hallway.

Rose had woken and eaten her dinner, then fallen asleep again by the time I again picked up the phone in her room, dialing zero for the hospital operator.

"Hi, I'm trying to make a call," I said, my credit card in hand.

My father answered on the first ring. I supposed that there was something about calling from a hospital that got people to pay attention.

"Stewart Parsons." His greeting was alert and ready, tinged with concern.

"Dad, it's Jenna."

"Hey, kiddo," he said. "What's wrong? Why are you at Hewn?"

"Listen, Dad," I said. "We need to talk."

"What's going on?" he asked, his voice increasing in gravity. I could hear him shutting a door. "Have there been any developments with Warren?"

I took a deep, steadying breath, but my words still came out sounding sodden with emotion. "You could say that."

"What happened?"

Maybe I savored for a moment the fact that my father was assuming the worst. Maybe I wanted to make him wait. To let him think that Warren was guilty and had been caught. Maybe I wanted him to regret everything that he was thinking about Warren and have to take it all back. Just like I did.

"Warren saved Rose's life," I finally said.

"What?!"

"She fell in the pond in the park and she could have drowned. But Warren saved her life." And from that dim little room, humming with the breath of the hospital, with its machines and generators, I said, "Mine, too, really." I hadn't known it was true until that moment.

"You know, Mom really needs more support from you," I said.

There was bitterness in my father's voice when he spoke again. "Jenna, I've been supporting your mother for twenty years."

I pictured Mom, her hand on Warren's back as she walked him into the auditorium for our high school graduation, into the restaurant for our grandfather's retirement party, into the church for his funeral. I pictured Mom with her hand on Warren's back as she walked him into Hewn Memorial, bleeding and hurt. "I don't mean financially, Dad."

In reply, I heard only my father's breath.

"They arrested a kid down the street for the thefts. Warren didn't have anything to do with them," I said. Then I added, a concession to his cooperation, "He actually helped the police in their investigation."

"You're kidding," he said, without thinking first.

"No, Dad. I'm not kidding."

I watched the tidy lines of advancing white headlights and≈retreating red taillights. "You know, Warren's your son, too."

His cracked voice came through the line. "I know."

"I realize that he's not who you wanted him to be, but . . ." I paused, remembering the look on Warren's face when I came home, on that very first night all those weeks ago. "He's actually amazing."

"I know," Dad said again.

"No, you don't, Dad. But I really hope you will."

And then I told him that I loved him. And then I said good night.

My mouth was dry and so I gently opened Rose's door and, shutting it behind me, walked to the little kitchen in the hallway where nurses filled cups of apple juice and parents microwaved their coffee. Blinking against the permanent artificial day of the fluorescent lights, I pulled a foam cup from a sleeve and filled it with ice from an enormous machine that spat frozen shards with such force that my cup over-flowedin just three seconds. Then, opening the fridge, I pulled out a carton of cranberry juice cocktail and poured myself a glass.

I was slugging it down as I walked back to Rose's room, the bottom of the cup lifted past my chin, when I saw Bobby coming toward me from the opposite end of the hallway. My pace slowed and his eyes met mine. In his hands were two plastic clamshell containers, each containing a sandwich. He was still in his scrubs and the skin beneath his eyes looked like the shadowed portion of a half-moon. His chin was darkened with stubble and his body seemed to be bearing a weight greater than his own. We both stopped, almost simultaneously, in front of Rose's door.

"Hey," I said, my eyes already wet, my voice shaking.

"I figured you were probably hungry," he said, lifting the sandwiches.

"Bobby, thank you," I said. I swallowed and started again. "For what you did for Rose."

He tilted his head back down the hall. "Do you want to go somewhere . . . and talk?" he asked.

I hesitated, glancing at Rose's door.

"After the day she's had, she'll sleep till noon," he said. "And if she does wake up, the nurses are here. A lot of parents go home at night."

"Okay," I said, nodding.

After Bobby asked me his clinical questions about Rose's recovery, we were mostly silent as we walked. He led me through the hospital's narrow corridors. "It's just over here," he said, pointing to a wide doorway above which hung silver letters. VINCENT C. SMITH ATRIUM.

I followed Bobby into the space, its soaring glass walls revealing the night outside. Around the room were banks of slender trees. *It's bamboo,* Warren would say. *Which is actually a member of the grass family.*

"This is beautiful," I said, looking at the stars and moon visible beyond the clear ceiling.

"Yeah," said Bobby. He seemed leached of energy. "No one ever comes in here at night." In front of a love seat was a low coffee table scattered with faded old magazines. He lifted his chin toward it. "Do you want to sit?"

We each took a place on the small couch and Bobby lifted the sandwich containers, peering into them. "They're both turkey," he said. "I hope that's okay."

"It's great," I said, trying to be cheerful.

He slid one to me and then opened his own only to stare down at the dismal little meal, the white bread sliding off a limp leaf of iceberg lettuce.

"Bobby," I started awkwardly, "I'm sorry I haven't called." He didn't move. He sat there with his forearms resting on his knees. "I just want you to know that it's not because I didn't . . . really want there to be something between us." I took a breath.

Bobby was listening. He wasn't going to say a word until I had finished. "I know I haven't told you much about Duncan, but he left when I was seven and a half months pregnant with Rose. He moved to Japan. And it wasn't like we were going to try and stay together or try to work it out. He just left." I felt my face redden, my eyes rim with tears. "And it was hard." I was going sentence by sentence, thought by thought, trying to move them past my lips one at a time. "And so when you said you were going to California, I just . . ." I stopped. Then, seeing his expression soften, I began again. "I thought it would be better, you know? For you, too."

Bobby's whole body seemed to exhale and he slung his arm around my back. "Come here," he said. He leaned into the sofa and I angled my body into his, feeling its solidity, its mass. "You could have told me," he said.

"I know. I should have," I said, curling my arm across his chest.

After a minute or two of silence, I felt him grow stone still with thought. "You know, I don't really want to go to California." I kept my head on his chest, listening to his heartbeat. "Mia and I . . . ," he started, his words tapping into a vein that was painful and deep. "We split up because she was having an affair." He let that sit there for a moment. "She wanted out of our marriage so badly she said that I could have custody of Gabby. But now she's remarried and pregnant. And I got a call from her lawyer saying that she wants to talk about the custody arrangement."

"Oh, God, Bobby," I said, realizing that there were worse things than neglectful, irresponsible Duncan. "I am so sorry."

Bobby put his hand on my shoulder, pulling me back again.

"It's all right. There really isn't anything she can do. Legally, I mean. They don't change custody agreements just like that. But . . ." I felt his hand tap once on my shoulder. "I thought my moving there might make things easier. Stop it from getting ugly."

We sat for what felt like a long time, gazing up at the feathery tops of the bamboo extending toward the stars, as the tips of his fingers ran up and down my arm. "How is this going to work?" I finally asked.

Bobby turned to me, looking at my face as if searching for an answer. "I don't know," he said finally. Then he pushed the hair off my forehead and brought his mouth to mine.

· · ·

CHAPTER FORTY

Birthday

Seven months later

I lay in the thick grass at the top of the hill, seeing the sun through my closed eyes. My shoulders were bare and I had kicked my flip-flops off, letting my toes run back and forth over the grass. Bobby reached over and took my hand. I could hear Gabby's and Rose's voices beside us, oblivious and giddy. From the sky came the hum of a small plane. Today was my and Warren's thirty-seventh birthday. My mother was clearing the cake plates from the picnic table she had set up in the backyard, while Gordo canvassed the ground in search of frosting and hamburger buns.

"Hey, War!" I called. "What time is it?"

I opened one eye to look at my brother. He glanced down at his slender wrist, his plane's controls still in his hands. "Four twenty-eight," he replied.

I had been waiting to ask him the time since our father had handed him a small box. Since Warren had carefully removed its wrapping. Since he had lifted off the lid and froze, staring down at our grandfather's watch. His head had jerked up to my father's face, his eyes wide.

"That was your grandpa's," said our father. But Warren knew what he had been given. Warren looked down at its gold face, then up again. "Try it on."

Warren set the box down on the picnic table, then slid on the watch that had been passed from Parsons son to Parsons son. His chest puffed with pride as he admired it, angling it so that the light hit it just right. "Yeah," he said. "That's nice." During the rest of the party, he stole glances at it.

After Maggie and her family had said good-bye and Mrs. Vanni had helped Mr. Vanni back home; after the Kotches had gone on their way and Fung had headed back to Pizzeria Brava; after my father had gotten into his car and driven back to Lydia, Bobby suggested we take the girls to the park.

"Want to come with us?" I had asked Mom. Her eyes were closed and her face was tilted up toward the sun. In her hand, she loosely gripped a white trash bag.

"You go ahead," she said, her eyes still closed. Her chest rose and fell with a contented breath. "I'm going to finish cleaning up."

Mom, Rose, and I had gone to Hattie's funeral, one week after Rose had slipped into the pond. We stood next to each other in the small chapel down the street from the home in which Hattie had died. We were the only ones in attendance. I watched as soundless tears slipped from my mother's eyes.

There was sadness to them but also release. And I often thought back to the timing of Hattie's death. It was as if Hattie took her last breath the moment after Lydia first spoke of what happened to my grandmother. Lydia hadn't meant to help my mother, but she had. Mom was now free to reconcile with her origins. She was free to move on. The past had shaped her, but it would no longer define her. After more than half a century, my mother was free.

Above us, Warren's plane hovered in the sky and Bobby brought his hand to his brow to shade his eyes. "How many of those things have you sold?" he asked my brother.

"Eighty-nine," answered Warren, without taking his eyes off the plane.

Bobby lifted his eyebrows. "At two hundred dollars a pop."

"Warren Parsons," I said, squinting into the sun. "Model Aeronautics Entrepreneur." I watched the plane dive and then burst back up into the sky. "Hey, you know what I read?" Though only Bobby turned his head, I was really talking to Warren. "That the light hitting our earth right now is thirty thousand years old."

"Really?" asked Bobby. Rose and Gabby burst into laughter that was private and their own.

"Yeah," I said, loud enough for Warren to hear. "It starts out in the sun's core, but its surface is so huge and dense that the light takes thirty *thousand* years to break through. It only takes like eight minutes to hit the earth once it's free."

"That's just an estimate," said Warren. "They don't know the exact age." And I fell back into the grass smiling, feeling the ancient light of sun meet my skin, knowing that it had existed before I had. Before my mother or my grandmother. That it had known our stories before they were told. That it had raced through space and time to illuminate them.

We stayed in the park until the sun began to hang heavier and begin its descent in earnest. Then we all walked together back to my mother's deck, Gordo trotting out to meet us as we approached. I stood on the bottom step so that I was taller than Bobby, then turned to face him. He wrapped his arm around my waist and rested his head against my chest. "So, we'll see you tomorrow?" he asked. It was going to be our last night all together before he and Gabby left for California. He was starting at San Diego General in two weeks.

"Come early," I said, running my hands over his hair. "We'll be back around noon." Warren had an appointment with the therapist he had been seeing and we often went together. Many of the sessions were spent just telling stories.

Bobby's lips found my neck and he said good-bye.

Warren sat on the steps next to Rose as I picked up a few cups that had blown into the forsythia bushes. As I bent down, I heard the door to the deck open and shut. Mom's slow steps made their way over to the railing. "You know, I was thinking that maybe we should have a garage sale," she said, leaning against the railing. "Get rid of some stuff."

"Oh, yeah?" I said, nestling the cups into each other.

She looked out over the park. "Warren and I have been talking," she said. "We think maybe it's time to leave Harwick."

I stopped at the base of the deck, looking from my mother to my brother.

"Where would you go?" I asked.

"I don't know," said my mother as her gaze rested on the

spot where the maple tree had stood. "I hear Southern California is nice."

Rose's giggles bubbled up until she clamped her hands over her mouth. "You guys would move there?" I asked, as I stared at the cups in my hands.

"Why not?" said my mother. "There's nothing keeping us here anymore." With her head tilted and her face soft, she looked at me. "Any of us."

"Yeah," mused Warren, *"California."* As if the idea had just occurred to him, as if he and my mother hadn't rehearsed this scene again and again. Then my brother looked at me, his eyes mischievous and brilliant as he said, "I bet Warren will fit right in there."

ACKNOWLEDGMENTS

. . .

My wonderful agent, Stephanie Kip Rostan, had to endure more than her fair share of less than perfect manuscript reading for this book, and provided honest and invaluable feedback with each version. She is a true professional.

My editor, Ellen Edwards, refused to accept anything less than my very best work, and for that, I am extremely grateful.

Jennifer Enderlin Blougouras and Erin Enderlin Bloys are not only my most steadfast, exacting, and valued readers, but also my sisters. I trust their opinions on literature, if not processed cheese products, wholly. My brother Jonathan Enderlin saved me from certain peril when, as a kid, I set myself adrift on the Gulf of Mexico in a vessel known as the "Party Tuber." And my brother Matthew Enderlin was my compatriot in childhood. I'm fortunate to call the lot of them family.

Several people helped with advice and information along the way. Olivier Sakellarios, Esq., provided input on my first draft so long ago that he probably doesn't even remember it, but let's still consider any errors or inaccuracies in this book entirely his fault. My friend Kristen Deshaies has a wonderful mind and heart, so we must forgive her for handing out raisins on Halloween. Sean W. Craine is a human being of the finest order. And I'm glad Stephen Moore is on my side.

I'd like to thank Sheila White Moore, James White, Marlow White Jr., Audrey Healy, Tom Healy, Phyllis Donohue, and all of my extended family—Whites, Moores, Francises, and Healys—for being such enthusiastic supporters.

It was my father, Peter Enderlin, who taught me the importance of telling the truth and my mother, Maureen Enderlin, who taught me to do so with compassion—which I think is a good way to try to live and write.

And finally, my husband, Dennis Healy, has seen me through the writing of this book and so much more. He and our three sons, Noah, Max, and Oliver, are my reasons for everything. I love them boundlessly.

Photo by Shem Roose

Sarah Healy lives in Vermont with her husband and three sons, where she works in marketing consultancy.

HOUSE of WONDER

. . .

SARAH HEALY

A CONVERSATION
WITH SARAH HEALY

Spoiler Alert: The Conversation with Sarah Healy and Questions for Discussion that follow tell more about what happens in the book than you might want to know until after you read it.

Q. You've said that House of Wonder *is, above all, a novel about family. Can you explain what you mean and what inspired you to write it?*

A. I've always been drawn to stories about families because there is something so universal about having to reconcile with your upbringing. Almost everyone I know, no matter how old, regresses a bit when around family and assumes the roles that they've always tended to play. I'm very fortunate that my own family is made up of some of my favorite people in the world, but I think it's always a process to figure out how to relate to your parents and siblings as an adult. And that process lies at the core of Jenna's narrative.

Q. *Both Priscilla's mother and Warren suffer from an undiagnosed condition or disability, but their experiences fifty years apart are very different. Why was it important to you to include both characters? And why did you want to show a family history, rather than make Warren's condition unique to him?*

A. In part, I wanted to explore the impulse to try to fit both Warren and Martha into the box of a diagnosis. Our culture tends to pathologize any behavior that deviates from the norm. Often, this is for a very good reason—because it can help us understand an individual and determine a treatment protocol. However, I don't think we can ignore the fact that treatments that were once acceptable can look misguided or even barbaric from a modern perspective—as is the case with the lobotomy to which Martha Harris was subjected.

Also, Priscilla is so central to this story that I wanted to afford the reader a deeper insight into both her devotion to her son and the conditions in which she allows herself to live through glimpses of her childhood and the loss of her mother.

Q. *Your description of the beauty pageants Priscilla competes in reminded me of pageants I watched on TV while growing up in the sixties, when—I'm chagrined to admit it—I found nothing objectionable in comparing women's breast, waist, and hip sizes. How my attitude has changed! Can you comment on how we viewed beauty pageants then, and how we do now, and what you wanted to convey about them in the novel?*

A. It seems that pageants used to be much more in the cultural fore than they are today. When I was growing up, the Miss America franchise was still a very big deal. But as the arenas and fields in which women could compete broadened, pageants lost some relevancy. Priscilla, though, is a product of a time and a place when "pretty" is one of the most important things a girl can aspire to be. That shapes her life in significant ways.

Q. *Your description of the suburban neighborhood in which Jenna grew up, where her mother still lives, struck a note of recognition in me, and I suspect it will in many readers. Is this the kind of place where you grew up? Did it have Maglons?*

A. I didn't grow up in a neighborhood like King's Knoll, but I did grow up in suburban New Jersey. The suburbs seem like such a perfect metaphor for adolescence, because they have always struck me as a place where fitting in is valued above almost all else.

My town didn't have "Maglons," but if it had, I would have been ready with my forsythia branches! I could have only hoped to have Howard Li at my side. . . .

Q. *The neglect and outright abuse that Priscilla suffers as a child seems to me to have been more prevalent in the fifties than it is now—or is that a misconception?*

A. I would be so happy to say that mistreatment like what Priscilla endured doesn't happen anymore, but unfortunately, I just don't think that's the case. Humanity has not evolved past cruelty. But humanity has not evolved past kindness either and on balance, I think we have a much greater capacity for the latter.

Q. *What do you hope that readers will take away from* House of Wonder, *and remember long after they finish reading?*

A. I hope my characters stay with people—Jenna, Silla, and especially Warren. Warren has been marginalized and dismissed for most of his life, but he has a wonderful, unique soul. I felt privileged to get to know him through the writing of this book. And there are probably more Warrens out there in the world than any of us realize.

Q. House of Wonder *is your second novel, following* Can I Get an Amen?, *which also takes place in suburban New Jersey. Are there any other similarities between the two novels?*

A. In some ways, they are both coming-of-age novels. . . . My protagonists just happen to be a bit older than is usual for the genre! But I've always found it funny that in typical coming-of-age novels, all these self-aware sixteen-year-olds are figuring out exactly who they are, when most of the adults I know are still a work in progress.

Q. *Where do you keep the pile of books you would like to read, and what is currently in it?*

A. I have a giant pile of books on the floor by my side of the bed, and at any given time, all but the few on the top have been read.

Those that I've finished will eventually find their way over to my bookshelves, but only after serving for a while as a repository for ponytail holders and teacups. What's in that pile runs the gamut; right now it contains titles by J. Courtney Sullivan, Junot Díaz, Meg Wolitzer, Elizabeth Gilbert, Maria Semple, Dave Eggers, and Carol Rifka Brunt.

Q. *In addition to writing novels, you work as a consultant and are raising three sons. How do you manage to do so much, and do you have any tips for readers who might be struggling with the age-old concern of too much to do, and too little time?*

A. Well, I don't know that I always manage it well. But I do try to take the long view, and think about how I'll feel about the way I prioritized my time twenty or thirty years from now. Some things just don't fit into my life at present—television watching being one of them. But before starting my next book, I plan to indulge in a full-on TV binge session.

Q. *What have you planned for your next book?*

A. It's in the incubation stage right now, but I would describe it as a book about sisters and unlikely friendships.

QUESTIONS FOR DISCUSSION

1. What did you most enjoy about *House of Wonder*?

2. The novel opens with Jenna returning to her family home after having avoided it for a number of years. What do you think draws her back? Did you, or other members of your family, go through a period of moving away from the family home and then returning to it?

3. Jenna's twin brother, Warren, is treated differently as an adult than as a child. Why is that? Was there someone like Warren where you grew up? How was he treated? Would he be treated differently today?

4. Warren notices things that other people miss. Discuss what they are and perhaps why he sees them while others do not.

5. In some ways, Warren is the facilitator of the story. Why do you think he's the one who brings Jenna home? What role does he play in Jenna's growth throughout the novel?

6. Is Priscilla exploited by the beauty pageants she participates in, or do they provide an opportunity for her to widen her prospects and fulfill her talents?

7. Discuss how Priscilla's upbringing, and the major events in her life since then, have made her the woman she is today.

8. Why does Priscilla keep secret her mother's history, and why does she finally share it with Jenna? Does revealing the truth change their mother/daughter relationship, or each of them individually?

9. How is Jenna's relationship with Bobby Vanni shaped by their history together, as kids in the neighborhood and then as teenagers? How might their relationship be different if they didn't have that shared past?

10. Bobby was Jenna's high school crush. Did you ever encounter your high school crush many years later? What did you learn about him? What kind of new relationship did you develop?

11. What changes does Jenna notice in the neighborhood she grew up in? Discuss the changes to your own neighborhood over the years. What factors do you think influence the identity of a neighborhood?

12. The novel suggests that Priscilla's need to buy and keep "stuff" arises from the emotional void she suffered from as a child, which has never fully healed. What role might our consumer-oriented society also play in her compulsion?

13. The thefts in the neighborhood create tension among the neighbors, and some people jump to the conclusion that Warren is guilty. Can you recall an incident from your own life when someone was unjustly accused? What was the outcome?

14. What do you think you'll take away from having read the novel? What will leave the most long-lasting impression?